Ben Jonson's Volpone, or the Fox: A Retelling

David Bruce

Published by David Bruce, 2022.

Ben Jonson's *Volpone, or the Fox*: A Retelling

***

***

Cover Photo: Patrice Audet (Public Domain)
  https://pixabay.com/en/fox-animal-wild-nature-animals-634307/

***

Ben Jonson was a master of satire who ranks with Jonathan Swift and Voltaire. In *Volpone*, he tackles greed. The wealthy Venetian gentleman Volpone is as cunning as a fox, and he pretends to be very ill and dying in order to entice legacy-hunters to give him valuable gifts in hopes of being named his heir. This works well for three years, but then …

BEN JONSON'S VOLPONE, OR THE FOX: A RETELLING

First edition. July 10, 2022.

Copyright © 2022 David Bruce.

ISBN: 979-8201351908

Written by David Bruce.

Table of Contents

Educate Yourself
Read Like A Wolf Eats
Be Excellent to Each Other
Books Then, Books Now, Books Forever

***

In this retelling, as in all my retellings, I have tried to make the work of literature accessible to modern readers who may lack the knowledge about mythology, religion, and history that the literary work's contemporary audience had.

Do you know a language other than English? If you do, I give you permission to translate this book, copyright your translation, publish or self-publish it, and keep all the royalties for yourself. (Do give me credit, of course, for the original retelling.)

I would like to see my retellings of classic literature used in schools, so I give permission to the country of Finland (and all other countries) to give copies of any or all of my retellings to all students forever. I also give permission to the state of Texas (and all other states) to give copies of any or all of my retellings to all students forever. I also give permission to all teachers to give copies of any or all of my retellings to all students forever. Of course, libraries are welcome to use my eBooks for free.

Teachers need not actually teach my retellings. Teachers are welcome to give students copies of my eBooks as background material. For example, if they are teaching Homer's *Iliad* and *Odyssey*, teachers are welcome to give students copies of my *Virgil's* Aeneid: *A Retelling in Prose* and tell them, "Here's another ancient epic you may want to read in your spare time."

CAST OF CHARACTERS

The Main Man and His Main Servant

VOLPONE, a *Magnifico*. *Volpone* is Italian for "fox." Volpone is crafty, is sly, and lacks morals. A *magnifico* is a wealthy, distinguished gentleman. *Magnifico* is Italian for "magnificent." In particular, a *magnifico* is a plutocrat — his power comes from his wealth.

MOSCA, Volpone's Parasite. *Mosca* is Italian for "fly." Mosca is a human parasite: He lives on other people. Many parasites are flatterers and hangers-on, but Mosca works hard at making himself indispensable to Volpone.

The Legacy-Hunters

VOLTORE, an Advocate. *Voltore* is Italian for "vulture." An advocate is a lawyer. Voltore is a legacy-hunter: He wants to inherit Volpone's wealth. Vultures feed on dead animals.

CORBACCIO, an Old Gentleman. *Corbaccio* is Italian for "raven." Corbaccio is a legacy-hunter: He wants to inherit Volpone's wealth. Ravens feed on dead animals. Ravens were also believed to neglect their young.

CORVINO, a Merchant. *Corvino* is Italian for "crow." Corvino is a legacy-hunter: He wants to inherit Volpone's wealth. Crows feed on dead animals. Merchants sell things, and Corvino is willing to sell his wife's honor.

Two People with Good Morality

BONARIO, Son to Corbaccio. *Bonario* is Italian for "good-tempered."

CELIA, Corvino's Wife. The Latin word "*caelia*" means "the Heavenly, aka celestial, one."

Volpone's Less Important Servants

NANO, a Dwarf. *Nano* is Italian for "dwarf." Many dwarves made their living as entertainers.

CASTRONE, a Eunuch. He has been castrated; some boys were castrated to preserve their high singing voice.

ANDROGYNO, a Hermaphrodite. His name is based on "androgynous" — both male and female. Volpone calls Androgyno his Fool — his jester.

Travelers

SIR POLITIC WOULD-BE, an English Knight and wanna-be VIP. He wants to be thought to be important in affairs of state. "Pol" is a name for a parrot. A poll parrot chatters. "Politic" refers to statesmanship and diplomacy.

LADY POLITIC WOULD-BE, Sir Politic Would-Be's Wife. Also known as FINE MADAME WOULD-BE. She is in Venice to learn the womanly arts by studying the well-regarded Viennese prostitutes.

PEREGRINE, an English Gentleman Traveler. A peregrine falcon is a kind of hawk. A peregrine falcon is a predatory bird.

Law Officials

COMMANDATORI: Police Officers, aka Officers of Justice.

ADVOCARI: Judges, four Magistrates.

NOTARY, the Registrar to the court, aka Clerk of Court.

Other Characters

THREE MERCHANTS. Three merchants help Peregrine fool Sir Politic Would-be.

CROWD. A crowd of people watch the mountebank's performance.

WOMEN: Lady Politic Would-be's female attendants.

SERVANTS.

SCENE

VENICE, ITALY. To the Elizabethans, Venice was wealthy, sophisticated, and immoral.

DATE

Probably February or March 1606.

THE ARGUMENT

Volpone, childless, rich, feigns sick, [feigns] despair,
*   **O**ffers his estate to hopes of several heirs,*
*   **L**ies languishing: his parasite receives*
*   **P**resents from all, assures, deludes; then weaves*
*   **O**ther cross plots [counter-plots], which open themselves [unfold and reveal*
themselves and] are told [exposed].
*   **N**ew tricks for safety are sought; they thrive: when bold,*
*   **E**ach tempts the other again, and all are sold [betrayed, ruined].*

***

The "argument" of the play is a brief summary of the plot. This argument is an acrostic; the first letter of each line spells out VOLPONE.

Volpone is a rich man who has no children. Other rich people would like to inherit his property, so Volpone pretends to be sick and near death. The other rich people give him many expensive presents, hoping to be named his heir in his will. Characters immorally compete with each other, and in the end, all guilty persons are punished.

A parasite is a person who lives off another person. Mosca is Volpone's parasite, his main servant.

PROLOGUE

Now, if God will send us a little luck, a little wit will serve to make our book a hit, according to the tastes of the literary season and audiences. However, here in this book is rhyme, and the rhyme is not empty of reason.

This we were bid to believe from our author, Ben Jonson, whose true intention, if you would know it, in all his books always has been this measure: to mix profit with your pleasure.

His intention has not been that of some authors, whose throats fail because of their envy as they cry hoarsely, "All he writes is excessively critical." And when his books come out, these overly prolific authors think that they can insult his books by saying that he took a year to write each of them.

To this Mr. Jonson need not say that it is a lie because all he needs to do is to point to this work of art, which did not exist two months before it was first seen — Mr. Jonson wrote it in less than two months.

And although Mr. Jonson dares to give them five lives to mend his book — depending on your opinion of his value as an author, that's five lives to look for non-existent errors to correct, or five lives to correct all the numerous errors — let it be known that it took him only five weeks to fully write it. He did not use the services of a co-author, a journeyman author paid to write some of the scenes, a beginning author working under his direction, or a tutor to provide direction to him.

Yet thus much I can give you as a token of his play's worth: No eggs are broken, nor are there quaking custards — quivering cowards — frightened by fierce teeth. This book contains no slapstick of the kind that delights the ordinary crowd of ordinary people.

Nor does the author drag in a fool who recites clichés and stale jokes to stop gaps in loose, badly constructed writing, and nor does the author drag in characters who engage in a great many monstrous and forced actions — such things might make the book a hit at Bedlam, the hospital for the insane. Nor has he made his book out of jests stolen from each table where joke-tellers eat, but instead he has written his own jokes as they appear naturally and fit the events that occur in this book.

The author presents quick, lively, refined comedy, in accordance with the best critics: Aristotle and Horace. He observes the laws of time, place, and persons. This book can be read in a day, and the events take place in a day. The events also take place in locations that can be reasonably reached in a day. Also, the characters remain consistent in character: Greedy characters stay greedy, and good characters stay good. Any changes that occur are those that can realistically occur.

From no needful rule does the author stray. An unnecessary rule — to be followed only sometimes — is the law of action: The book should have only one plot. This book has a main plot and a sub-plot related to the theme of the main plot, and so the law of action is obviously not a needful rule.

All gall and copperas, aka sulphuric acid — from his ink the author has drained, and only a little salt — sediment — remains, wherewith he'll rub your cheeks, so that red with laughter, they shall look fresh for the upcoming week.

Yes, bitter gall and acid shall be absent from this book, although a little salty wit shall be present so that you shall laugh and be cheerful for a week.

CHAPTER 1
— 1.1 —

Volpone and Mosca were talking one morning in a room in Volpone's house in Venice.

Volpone said, "Good morning to the day; and next, good morning to my gold. Open the shrine, so that I may see my saint."

Mosca opened a treasure chest, revealing gold and other precious metals, jewels, etc. Volpone was a very wealthy man.

Some religious people believe in beginning the day with a prayer to what the people most value. Many Christians begin the day with a prayer to God. Volpone valued seeing the Sun — that is, being alive — and he valued material wealth. He now parodied a Christian's morning prayer.

Looking at the treasure, Volpone said, "Hail the world's soul, and my soul!"

Some systems of thought regard the *anima mundi* — the world's soul — as the most vital force in the universe.

He continued, "The teeming — pregnant — earth is glad to see the longed-for Sun peep through the horns of the celestial Ram."

In astrology, the Sun enters the astrological sign Aries, the Ram, at the beginning of spring in the Northern hemisphere. With the arrival of more minutes of sunshine, the Northern hemisphere is able to give birth to the many potential plants in seeds in the earth.

Volpone continued, "But I am even gladder than the teeming earth seeing the Sun when I see my treasure's splendor darkening the splendor of the Sun by contrast. My treasure, lying here among my other hoards of treasure, appears as bright as a flame by night, or like the first day of creation, when God created the Sun and the Moon out of chaos, and all darkness fled to Earth's center, where Hell is located."

In Exodus 13, God had appeared as a pillar of fire in order to lead the Israelites to the Promised Land.

Volpone then referred to the son of Sol; Sol is the Sun, and alchemists referred to gold as the son of Sol.

"Oh, you son of Sol, but brighter than your father, let me kiss you with adoration, and let me kiss every relic of sacred treasure in this blessed room.

"Well did wise poets, by your glorious name, title that age which they would have the best."

He was referring to the Golden Age, the best age, an age in which men lived easy lives. Life in the classical Golden Age is comparable to life in the Garden of Eden. Greed for gold, however, was not known in the Golden Age. Love of gold often leads to sin.

1 Timothy 6:10 states, *"For the love of money is the root of all evil: which while some coveted after, they have erred from the faith, and pierced themselves through with many sorrows"* (King James Version).

Referring to gold, Volpone said, "You are the best of all things, and you far transcend all kinds of joy — joy in children, parents, friends, or any other waking dream on Earth. I would rather have gold than any of these other things.

"People talk about golden Venus, the most beautiful goddess. They should have given Venus twenty thousand Cupids — such are your beauties and our loves! Gold is so beautiful that if Venus is golden, she should have been made pregnant twenty thousand times and given birth to twenty thousand Cupids, the god of cupidity.

"Gold, you are my dear saint. Riches are the dumb God that gives all men tongues. Gold cannot speak, yet all men will speak volumes — including volumes of lies — to acquire gold.

"Gold, you can do nothing, and yet you make men do all things — including evil things — to acquire you. Gold, you are the Unmoved Mover.

"Think of the price of souls. The Son of God gave his life to redeem the souls of sinners. But if a sinful life contains gold, sinners will consider Hell to be worth as much as Heaven. Gold is as valuable as the blood of Christ because both gold and the blood of Christ buy souls.

"Gold, you are virtue, fame, honor, and all other things. Whoever can get you shall be regarded as noble, valiant, honest, wise —"

Mosca interrupted, "And whatever else he wishes to be regarded as, sir. Riches are in fortune a greater good than wisdom is in nature. It is better to be lucky enough to acquire riches than it is to be born with wisdom."

Proverbs 16:16 states, "*How much better is it to get wisdom than gold! and to get understanding rather to be chosen than silver!*" (King James Version). Mosca — and Volpone — disagree.

"True, my beloved Mosca," Volpone said. "Yet I glory more in the cunning acquisition of my wealth than in its glad possession, since I gain wealth in no ordinary, common way.

"I don't engage in business. I don't engage in risky speculations. I wound no earth with plows, I fatten no beasts to feed the slaughterhouses. I have no mills for iron, olive oil, corn, or men, to grind them into powder."

Men can be ground down through excessively hard work.

Volpone continued, "I blow no subtly conceived glassware. I expose no ships to the threats of the furrow-faced — wave-wracked — sea. I make no monetary speculations in the public bank, nor am I a private moneylender —"

Mosca interrupted, "No sir, nor do you devour soft, easily manipulated prodigal sons who spend their money before they inherit it. Some people will swallow a melting heir — an heir whose wealth melts wastefully away — as glibly as your Dutch will swallow pills — mouthfuls — of butter, and never purge — take an emetic or a laxative — for it. They digest the heir so thoroughly that there is no need for such remedies, and they are able to do so without purging — being punished for — their actions.

"Such people tear forth the fathers of poor families out of their beds, and coffin them alive in some kind, clasping — fetters are clasping — prison, where their bones may be forthcoming, when the flesh is rotten. In other words, they won't leave the debtors' prison alive.

"But your sweet nature abhors these courses of action. You loathe the widow's or the orphan's tears that would then wash your pavements, and their piteous cries that would ring in your roofs, and beat the air for vengeance."

"You are right, Mosca," Volpone said. "I do loathe it."

He had seen the tears and had heard the cries of distress.

Mosca continued, "And besides, sir, you are not like a thresher who stands with a huge flail, watching a heap of corn, and, although he is hungry, he dares not taste the smallest grain, but instead feeds on mallows — vegetation that is eaten during famines — and other such bitter herbs.

"Also, you are not like the merchant who has filled his vaults with fine wines from Greece and rich wines from Crete, yet drinks the dregs of bad, vinegary wine from Lombardy.

"You will not lie in straw while moths and worms feed on your sumptuous hangings and soft beds."

In other words, Volpone knew how to spend money and enjoy himself. He was a *bon vivant*, not a miser.

Mosca continued, "You know the use of riches, and dare give now from that bright heap, to me, your poor servant, or to your dwarf, or your hermaphrodite, your eunuch, or what other household-trifle — menial servant — your pleasure permits to work for you."

Volpone's servants included a dwarf, a eunuch, and a hermaphrodite. He had hired these people to keep him entertained.

"Stop, Mosca," Volpone said.

He took a coin from his treasure chest and held it out to Mosca, saying, "Take this from my hand."

Mosca took the coin.

Volpone then said, "You strike on the truth in all things, and those people who call you a parasite are envious of you.

"Bring here my dwarf, my eunuch, and my Fool, and let them entertain me."

Mosca exited to summon Nano the dwarf, Castrone the eunuch, and Androgyno the hermaphrodite, who was also Volpone's Fool, aka professional jester.

Alone, Volpone said to himself, "What should I do, but cocker up my genius, and live free to all delights my fortune calls me to?"

By "cocker up my genius," Volpone meant "indulge my appetites." "Cocker up" was a fitting term because many of his appetites were sexual.

Volpone continued, "I have no wife, no parent, child, or relative to give my possessions to, so whomever I choose must be my heir, and this makes men flatter and pay attention to me. My lack of an heir draws new flatterers daily to my house, women and men of all ages, who bring me presents, send me gold and silver vessels and utensils, money, and jewels in the hope that when I die (which they expect each greedy minute) their gifts shall then return ten-fold to them.

"And some, greedier than the rest, seek to have a monopoly of me and inherit all I have, and they work to undermine their competitors who would also like to inherit all I have. They compete in giving gifts because the bigger the gift, the bigger appears to be their love for me.

"All of these things I allow to happen. I play with their hopes, and I am happy to turn their hopes into my profit. I am happy to look upon their kindness, and accept more of the gifts they bring, and look upon those gifts. All the time I take these flatterers in hand and manipulate them. I tie a cherry to a string and let the cherry knock against their lips, and I let it get close to their mouths, and then I draw the cherry back before they can bite it."

Hearing a noise, he said, "What's that?"

Mosca arrived with Nano the dwarf, Castrone the eunuch, and Androgyno the hermaphrodite. The three had been summoned to entertain Volpone. Nano was holding a paper.

Nano the dwarf said, reading from his notes, "*Now, make room for fresh performers, who want you to know, they bring you neither play, nor university show.*"

They were giving a performance, but it was not like a play in a theater, nor was it like a university show that would display vast learning. Actually, their show would display vast learning, but it would do so in a satiric manner. They would mock the belief in progress, using the Pythagorean idea of reincarnation, or the transmigration of souls.

Nano the dwarf held the notes as he recited, "*Therefore we entreat you that whatsoever we performers rehearse, may it not fare a whit the worse, for the false pace of the verse.*"

By "rehearse," he meant "recite," but sometimes performers regard each performance as the rehearsal for the next performance.

Nano the dwarf recited, "*If you wonder at this, you will wonder more before we pass, for know, here in the body of Androgyno the hermaphrodite is enclosed the soul of Pythagoras, that divine trickster, as hereafter shall follow.*"

Nano the dwarf now explained the origin of this particular soul and how through the process of reincarnation it came to be Pythagoras' soul and eventually became Androgyno the hermaphrodite's soul.

Nano the dwarf recited, "*Pythagoras' soul, fast and loose, sir, came first from the god Apollo.*"

Apollo was the classical god of prophecy, music, archery, medicine, plague, and more.

The soul was fast and loose. In reincarnation, it was connected fast to a body and then became loose and so was able to travel to another body. "Fast and loose" was also a con game in which a chain or string was placed on a table with the chain or string making loops. The sucker was supposed to pick the loop that was fast, but the con man could arrange the chain or string in such a way that whichever loop the sucker picked, the loop would be loose. Similarly, since humans are mortal, the soul always eventually comes loose from the body.

Nano the dwarf recited, "*And then the soul was breathed into Aethalides, Mercury's son, where it had the gift to remember all that ever was done.*"

Aethalides was the herald of Jason and the Argonauts, who are famous for traveling to acquire the Golden Fleece. Mercury was the herald of the gods, and he gave Aethalides perfect memory. Because of this, all who had the soul, including Pythagoras, were able to remember all his or her previous incarnations.

Nano the dwarf recited, "*From Aethalides the soul fled forth, and made quick transmigration to goldy-locked Euphorbus, who was killed in good fashion, at the siege of old Troy, by the cuckold of Sparta.*"

Euphorbus, who decorated his hair with gold clips, was the first warrior to wound Patroclus, the beloved friend of Achilles, the greatest warrior of the Trojan War. Euphorbus was killed by Menelaus, who was cuckolded by Paris, Prince of Troy, who ran away with Menelaus' wife, Helen, the most beautiful woman in the world.

Nano the dwarf recited, "*Hermotimus was next (I find it in my notes) to whom the soul did pass, where no sooner it was missing but with one Pyrrhus of Delos it learned to go a fishing, and from him did it enter the sophist of Greece.*"

Hermotimus was a philosopher, and Pyrrhus was a fisherman. The sophist of Greece was Pythagoras himself, who is famous for the Pythagorean theorem, among other things.

Nano the dwarf recited, "*From Pythagoras, the soul went into a beautiful piece of ass named Aspasia, who was a* meretrix, *which is Greek for 'prostitute.' She was a* meretrix *who performed merry tricks and who was the mistress of the Greek statesman Pericles. And the next toss of her — the soul — was from a whore to a philosopher again.*"

The "next toss" meant both "next sexual bout" and "next reincarnation."

Nano the dwarf recited, "*As the soul itself does relate, the soul became Crates the Cynic, a disciple of the Cynic philosopher Diogenes. Since then the soul has resided in kings, knights, and beggars, knaves, lords and fools, and the soul has resided in ox and ass, camel, mule, goat, and badger, in all which it has spoken, as it has in the cobbler's cock.*"

Lucian of Samosata was a satirist who wrote in Greek. In his work "The Dream, or the Cock," he wrote about a cock — a rooster — that claimed to be the reincarnation of the soul of Pythagoras. The cock also recounted many other reincarnations of the soul. The work is a Cynic sermon that praises poverty and argues that wealth does not necessarily lead to happiness. In this work, a cock awakens Micyllus the cobbler. He threatens to kill the cock, but the cock makes him invisible and shows him how the rich live in private, proving that he, a cobbler, is better off than the wealthy.

Nano the dwarf recited, "*But I didn't come here to discourse about that matter of reincarnation, or his one, two, or three, or his great oath, BY QUATER! Nor did I come here to discourse about his musics, his trigon, his golden thigh, or his telling how elements shift.*"

Pythagoras believed in the importance of mathematics in understanding reality. The quaternion consisted of the first four whole numbers (1, 2, 3, 4). These numbers added up to ten, an important number. These numbers also could be used to construct a trigon, an equilateral triangle with four dots as the bottom level, three dots as the next level, two dots as the next level, and one dot as the top level. Each side would have four dots.

Pythagoras used numbers and ratios to investigate such things as the musical scale.

According to myth, Pythagoras had a golden thigh, and he believed that the four elements — air, fire, water, and earth — were constantly changing into each other.

Nano the dwarf recited to Androgyno the hermaphrodite, "*But I would ask, how of late have you experienced transformation and how have you shifted your coat in these days of reformation.*"

The days of reformation referred to the Protestant Reformation; the most radical of the Protestants were the Puritans. "Shifted your coat" meant "changing sides" — leaving Catholicism to become Protestant.

Androgyno the hermaphrodite recited, "*Like one of the reformed, I am a fool, as you see, accounting all old doctrine as heresy.*"

Androgyno the hermaphrodite was wearing the costume of a Fool, a professional jester. As a Fool, he regarded the old doctrines — such as those of Catholicism — as heretical.

Nano the dwarf recited, "*But have you eaten food that is forbidden to you?*"

Pythagoreans were forbidden to eat meat, fish, and beans.

Androgyno the hermaphrodite recited, "*My soul dined on fish, when first my soul entered a Carthusian.*"

Carthusians were members of a religious sect that allowed devotees to eat fish.

Nano the dwarf recited as he asked about the soul, "*Has your dogmatical silence ever left you?*"

Pythagoreans — and Carthusians — made a vow of silence for a number of years.

Androgyno the hermaphrodite recited, "*Of that an obstreperous lawyer bereft me.*"

The soul had once entered a loud lawyer.

Nano the dwarf recited, "*Oh, what a wonderful change, when Sir Lawyer forsook the soul! For Pythagoras' sake, what body then did the soul take?*"

Androgyno the hermaphrodite recited, "*A good dull mule.*"

Lawyers rode mules.

Nano the dwarf recited, "*What! And by that means you were brought to allow yourself to eat beans?*"

Although Pythagoreans were forbidden to eat beans, mules were fed them.

Androgyno the hermaphrodite recited, "*Yes.*"

Nano the dwarf recited, "*But from the mule into whom did the soul pass?*"

Androgyno the hermaphrodite recited, "*Into a very strange beast, by some writers called an ass. By other writers, the very strange beast is called a precise, pure, illuminate brother, one of those who devour flesh, and sometimes one another, and who will drop you forth a libel, or a sanctified lie, between every spoonful of a nativity pie.*"

The very strange beast was a Puritan. Puritans are "precise" because they are strict, and they are "illuminate" because they have seen religious light. The name "Puritan" comes from their claim to be "pure."

Puritans literally ate the flesh of animals, and they metaphorically ate the flesh of their fellow human beings through their sharp business dealings.

Puritans were fond of publishing libelous pamphlets denouncing their enemies.

Due to a hatred of Catholicism, including Catholic masses, Puritans avoided the use of the syllable "mas" and so they ate what they called nativity pie rather than Christmas pie, which was the same thing except for the name.

Nano the dwarf recited, "*Now move on, out of respect for Heaven, from that profane sect of Puritanism, and gently report your next transmigration.*"

Androgyno the hermaphrodite recited, "*I, the soul, then entered the body you see before you. I am in the body of Androgyno the hermaphrodite.*"

Nano the dwarf recited, "*This body is a creature of delight, and, what is more than a Fool, it is a hermaphrodite! Now, please, sweet soul, in all your variation, which body would you choose to be in to keep up your station?*"

Androgyno the hermaphrodite recited, "*Truly, I prefer this body I am in. This is the body in which I would tarry.*"

Nano the dwarf recited, "*Because here the delight of each sex you can experience? As a hermaphrodite, you can experience sex as a man and as a woman.*"

Androgyno the hermaphrodite recited, "*Unfortunately, those pleasures are stale and forsaken. No, it is your Fool wherewith I am so taken. The Fool is the one and only creature that I can call blessed. For all other forms I have taken have proven to be most distressed.*"

Nano the dwarf recited, "*That is spoken truly, as if you were still in Pythagoras. This learned opinion we will celebrate, fellow eunuch, as behooves us, with all our wit and art, to dignify that whereof ourselves are so great and special a part.*"

Nano the dwarf and Castrone the eunuch were part fool, as are we all.

Volpone said, "Now, that was very, very pretty! Mosca, was this your invention? Did you write this?"

Mosca said, "If it pleases you, my patron, I admit that I wrote it. But if you don't like it, I did not write it."

"It does please me, good Mosca," Volpone said.

"Then I wrote it, sir," Mosca said.

The skit was cynical. A god created the soul, but the bodies the soul inhabited varied greatly and did not progress, but if anything, regressed. Nothing was learned from ascetic and religious practices, as these varied from body to body with no consistency. The skit pointed out the soul's lack of progress.

Readers could argue that although this is cynical, it is true. Despite millennia of religious education, many people of Ben Jonson's day and our own seem determined to turn themselves into animals.

Nano the dwarf and Castrone the eunuch then sang this song about Fools:

"Worth men's envy, or admiration,

"Free from care or sorrow-taking,

"Selves and others merry making,

"All that Fools speak or do is sterling.

"Your Fool is your great man's darling,

"And your ladies' sport [entertainment] and pleasure;

"Tongue and bauble are his treasure."

A Fool's bauble is the court jester's baton, which has a face carved at the top. "Bauble" was also a slang word for "penis," and a Fool could use his tongue and penis to entertain the ladies.

"Even his face begets laughter,

"And he speaks truth free from slaughter."

Professional Fools were given free speech. They could almost always say insulting things without being punished as long as they were witty.

"He's the grace of every feast,

"And sometimes the chiefest guest."

Sometimes, the Fool sat in the seat of honor: at the top of the table, beside the host.

"He has his trencher [plate] and his stool,

"When Wit waits upon the Fool."

The master of the house, who is presumably intelligent — "wit" means "intelligent person" — waits on the Fool. Also, the god of Wit serves the Fool by making the Fool witty.

"Oh, who would not be

"He, he, he?"

As Nano the dwarf and Castrone the eunuch laughed *"he, he, he,"* they pointed to Androgyno the hermaphrodite, who was wearing a Fool's costume and who carried a Fool's bauble.

Knocking sounded on the door.

Volpone asked, "Who's that?"

He then ordered the entertainers to leave: "Away!"

Nano the dwarf and Castrone the eunuch exited.

Volpone said, "Look and see who it is, Mosca."

Seeing Androgyno the hermaphrodite, Volpone ordered, "Fool, begone!"

Androgyno the hermaphrodite exited.

Mosca said, "It is Signior Voltore, the lawyer. I know him by his distinctive knock."

Voltore is Italian for "vulture."

Volpone needed to appear to be ill and bedridden when he saw Voltore, so he ordered, "Fetch me my gown, my furs, and my caps. Tell him that my bed is being changed, and let him entertain himself for a while outside in the gallery."

The caps were worn for warmth. One cap buttoned under the chin and covered hair and ears. The other cap was a skullcap with ear flaps.

Mosca exited.

Volpone said to himself, "Now, now, my clients begin their visitation!"

Clients would visit their patron in the early morning as a form of respect.

Volpone continued, "Vulture, kite, raven, and carrion-crow, all my birds of prey who think that I am turning into a carcass, now they come."

Voltore was the vulture, Corbaccio was the raven, and Corvino was the crow. These birds all ate carrion, but did not usually kill it — they waited for it to die. Voltore, Corbaccio, and Corvino were all waiting for Volpone to die. The kite really is a bird of prey, and if anyone is the kite, events would show that Mosca is.

Volpone said, "I am not for them yet."

He was not yet ready to meet them, nor was he yet a corpse.

Mosca returned with the gown and other items.

Volpone asked, "What is the news?"

Mosca said, "Voltore has brought a piece of plate, sir."

The plate was a gold utensil.

"How big?" Volpone asked.

"Huge, massy, and antique, with your name inscribed and your coat of arms engraved," Mosca replied.

"Good!" Volpone said. "And doesn't it show a fox stretched on the earth, with fine delusive sleights, mocking a gaping crow?"

He was imagining that a sly fox would be a suitable image to engrave on the plate. Foxes would sometimes pretend to be dead. When scavenging birds came near the fox, the fox would spring up and kill a bird and feed on it. Volpone pretended to be near death so that suckers would give him expensive gifts such as this huge plate.

Volpone was also referring to one of Aesop's fables. A crow had a piece of cheese in its beak, and a fox wanted to eat the cheese. The fox began to praise the crow, and when the fox praised the crow's singing voice, the crow opened its beak to caw. The cheese fell out of the crow's mouth, and the fox gobbled it up.

Volpone laughed, "Ha, Mosca?"

He replied, "Your wit is sharp, sir."

Volpone said, "Give me my furs."

The furs were meant to keep an ill man warm.

Volpone, putting on his invalid's clothing, asked Mosca, "Why are you laughing so much, man?"

"I cannot refrain from laughing, sir," Mosca replied, "when I think about what thoughts Voltore has now, outside, as he walks. He thinks that this might be the last gift he will give to you. He thinks that this gift might be the one that will convince you to make him your heir. He is thinking that if you die today, and give him all you own, what a wealthy man he will be tomorrow. He thinks about what a large return he would get from all his gifts to you. He thinks about how he would be worshiped, and reverenced, by other people. He thinks about how he would ride with his furs on a horse wearing an ornamental cloth that reaches its hooves. He thinks about how he would be waited on by herds of fools and clients. He thinks about how he would have a way cleared for his mule that is as lettered — educated — as himself. He thinks about how he would be called the great and learnéd lawyer, and then he concludes that there's nothing impossible."

Volpone said, "Yes, one thing is impossible: to be learnéd, Mosca."

"Oh, no — you are wrong," Mosca said. "Being rich implies being learnéd. Hood an ass with reverend purple, so you can hide its two ambitious ears, and it shall pass for a cathedral doctor."

Doctors wore purple hoods to show that they were learnéd. Hide an ass' ears with such a hood, and people will think that the ass is learned.

An ambitious man aspires to a high position; an ass' ears have a high position.

"My nightcaps, my nightcaps, good Mosca," Volpone said.

He put on the two nightcaps and then said, "Bring Voltore in."

"Wait, sir," Mosca said. "You need your ointment for your eyes."

The ointment made Volpone's eyes appear to be those of a sick man. Volpone would act as if he were nearly blind, nearly deaf, and nearly dead.

"That's true," Volpone said. "I need to use that ointment. Hurry, hurry."

Mosca helped him by applying the cosmetics and ointment that made him appear to be ill.

Volpone said, "I long to have possession of my new present."

"That, and thousands more, I hope to see you lord of," Mosca said.

"Thanks, kind Mosca," Volpone said.

Mosca began, "And that, when I am dead and lost in blended dust, as are a hundred such servants as I am, in succession —"

He was wishing Volpone an incredibly long life, one in which Volpone would outlive him and one hundred other servants who would, one at a time, take Mosca's place.

"No, that would be too much, Mosca," Volpone said.

"You shall live, continually, to delude these Harpies," Mosca said.

Harpies are half-women, half-birds who torment people by eating their food and fouling the food that they do not eat. Sometimes, they are sent to bedevil sinners. They are also a symbol of greed.

"Loving Mosca!" Volpone said. "My disguise is well done now. Give me my pillow, and let Voltore enter."

Mosca exited to bring in Voltore.

Poets such as Homer and Virgil began their epics with an invocation to a god or gods to help them with their epic poems. For example, Homer began his *Iliad* in this way:

Rage.

Goddess, use me to tell the story of the rage of Achilles, a Greek warrior who had the rage of a god. The rage of the son of Peleus made corpses of many men and sent their souls to the Land of the Dead. Dogs and birds feasted on warriors' flesh, all because of Achilles and the will of Zeus, king of gods and men.

Volpone now parodied these invocations by praying not to a god or goddess for help but by praying to a number of feigned illnesses for help.

He prayed, "Now, my feigned cough, my feigned tuberculosis, and my feigned gout, my feigned paralysis, feigned palsy, and feigned watery discharges from my nose and eyes, with your artificially induced functions help this my imposture, wherein, these past three years, I have milked their hopes.

"Voltore comes; I hear him."

Volpone then faked some weak coughs and a groan.

— 1.3 —

Mosca returned, leading Voltore, who was holding a large piece of plate.

Mosca said to Voltore, "You still are what you were in Volpone's affections, sir. Only you, of all the rest, are the man who commands his love, and you do wisely to preserve it thus, with visits early in the morning, and kind gifts that show your good intentions to him, which, I know, cannot but be accepted most gratefully."

He then said loudly to Volpone, "Patron! Sir! Signior Voltore has come —"

Volpone interrupted with a weak voice, "What did you say?"

Mosca said, "Sir, Signior Voltore has come this morning to visit you."

"I thank him," Volpone said.

"And he has brought you the gift of a piece of antique plate, bought from a goldsmith's shop in the Piazza di San Marco."

"He is welcome," Volpone said weakly. "Ask him to come more often."

"Yes," Mosca said.

Voltore asked, "What did he say?"

Mosca replied, "He thanks you, and he wants you to see him often."

"Mosca," Volpone said.

"My patron!" Mosca replied.

"Bring Voltore near to me," Volpone said. "Where is he? I long to feel his hand."

Knowing what Volpone was really interested in, Mosca said, "The plate is here, sir."

Voltore asked, "How are you, sir? How is your health?"

"I thank you, Signior Voltore," Volpone said. "Where is the plate? My eyes are bad."

Voltore put the plate into Volpone's hands and said, "I'm sorry to see you still this weak."

Mosca thought, *He's sorry that Volpone is not weaker.*

Volpone said, "You are too munificent — too generous."

"No, sir," Voltore said. "I wish to Heaven that I could give health to you as well as that plate!"

"You give, sir, what you can," Volpone said. "I thank you. Your love shows judgment in this, and it shall not be unrewarded. I ask that you see me often."

"Yes, I shall, sir," Voltore said.

"Be not far from me," Volpone said.

"Do you observe that, sir?" Mosca asked Voltore.

Volpone said, "Listen to me carefully; it will concern you."

Mosca said to Voltore, "You are a happy man, sir; know your good. Know what good thing will happen to you."

Volpone said, "I cannot now last long —"

Mosca said to Voltore, "You are his heir, sir."

Voltore asked, "Am I?"

"I feel me going," Volpone said.

He faked some coughs and groans.

He added, "I'm sailing to my port."

He faked some more coughs and groans.

He added, "And I am glad I am so near my haven."

The haven is Heaven, although Volpone may have been optimistic when he called it "my haven."

"Alas, kind gentleman!" Mosca said, "Well, we must all go —"

Voltore interrupted, "But, Mosca —"

Mosca ignored him and continued, "Age will conquer."

Voltore said, "Please listen to me. Am I officially made his heir for certain?"

"Are you?" Mosca said. "I beg you, sir, to be pleased to write my name in your list of servants and dependents. All my hopes depend upon your worship: I am lost once Volpone is dead, unless the rising Sun shines on me."

Volpone's wealth would make the Sun — Voltore — rise.

"It shall both shine on and warm you, Mosca," Voltore said.

"Sir, I am a man who has not done your love all the worst services," Mosca said. "Here I serve you. It is as if I am trusted with your keys so that I can see that all your coffers and all your caskets are locked, and so that I can keep the poor inventory of your jewels, your plate, and your monies. I am your steward, sir. I husband your goods here."

Mosca claimed to have Volpone's keys and to take care of Volpone's wealth — wealth that according to Mosca would soon belong to Voltore.

"But am I the sole heir?" Voltore asked.

"You are the heir without a partner, sir," Mosca replied. "This was confirmed this morning. The wax of the seal is still warm, and the ink is scarcely dry upon the parchment."

"Happy, happy me!" Voltore said. "For what reason did he make me his sole heir, sweet Mosca?"

"Your merit, sir," Mosca said. "You deserved it. I know no second reason."

"Your modesty won't allow you to know it," Voltore said, "but I know the help that you have given to me. Well, I shall requite it."

He may have meant that Mosca will be well rewarded for his services, but given his greed, he may have simply meant that Mosca would receive a small reward.

Mosca said, "Volpone has always liked your manner of acting, sir. That was what first took his fancy and made you his favorite. I often have heard him say how he admired men of your large profession, who promise much and advocate for every side, right or wrong, and who advocate for things that are complete contradictions, until the lawyers are hoarse again, and yet all that they say is lawful to be said. They take any case and argue any position. Men of your large profession, with very quick agility, are men who turn and re-turn, and who make knots and undo them. Men of your large profession give forkéd-tongued, ambiguous counsel. They take provoking gold [Mosca thought, *Either they take a bribe, or they take money to petition a judge to take up a case*] from either side of a dispute, and put it away in their pocket. These men, he knew, would thrive with their humility [Mosca thought sarcastically, *They must be humble because, like beggars, they accept money from anyone*], and for his part, he thought he would be blest to have his heir of such a suffering spirit, so wise, so grave, of so perplexed a tongue, and also so loud, which would not wag, nor scarcely lie still, without a fee, when every word your worship lets fall is a chequin!"

Mosca's "praise" of the legal profession was hardly praise. A lawyer's tongue would scarcely lie still — either not move at all or be constantly lying — without a fee. A chequin is a Venetian gold coin.

Loud knocking sounded at the door.

Mosca said, "Who's that? Someone is knocking. I would not have you seen, sir. And yet — pretend you came and went in haste. I'll make up an excuse.

"And, gentle sir, when you come to swim in golden lard, up to the arms in honey, so that your chin is held up stiff, with the fatness — richness — of the flood, think about me, your vassal. Just remember me. I have not been your worst of clients."

Mosca was telling Voltore that soon Voltore would be up to his chin in riches and that he hoped that Voltore would remember him. Once Voltore inherited Volpone's wealth, Mosca would be out of a job.

Voltore said, "Mosca!"

Mosca asked, "When will you have your inventory brought, sir? Or see a copy of the will?"

The inventory was of Volpone's goods, goods that Voltore thought he would soon inherit.

The knocking continued, and Mosca shouted, "Coming!"

Mosca then said to Voltore, "I will bring them to you, sir. Leave, be gone, look serious as if you were doing business here."

Voltore exited.

Volpone jumped out of bed and said, "Excellent Mosca! Come here, and let me kiss you."

"Keep still, sir," Mosca said, looking out of a window. "Corbaccio is here to see you."

Volpone said, "Put the plate away. The vulture's gone, and the old raven's come!"

Mosca put the plate on the treasure chest, where it was visible, and said to the plate, "Betake you to your silence, and your sleep. Stand there and multiply."

Mosca was parodying part of Genesis 1:28:

And God blessed them, and God said unto them, Be fruitful, and multiply, and replenish the earth, and subdue it: and have dominion over the fish of the sea, and over the fowl of the air, and over every living thing that moveth upon the earth. (King James Version)

One meaning of "stand" in Elizabethan and Jacobean English was "to have an erection."

Mosca thought, *Now, we shall see a wretch who is indeed more impotent than this wretch — Volpone — can feign to be, yet the first wretch hopes to hop over the second wretch's grave.*

Volpone was pretending to be so ill that he was impotent, but Corbaccio was an old man who really was impotent.

If Corbaccio were more intelligent, he would realize that he was much more likely than Volpone to die first.

Corbaccio entered the room. *Corbaccio* is Italian for "raven."

Mosca greeted him: "Signior Corbaccio! You're very welcome, sir."

Corbaccio asked, "How is Volpone, your patron?"

"Indeed, just as he was before," Mosca said. "He has not gotten better."

Corbaccio, an old man who was hard of hearing, asked, "What! Is he getting better?"

"No, sir. He's rather worse," Mosca said.

Corbaccio, who hoped to inherit Volpone's goods, said, "That's good. Where is he?"

"Upon his couch, sir, newly fallen asleep," Mosca said.

Volpone was using the couch as a daybed.

"Does he sleep well?" Corbaccio asked.

"Not a wink, sir, all this night," Mosca said. "Nor did he sleep yesterday. He only dozes."

"Good!" Corbaccio said. "He should take some advice from physicians. I have brought him an opiate here, from my own doctor."

"He will not hear of drugs," Mosca said. "He refuses to take them."

"Why?" Corbaccio said. "I myself stood by while it was made, I saw all the ingredients, and I know that it cannot but most gently work. I would bet my life against his that the purpose of this potion is just to make him sleep."

Lying on the couch, Volpone thought, *Yes, to make him sleep his last sleep — the eternal sleep — if he would take it.*

"Sir," Mosca said, "he has no faith in medicine."

"What did you say?" Corbaccio asked. "What did you say?"

"He has no faith in medicine," Mosca repeated. "He thinks that doctors are the greater danger, and the worse disease, to escape. I often have heard him protest that a physician should never be his heir."

A proverb stated that only a fool would make his physician his heir.

The hard-of-hearing Corbaccio asked, "I won't be his heir?"

"No, a physician will not be his heir, sir," Mosca said.

"Oh, no, no, no," Corbaccio said. "I do not intend for a physician to be his heir."

"No, sir," Mosca said, "and he says that he cannot endure their fees. He says that they financially flay a man before they kill him."

"Right," Corbaccio said. "I understand you."

"And then they do it by experimenting with 'cures' on the patient," Mosca said, "for which the law not only absolves them, but gives them great reward, and he is loath to pay a doctor to kill him."

"It is true," Corbaccio said. "Doctors kill with as much license as a judge."

"No, with even more license than a judge," Mosca said. "A judge kills, sir, only when the law condemns a man to death, but a doctor can kill even a judge when the judge is the doctor's patient."

"Yes," Corbaccio said, "or the doctor can kill me or any other man."

He then asked about Volpone's health, "How is his apoplexy? Is that strong on him still?"

Apoplexy is the condition of incapacity that follows having suffered a stroke. Strong apoplexy is deadly.

"Very violent," Mosca said. "His speech is broken, and his eyes are set and staring. His face is drawn longer than it was accustomed to be."

"What? What? He is stronger than he was accustomed to be?" Corbaccio asked, mishearing.

"No, sir," Mosca said. "His face is drawn longer than it was accustomed to be."

"Oh, good!" Corbaccio said. He wanted Volpone to die soon.

Mosca said, "His mouth is always open and gaping, and his eyelids hang."

"Good," Corbaccio said.

"A freezing numbness stiffens all his joints," Mosca said, "and makes the color of his flesh like lead."

"That is good," Corbaccio said.

"His pulse beats slowly, and dully."

"These are all good symptoms, still," Corbaccio said.

Mosca said, "And from his brain —"

"I understand you," Corbaccio interrupted. "Good."

Mosca continued, "— flows a cold sweat, with a continual watery discharge from the sagging corners of his eyes."

Discharge from the brain was a sign of imminent death.

"Is it possible?" Corbaccio said. "Despite my old age, I am in better shape than he is, ha!"

He then asked, "How fares Volpone with the swimming of his head?"

"Oh, sir, he has gone past the dizziness and dimness of vision," Mosca said. "He has gotten worse. He now has lost his feeling, and he has stopped snoring. You can hardly perceive that he breathes."

"Excellent, excellent!" Corbaccio said. "Surely I shall outlast him. This makes me young again by a score of years. I feel twenty years younger."

"I was coming for you, sir," Mosca said.

This could mean that he was coming to bring Corbaccio to Volpone's deathbed, or that he was setting a trap for Corbaccio.

"Has Volpone made his will?" Corbaccio asked. "What has he given me?"

"No, sir," Mosca said, answering the first question.

Thinking that Mosca was answering the second question, the hard-of-hearing Corbaccio said, "Nothing! What!"

Mosca clarified, "Volpone has not made his will, sir."

"Oh! Oh! Oh!" Corbaccio said. "But why was Voltore, the lawyer, here?"

"He smelled a carcass, sir, when he heard that my master was thinking about his testament," Mosca said. "I urged Volpone to make his last will and testament for your good."

"Voltore came to Volpone, did he?" Corbaccio said. "I thought so."

"Yes," Mosca said, "and Voltore presented Volpone with this piece of plate."

"In order to be his heir?" Corbaccio asked.

"I do not know, sir," Mosca replied.

"True," Corbaccio said, mishearing. "I know it, too."

Mosca thought, *Yes, you would think that Voltore gave the plate in order to become Volpone's heir. You are judging Voltore by your own scale. You are thinking that Voltore is doing what you are doing. Of course, you are correct.*

Corbaccio said, "Well, I shall yet prevent him from succeeding. See, Mosca, look. I have brought here a bag of bright chequins that will quite weigh down his plate."

He meant that the bag of gold coins was more valuable than the plate that Voltore had given to Volpone.

Taking the bag of gold coins, Mosca said, "Yes, indeed, sir. This is truly health-giving; this is your sacred medicine. Opiates do not compare to this great elixir!"

An elixir was a health potion. Alchemists sought to create the Elixir of Life, which was thought to make humans live very long lives, and perhaps forever.

Corbaccio said, "It is *aurum palpabile*, if not *potabile*."

These are Latin terms. *Aurum palpabile* is touchable gold; *aurum potabile* is drinkable gold. *Aurum potabile* was a drink containing gold; it was thought to promote health.

Mosca joked, "It shall be administered to him in his bowl."

He was joking that he would pour the gold coins into Volpone's bowl so that Volpone could eat them and restore his health.

"Yes, do, do, do," Corbaccio said.

"This is a very blessed cordial!" Mosca said. "This will restore his health."

"Yes, do, do, do," Corbaccio said.

"I think it were not best, sir," Mosca said.

"To do what?" Corbaccio asked.

"To restore Volpone's health."

"Oh, no, no, no," Corbaccio said. "By no means."

Mosca said, "Why, sir, this bag of gold coins will work some strange effect on Volpone, if he would feel it."

"That is true," Corbaccio said. "Therefore, let's not let him feel it. I'll take my bag of gold coins. Give it back to me."

"By no means," Mosca said, "pardon me."

He meant for "By no means" to be an introductory element, but "By no means pardon me" was good advice.

He added, "You shall not do yourself that wrong, sir. I will so advise you that you shall inherit *all* of Volpone's wealth."

"What!" Corbaccio asked.

"All of it, sir," Mosca said. "It is your right, your own. No man can claim a part of Volpone's wealth. It is yours, without a rival, and decreed by destiny."

"How, how, good Mosca?" Corbaccio asked.

"I'll tell you, sir," Mosca said. "He shall recover from this fit."

"I understand," Corbaccio said.

"And, at the first opportunity after he has regained his senses, I will importune him to make his last will and testament, and I will show him this bag of gold coins."

"Good, good," Corbaccio said.

"It will be better yet," Mosca said, "if you will listen to me, sir."

"Yes, with all my heart," Corbaccio said.

"Now, I advise you to speedily go home. There, make a will in which you shall inscribe my master as your sole heir."

"And disinherit my son!" Corbaccio said.

"Oh, sir, it is all for the better," Mosca said. "This new will shall have an outward appearance that conceals the truth in order to make this trick much more plausible."

"Oh, so the new will is only a trick?" Corbaccio said.

Mosca said, "This will, sir, you shall send to me. Now, when I come to emphasize, as I will, your cares, your watchings at Volpone's sickbed, and your many prayers for him, your more than many gifts, and your this day's present, and finally, I produce your will — where, without thought or the least regard for your legitimate son, a son so brave and highly meriting, the stream of your diverted love has thrown you upon my master and made him your heir, Volpone cannot be so stupid, or stone dead, but out of conscience, and complete gratitude —"

Corbaccio interrupted: "— he must pronounce me his heir."

"That is true," Mosca said.

Corbaccio said, "I have thought of this plot previously."

"I believe it," Mosca said, flattering Corbaccio.

The hard-of-hearing Corbaccio asked, "Don't you believe it?"

"Yes, sir," Mosca said. He really did not believe it.

"My own plot," Corbaccio said.

Mosca said, "Which, when he has done, sir —"

Corbaccio interrupted, "Made me his heir?"

Mosca said, "And you so certain to survive him —"

"Yes," Corbaccio said.

Mosca said, "Being so lusty a man —"

One meaning of "lusty" was healthy; the other meaning definitely did not apply to Corbaccio because he was impotent.

"That is true," Corbaccio replied to Mosca.

"Yes, sir," Mosca said.

Corbaccio said, "I thought of that, too. You, Mosca, are the exact instrument that expresses my thoughts!"

Mosca began, "You have not only done yourself a good —"

Corbaccio interrupted: "— but multiplied it on my son."

Corbaccio thought that he would outlive Volpone, and so Corbaccio's son would inherit Volpone's wealth as well as Corbaccio's wealth.

"That is right, sir," Mosca said.

"This is still what I have plotted previously," Corbaccio said.

Mosca said, "Alas, sir! Heaven knows that it has been all my concern, all my care — I even grow gray from it — how to work things —"

"I understand, sweet Mosca," Corbaccio said.

"You are the man for whom I labor here," Mosca said.

"Yes, do, do, do," Corbaccio said. "I'll see to the will immediately."

He started for the door.

Mosca said quietly so that Volpone but not Corbaccio could hear him, "May a rook go with you, raven!"

This meant, *May you — who are the raven — be rooked, aka cheated.*

Corbaccio said to Mosca, "I know that you are honest."

Mosca said quietly so that Volpone but not Corbaccio could hear him, "You lie, sir!"

Corbaccio said, "And —"

Mosca finished the sentence quietly so that Volpone but not Corbaccio could hear him, "— your knowledge is no better than your ears, sir."

Corbaccio said, "I do not doubt that I will be a father to you."

Corbaccio was a father who was going home to write a will that disinherited his son.

Mosca said quietly so that Volpone but not Corbaccio could hear him, "Nor do I doubt that I will cheat my brother out of his blessing."

Mosca intended to cheat Corbaccio's son out of his inheritance, and so if Corbaccio were Mosca's father, then Mosca would be cheating his brother out of his inheritance.

In Genesis 27, Jacob cheats Esau, his brother, out of their father's blessing.

Corbaccio said, "I may have my youth restored to me. Why not?"

Mosca said quietly so that Volpone but not Corbaccio could hear him, "Your worship is a precious ass!"

"What did you say?" Corbaccio asked.

Mosca replied, "I desire your worship to make haste, sir."

"It is done," Corbaccio said. "It is done. I am going."

He exited.

Volpone leapt out of bed and said, "Oh, I shall burst with laughter! Loosen my clothing so I can laugh! Loosen my clothing!"

Mosca said, "Contain your flux of laughter, sir."

"Flux" means both "flood" and "dysentery." The illness dysentery results in a flood of bloody diarrhea.

Mosca added, "You know this hope of inheriting all your wealth is such a bait that it covers any hook."

Volpone said, "Oh, but the way you work with the bait, and the way that you place it in front of them! I cannot hold back my good feelings. Good rascal, let me kiss you. I have never known you to be in so rare a humor. I have never seen you be so effective in trapping suckers — you are in excellent form!"

"I do not deserve such praise, sir," Mosca said. "I am only doing as I have been taught. I follow your grave instructions: I trick them with words, I pour oily flattery into their ears, and I send them away."

"It is true! It is true!" Volpone said. "What a rare punishment is avarice to itself! A greedy man punishes himself!"

"Yes, with our help, sir," Mosca said.

Volpone said, "So many cares and worries, so many maladies, so many fears attend on old age, yes, that death is so often called on, as no wish other than for death can be more frequent with old men. Their limbs are weak, their senses are dull, and their seeing, hearing, and walking are all dead before them. Yes, even their teeth, their instruments of eating, fail them. Yet this is reckoned life!

"Just now, here was an old man, who has now gone home, who wishes to live longer! He does 'not' feel his gout or his palsy. He pretends to himself that he is younger by scores of years. He flatters his age by confidently lying about it. He hopes that he may, with the use of magic charms, like Aeson, have his youth restored."

Aeson was the father of Jason, leader of the Argonauts. Medea, a young witch, helped Jason get the Golden Fleece. Medea and Jason then married, and Medea used magic to restore Aeson's youth.

Volpone continued, "And with these thoughts he so fattens himself, as if fate would be as easily cheated as he himself, and all turns to air! He regards old age as a delusion!"

Knocking sounded at the door.

Volpone asked, "Who's that there, now? A third visitor?"

Mosca said, "Quiet. Get into your bed again. I hear the visitor's voice. He is Corvino, our spruce, dapper, well-dressed merchant."

Volpone lay down on the bed and said, "I am 'dead.'"

Mosca said, "Let's have another bout, sir, with your eyes."

He used the ointment again to make Volpone's eyes look like those of a very ill man.

Mosca asked loudly, "Who's there?

Corvino entered the room. *Corvino* is Italian for "crow."

Mosca said, "Signior Corvino! You have come when you were most wished for! Oh, how happy would you be, if you knew it, now!"

Corvino asked, "Why? What? Wherein?"

"The tardy hour has come, sir," Mosca said.

"Volpone is not dead, is he?" Corvino asked.

"He is not dead, sir, but he is as good as dead," Mosca replied. "He knows no man."

Corvino asked, "What shall I do then?"

"What do you mean, sir?" Mosca asked.

"I have brought him here a pearl as a gift," Corvino said.

If Volpone could not recognize Corvino, Corvino would get no credit for giving him a valuable gift.

Mosca said, "Perhaps he has enough remembrance left as to know you, sir. He continually calls for you. Nothing but your name is in his mouth.

"Is your pearl orient, sir?"

Pearls from the orient were the most valuable.

"Venice was never owner of the like," Corvino said.

Volpone said faintly, "Signior Corvino."

"Listen," Mosca said.

Volpone again said faintly, "Signior Corvino."

Mosca said, "He calls you; step over to him and give him the pearl."

Mosca said to Volpone, "Signior Corvino is here, sir, and he has brought you a rich pearl."

Corvino gave the pearl to Volpone, who grabbed it and held it tightly.

Corvino said to Volpone, "How are you, sir?"

He then said to Mosca, "Tell Volpone that the pearl doubles the twelfth carat."

The pearl's size was twenty-four carats; it was a very large and very valuable pearl.

"Sir, he cannot understand; his hearing's gone, and yet it comforts him to see you."

Corvino said, "Say that I have a diamond for him, too."

Mosca said, "It's best for you to show it, sir. Put it into his hand; it is only there he apprehends. He has his feeling, yet."

Volpone grabbed the diamond.

Mosca said, "See how he grasps it!"

"Alas, good gentleman!" Corvino said. "How pitiful the sight is!"

"Tut!" Mosca said, "You forget, sir. The weeping of an heir should always be laughter under a mask."

"Why, am I his heir?" Corvino asked.

Mosca replied, "Sir, I am sworn. I may not show you the will until Volpone is dead, but here has been Corbaccio, here has been Voltore, here have been others, too. I cannot number them because they were so many. All of them had their mouths open hoping for legacies: They all want to inherit Volpone's wealth. But I, taking the opportunity given by his calling for you — 'Signior Corvino, Signior Corvino' — took paper, and pen, and ink, and there I asked him whom he would have to be his heir? 'Corvino.' Who should be his executor? 'Corvino.' And, to any question he was silent to, I always interpreted the nods he made, through weakness and palsy, for consent, and I sent home the others, with nothing bequeathed to them, except a reason to cry and curse."

According to Mosca's story, Volpone's illness included palsy, which made him nod. Although the nods were involuntary movements caused by the palsy, Mosca had always interpreted them as being voluntary acknowledgments that Volpone wanted Corvino to be his heir and the executor of his will.

Corvino said, "Oh, my dear Mosca!"

He hugged him.

Corvino asked, "Doesn't he perceive us?"

"No more than a blind harper would," Mosca replied.

A blind harper such as the epic poet Homer, who strummed a lyre as he sang his poems, would perceive quite a lot.

Mosca continued, "He knows no man, no face of friend, nor name of any servant, nor who fed him last or gave him something to drink. Not even those he has begotten, or brought up, can he remember."

"Has he children?" Corvino asked.

"Bastards," Mosca said. "Some dozen, or more, whom he begot on beggars, gypsies, and Jews, and blacks, when he was drunk. Didn't you know that, sir?

It is the common talk of the town. The dwarf, the Fool, and the eunuch in this house are all his. He's the true biological father of his family, in all, except me — but he has given them nothing."

"That's good, that's good," Corvino said. "Are you sure he doesn't hear us?"

"Am I sure, sir?" Mosca said. "Why, look and listen, then give credit to your own senses."

Mosca shouted in Volpone's ear, "May the pox — syphilis — approach, and add to your diseases, if it would send you into the hereafter sooner, sir, because your sexual incontinence has deserved syphilis through and through, and thoroughly, and it deserves the plague to boot!"

What Mosca said about Volpone's sexual incontinence may be true, but Volpone was pretending to be so ill that he is incapable of sexual incontinence.

Mosca said to Corvino, "You may come close, sir."

Mosca shouted in Volpone's ear, "I wish that you would once and for all close those filthy eyes of yours that flow with slime like two frog-ponds, and I wish the termination of those same hanging cheeks that are covered with hide instead of skin —"

Mosca said to Corvino, "Help me, sir."

Mosca continued, "— and that look like frozen dishrags set on end!"

Corvino said loudly, "Or that look like an old smoked wall, on which the rain ran down in streaks!"

"Excellent! Sir, speak out," Mosca said. "You may be louder still. A firearm discharged in his ear would hardly penetrate it and make itself heard."

Corvino shouted, "His nose is like a common sewer, always running."

"That is good!" Mosca said. "And what about his mouth?"

"It is a complete cesspool," Corvino said.

"Oh, stop his mouth," Mosca said. "Suffocate him."

"By no means," Corvino said. "No way."

"Please let me do it," Mosca said. "Truly, I could stifle him excellently with a pillow — as well as any woman could who should look after him."

"Do as you will," Corvino said, "but I'll be gone."

Corvino did not want to witness the murder.

"Do as you wish," Mosca said. "It is your presence that makes him last so long."

"Please use no violence," Corvino said.

"No?" Mosca said. "Sir, why not? Why should you have such scruples, sir?"

"Use your discretion," Corvino said.

Mosca had called Corvino's bluff. Corvino did not mind if Mosca were to murder Volpone, but Corvino did not want to witness it or get in legal trouble for it.

"Well, good sir, leave," Mosca said.

Corvino said, "Shouldn't I trouble Volpone now and take my pearl back?"

Mosca said, "Pooh! Nor your diamond."

Mosca meant that Corvino should not trouble Volpone by taking his pearl and diamond back again.

Mosca said, "What a needless worry is this that afflicts you? Isn't everything that is here yours?"

If Corvino were Volpone's heir, as Corvino supposed, Corvino would inherit all of Volpone's wealth, including the diamond and pearl that Volpone was holding.

Mosca said, "Am not I here, whom you have made your servant? Am I not here, who owe my being to you?"

Mosca had stated that he was willing to murder Volpone for Corvino. If this happened, Corvino would get back his two jewels quickly.

"Grateful Mosca!" Corvino said. "You are my friend, my fellow, my companion, and my partner, and you shall share in all my fortunes."

"Excepting one," Mosca said.

"What's that?" Corvino said.

"Your gorgeous wife, sir."

Corvino immediately exited. He was a jealous man, and he was leaving to check up on his wife. Soon, however, he would be willing to allow Volpone to sleep with his wife if it would get him Volpone's wealth. Because he was willing to allow Volpone to cuckold him, it is appropriate that he gave Volpone a diamond and a pearl — two precious stones. In this society, testicles were called stones. They are still known as the family jewels.

Mosca said, "Now he is gone. We had no other way to shoo him away from here, but this."

"My divine Mosca!" Volpone said. "You have outdone yourself today!"

Knocking sounded on the door.

Volpone said, "Who's there? I will be troubled with no more visitors. Prepare for me music, dances, banquets, and all delights. The Turk is not more sensual in his pleasures than Volpone will be."

The Turk was Mahomet III, the Ottoman Sultan, who was also known as the Grand Turk. He was known for taking great delight in sensual, including sexual, pleasures.

Mosca exited.

Volpone looked over the morning's profits, saying, "Let me see. A pearl! A diamond! Plate! Gold coins! A good morning's haul! Why, this is better than robbing churches, even. Or getting fat, by eating, once a month, a man."

The eating of a man was metaphorical. He was referring to devouring a man by collecting the interest each month on usurious loans, or by grinding down the man through excessive hard work. One man's ruin can be another man's source of wealth.

Mosca returned.

"Who is it?" Volpone asked.

"'The beauteous Lady Politic Would-be, sir. Wife to the English knight, Sir Politic Would-be.' These are the exact words I have been demanded to say to you. She has sent a squire to learn how you slept last night and to ask whether you would be willing to entertain visitors."

"Not now," Volpone said. "She can visit me some three hours from now."

"I told the squire as much," Mosca said.

Volpone said, "When I am high with mirth and wine, then, then.

"Before Heaven, I wonder at the desperate valor of the bold English, that they dare let loose their wives to all encounters!"

Venetian men such as Corvino kept a close eye on their wives; in contrast, Englishmen such as Sir Politic Would-be gave their wives free rein.

Mosca said, "Sir, this knight had his name not for nothing. He is politic and cunning, and knows, however his wife may affect strange airs, she hasn't the face to be dishonest."

In other words, the knight's wife's face was not pretty enough to have an affair.

He continued, "But if she had Signior Corvino's wife's face ..."

"Has she so excellent a face?" Volpone asked.

"Oh, sir, her face is the wonder, the blazing star of Italy!" Mosca said. "She is a wench of the first year! She is a beauty as ripe as harvest! Her skin is whiter than a swan all over; it is whiter than silver, snow, or lilies! She has a soft lip that would tempt you to an eternity of kissing! And she has flesh that melts in the touch to blood!"

Touching her skin would make her blush — or grow hot with sexual passion.

Mosca continued, likening her to what Volpone loved best: "She is as bright as your gold, and as lovely as your gold!"

"Why haven't I known this before?" Volpone asked.

"Alas, sir," Mosca said. "I myself discovered it only yesterday."

"How might I see her?" Volpone asked.

"Oh, that is not possible," Mosca said. "She's guarded as warily as is your gold. She never goes out of doors and never gets fresh air except at a window. All her looks are sweet as the first grapes or cherries, and her looks are watched as closely as the first grapes or cherries are."

The first grapes or cherries are watched very carefully to ensure that the crop is harvested at the best time.

"I must see her," Volpone said.

"Sir, there is a guard of spies ten thick upon her," Mosca said. "The spies are Corvino's whole household. Each spy is set to spy upon his fellow, and all the spies have their orders to spy upon his wife. When Corvino leaves or enters his home, he has his spies report to him."

"I will go see her, though but at her window," Volpone said.

"If you do, wear some disguise, then," Mosca said.

"That is true," Volpone said. "I must maintain my pretense of being a seriously ill man. We'll think about which disguise I can use."

CHAPTER 2

— 2.1 —

At Saint Mark's Place, at a corner near Corvino's house, Sir Politic Would-be and Peregrine were talking. Both were travelers from England, and they had just met. In fact, Peregrine had just disembarked on this day.

Sir Politic Would-be said, "Sir, to a wise man, all the world's his soil, aka country."

A proverb states, "A wise man may live anywhere."

He continued, "It is not Italy, nor France, nor Europe, that must bound me, if my fates call me forth. Yet, I protest, it is no salty, wanton desire of seeing countries, changing my religious affiliation, or suffering any disaffection to the state of England, where I was bred and to which I owe my dearest projects, that has brought me out of England, much less Ulysses' idle, antique, stale, gray-headed project of knowing men's minds and manners!"

Ulysses was the Roman name of Odysseus, hero of Homer's *Odyssey*. In the beginning of the *Odyssey*, we learn that Odysseus has traveled to many lands and learned the minds of many men. Learning the minds of many men is a very good reason to travel.

Sir Politic Would-be continued, "Instead, a peculiar humor, aka inclination or whim, of my wife's laid for this height of Venice."

Venice is definitely at sea level; Sir Politic Would-be liked to use fancy language, and he was using "height" to mean "latitude."

He continued, "We came to observe, to make notes, to learn the language, and so forth."

He paused and then asked, "I hope you travel, sir, with license?"

English travelers were required to get a permit from the Privy Council to travel aboard. Some travelers did not do this.

"Yes," Peregrine replied.

"Since you have a permit, I dare the more safely to converse with you," Sir Politic Would-be said.

English travelers with licenses were not supposed to talk to English travelers without licenses.

He then asked, "How long, sir, has it been since you left England?"

"Seven weeks."

"You left so recently!" Sir Politic Would-be said. "You have not been with my lord ambassador?"

English travelers with permits were required to be presented to the English lord ambassador.

"Not yet, sir," Peregrine replied.

"Please," Sir Politic Would-be said, "tell me what news, sir, vents our climate?"

"Vents our climate" was a fancy way of saying "comes from England."

He continued, "I heard last night a very strange thing reported by some of my lord ambassador's followers, and I long to hear how it will be seconded."

By "seconded," he meant "confirmed."

"What was it, sir?" Peregrine asked.

Sir Politic Would-be whispered as if he were imparting a secret, "Indeed, sir, the news was of a raven that was said to have built a nest in a ship royal of the King's."

A raven was thought to be an omen of evil, and the building of a nest on a ship was also thought to be a bad omen. However, these were superstitions, and Peregrine marveled at how seriously Sir Politic Would-be was taking them.

Peregrine thought to himself, *This fellow, is he trying to trick me and make me look like a fool, or has he himself been tricked and made to look like a fool, do you suppose? Sir Politic Would-be is either trying to make me a fool, or he is a fool himself.*

He asked, "What is your name, sir?"

"My name is Politic Would-be."

Peregrine thought, *Oh, his name sums him up. He wants people to think that he is in the know about political matters, including political intrigues. But if he takes these superstitions seriously, he can't be in the know. He is a fool, and that gives me license to make fun of him.*

He asked, "Are you a knight, sir?"

Sir Politic Would-be wore spurs, although in Venice there was no use for spurs.

"I am a poor knight, sir," Sir Politic Would-be replied.

Peregrine was likely to agree.

Peregrine said, "Is your lady lying — staying — here in Venice to acquire knowledge of fashions of clothing, including headdresses, and behavior, among the courtesans? Is she the fine Lady Would-be?"

Venetian courtesans were renowned for their fashionable clothing and courteous conversation.

Sir Politic Would-be said, "Yes, sir; the spider and the bee often suck from one and the same flower."

He did not say which — his wife or the courtesan — was the spider and which was the bee, but apparently he meant that his wife could learn from the courtesans without having any of the reputation of the courtesans rub off on her. This may not be a good thing since in some circles the courtesans had an excellent reputation.

"Good Sir Politic Would-be," Peregrine said, "I beg your pardon. I have heard much about you. What you said about the raven is true."

"You know that for a fact?" Sir Politic asked.

"Yes," Peregrine replied, "and I know about the lion's whelping in the Tower of London."

Lions were kept in the Tower of London, and a lioness named Elizabeth whelped on 5 August 1604 and on 26 February 1605. Such births to cubs in the Tower of London were unprecedented.

"Another whelp!" Sir Politic Would-be exclaimed.

"Yes, another, sir," Peregrine said.

"Now, by Heaven, what prodigies are these? We have also had the fires at Berwick and the new star!"

On 19 July 1333, the Battle of Halidon Hill occurred, in which the army of King Edward III of England defeated the Scottish army of Sir Archibald Douglas. A letter written on 15 January 1605 described a recently witnessed spectral battle between two armies in the sky above Halidon Hill, which is near Berwick. Today, we think that superstitious people witnessed the aurora borealis.

On 30 September 1604, a supernova appeared in the sky and remained visible for seventeen months.

Superstitious people regarded such unusual things appearing in the sky as ominous.

Sir Politic Would-be continued, "All these things happened at the same time; this is strange and full of omen! Did you witness those atmospheric phenomena?"

"I did, sir," Peregrine replied.

"They are fearsome signs!" Sir Politic Would-be said. "Please, sir, confirm this for me, if you can. Were three porpoises seen above the London Bridge, as has been reported?"

On 19 January 1606, a porpoise was captured in a small creek where no one would expect a porpoise to be, but it was captured below London Bridge. Peregrine knew that only one porpoise had been captured, but he was willing to have fun at Sir Politic Would-be's expense.

Peregrine replied, "Six porpoises, and a sturgeon, sir."

Actually, sturgeons were commonly found in the Thames River at the time.

"I am astonished," Sir Politic Would-be said.

"Sir, don't be astonished," Peregrine said. "I'll tell you a greater prodigy than these."

"What should these things portend?" Sir Politic Would-be asked. "They must foretell important events."

Peregrine said, "The very day — let me be sure — that I put forth from London, a whale was discovered in the river, as high as Woolwich, that had waited there, few know how many months, for the subversion of the Stode fleet."

Ships belonging to the English Merchant Adventurer's fleet were at Stade (then known at Stode), located northwest of Hamburg, Germany. A few days after the porpoise mentioned previously was captured, a whale was sighted in the Thames River at Woolwich, eight miles from London. "To subvert" is "to destroy completely." What connection a whale in the Thames River could have with the complete destruction of a fleet of English ships at Stade, Germany, is something that needs explanation.

"Is it possible?" Sir Politic Would-be said. "Yes, believe that it is possible. The whale was either sent from Spain, or the archdukes. It is Spinola's whale, upon my life and my reputation! Won't the Spaniards cease these projects that attempt to destroy England?"

At this time, England and Spain were at peace, due to a peace treaty signed in 1604, but Sir Politic Would-be was still suspicious of Spaniards. He thought that the whale could have come directly from Spain or from the archdukes. The archdukes were Albert of Austria and his wife, the Infanta Isabella, who ruled the Spanish Netherlands. ("Infanta" means daughter of the King of Spain.) Ambrogio Spinola commanded the Spanish army that was located in the Netherlands. In reality he was a very successful commander, but some credulous people believed that he was a military mastermind who thought of having a whale swim up the Thames River to London, where it would take in water and then spout the water over London, drowning the city.

Sir Politic Would-be said, "Worthy sir, please give me some other news."

Peregrine said, "Indeed, Stone the Fool is dead, and the people he entertained lack a tavern fool extremely."

Stone the Fool, the court jester of King James I of England, had been whipped in the spring of 1605 for making jokes about the Lord Admiral, who had been part of the English delegation to end the Anglo-Spanish War, which had lasted for nineteen years. Professional Fools were supposed to have immunity to such punishment, but occasionally one went too far.

"Is Master Stone dead?" Sir Politic Would-be asked.

"He's dead, sir," Peregrine replied. "Why, I hope that you didn't think him to be immortal?"

He thought, *Oh, this knight, if he were well known, would be a precious thing to put on our English stage, but anyone who would write such a character would be thought to feign extremely, if not maliciously. Such a character as Sir Politic Would-be would not be believed.*

"Stone dead!" Sir Politic Would-be said.

"Dead," Peregrine said. "Lord, how deeply, sir, you apprehend it! You feel it deeply, sir. Was he a kinsman of yours?"

"Not that I know of," Sir Politic Would-be said. "Well! That same fellow was an unknown Fool."

He meant that people really did not know Stone the Fool; Stone the Fool kept his real character secret.

"And yet you knew him, it seems?" Peregrine asked.

"I did know him," Sir Politic Would-be said. "Sir, I knew him to have one of the most dangerous heads living within the state, and so I held him."

"Indeed, sir?"

"While he lived, he actively took action against the interests of England. He received weekly intelligence reports, upon my knowledge, out of the Low Countries, for all parts of the world, secreted in cabbages. And those intelligence reports he dispensed again to ambassadors, in oranges, melons, apricots, lemons, citrons, and such-like foods for the upper class. Sometimes he hid the intelligence reports in oysters from Colchester and cockles from Selsey."

"You make me marvel," Peregrine said.

"Sir, I say these things upon my knowledge," Sir Politic Would-be said. "I've observed him, at your public tavern, take his instructions in a plate of food from a traveller who was a secret agent, and immediately, before the meal was done, convey an answer in a toothpick."

"Strange!" Peregrine said. "How could this be done, sir?"

"Why, the meat was cut so like his code, and so laid, as he must easily read the cipher," Sir Politic Would-be said.

A fashion of the time was to cut food into strange shapes, sometimes including the shapes of letters. Sir Politic Would-be was claiming that Stone the Fool's food had been cut in such a way that it contained a secret message in the form of a cipher, aka secret code.

He didn't explain how an answer could be conveyed in a toothpick.

"I have heard," Peregrine said, "that Stone the Fool could not read, sir."

"That misinformation was cunningly spread as part of a plan by those who employed him," Sir Politic Would-be said, "but he could read, and he knew many languages, and to add to these things, he had as sound a noggin —"

Peregrine interrupted, "I have heard, sir, that baboons were spies, and that they were a kind of cunning nation near China."

Sir Politic Would-be agreed: "Yes, yes. They are known as the Mamuluchi. Indeed, they had their hand in a French plot or two, but they were so extremely given to women that they revealed everything, yet I received intelligence and news here, on Wednesday last, from someone on their side, that they were returned, made their reports, as the fashion is, and now stand ready for fresh employment."

Actually, the Mamuluchi had nothing to do with either baboons or China, but Sir Politic Would-be wanted to appear to be in the know. What he called the Mamuluchi were actually the Mamelukes; they were former slaves who in

1254 seized power in Egypt and who beginning in 1517 ruled Egypt under an Ottoman viceroy. Many powerful Mamelukes were eunuchs, not womanizers.

"By God's heart!" Peregrine said.

He thought, *This Sir Pol will admit to ignorance of nothing.*

"Pol" is short for "politician" or "parrot." A parrot speaks without understanding, as do many politicians.

Peregrine said, "It seems, sir, you know all."

"Not all, sir, but I have some general notions," Sir Politic Would-be said. "I love to note and to observe. Although I live outside of London, free from the active torrent, yet I wish to mark the currents and the passages of things for my own private use, and I want to know the ebbs and flows of state."

"Believe, sir," Peregrine said, flattering Sir Politic Would-be, "that I hold myself in no small obligation to my good fortune for casting me thus luckily upon you, whose knowledge, if your generosity in imparting it equal it, may do me great assistance in instruction for my behavior and my bearing, which are still so rude and raw."

"Why, have you come forth out of England without knowledge of the rules for travel?" Sir Politic Would-be asked.

"Indeed, I had some common rules from out of that vulgar grammar that he who cried Italian to me, taught me," Peregrine said.

The grammar was vulgar because it was written in the vulgar, aka common, language: Italian, not Latin. Peregrine said that the writer "cried" rather than "taught" Italian because Italian is an expressive language.

"Why, this is what spoils all our brave young bloods," Sir Politic Would-be said. "We entrust our hopeful gentry — our splendid young gentlemen — to pedants, who are fellows of exterior surface, and mere bark, aka shell. They have nothing worthwhile inside. You seem to be a gentleman of noble race. I do not teach my knowledge professionally, but my fate has been to be where I have been consulted with in matters of this high kind, touching some great men's sons, who are persons of good blood and honor."

He was saying that he had imparted his important knowledge to other young gentlemen.

Mosca and Nano the dwarf, wearing disguises, arrived, carrying material for erecting a temporary stage. Their disguises were those of zanies — the mountebank's assistants, who would also perform. Some curious people followed them.

Peregrine asked, "Who are these people, sir?"

He was either asking about the gentlemen to whom Sir Politic Would-be had claimed to impart his important knowledge, or he was asking about the newly arrived people.

Mosca said, "Under that window, there the stage must be."

Nano the dwarf pointed to a window, and Mosca said, "The same."

The window was part of Corvino's residence.

Sir Politic Would-be said, "These are fellows who will mount a bank. Didn't your instructor in the valuable languages ever discourse to you about the Italian mountebanks?"

A mountebank is someone like the proprietor of an American medicine show. The term "mountebank" originated in the late 16th century. It comes from the Italian *montambanco*, which in turn comes from *monta in banco!* This means, "Climb on the bench!" Often, the mountebank would stand on a bench or other raised platform while performing and while selling his medicine.

Mountebanks would mount a *bank* — climb upon a temporary stage, which was often made of a bench or benches — and entertain the crowd of people who would gather. The mountebanks would then sell the crowd of people quack medicines.

"Yes, sir," Peregrine replied.

"Why, here you shall see one," Sir Politic Would-be said.

"They are quacks," Peregrine said. "They are fellows who live by venting — loudly advertising and selling — oils and drugs."

"Was that the character he gave you of them?" Sir Politic Would-be asked. "Is that what sort of people he told you Italian mountebanks are?"

"That's what I remember," Peregrine said.

"Pity his ignorance," Sir Politic Would-be said. "Italian mountebanks are the only knowing — knowledgeable — men of Europe! They are great general scholars, excellent physicians, very admired statesmen, and the professed favorites and private advisors to the greatest princes. They are the only languaged men of all the world! They know the most languages, and they speak the most skillfully!"

Sir Politic Would-be believed the lies that mountebanks said while speaking to the crowds.

Peregrine said, "And, I have heard, they are most ignorant impostors, whose language consists of fancy words and bits of knowledge to use to baffle their audience with bullshit. They lie about being the favorites of great men just as much as they lie about their own vile medicines; they tell these lies while also making monstrous oaths. They will sell a drug for two-pence, before they depart, that they have valued at twelve crowns previously."

Sir Politic Would-be replied, "Sir, calumnies are answered best with silence. You yourself shall judge for yourself."

He asked the disguised Mosca and Nano the dwarf, "Who is it mounts, my friends? Who is the mountebank?"

Mosca replied, "Scoto of Mantua, sir."

Scoto of Mantua was a famous Italian mountebank who had performed juggling and sleight-of-hand tricks before Queen Elizabeth I in England around 1576.

"Is it he?" Sir Politic Would-be said.

He then said to Peregrine, "Now, then, I'll proudly promise, sir, you shall behold a different man than the man who has been fantasied to you. I wonder, though, that he should mount his bank — his stage — here in this undistinguished nook. After all, he has been accustomed to appear in the main part of the Piazza!"

Of course, "Scoto of Mantua" — actually, Volpone — was performing here because he wanted to see Corvino's wife at the window under which he would perform.

Sir Politic Would-be said, "Here he comes."

Volpone, disguised as a mountebank doctor, arrived. A crowd of people followed him.

Volpone said to the disguised Nano the dwarf, "Mount, zany. Climb up to the temporary stage."

Nano the dwarf climbed up on stage; he would perform.

The crowd made excited noises.

Sir Politic Would-be said, "See how the people follow him! He's a man who may write a check for ten thousand crowns on a bank here. He's wealthy."

The disguised Volpone now climbed up on the temporary stage.

Sir Politic Would-be said, "Observe closely how he moves. I always observe closely his stateliness as he climbs on stage."

"It is worth seeing, sir," Peregrine said.

The disguised Volpone said to the crowd, "Most noble gentlemen, and my worthy patrons! It may seem strange that I, your Scoto Mantuano, who was always accustomed to fix my bank, aka stage, in the main part of the public Piazza, near the shelter of the Portico to the Procuratia, where VIPs are seen, should now, after eight months' absence from this illustrious city of Venice, humbly retire myself and mount my stage in an obscure nook of the Piazza."

Sir Politic Would-be said, "Didn't I just now say the same thing?"

Peregrine shushed him, "Be quiet, sir."

The disguised Volpone said, "Let me tell you that I am not, as your Lombard proverb saith, cold on my feet, or content to part with my commodities at a cheaper rate than I am accustomed to sell them for. Don't look for bargain-basement prices."

The Lombard proverb about cold on one's feet meant that someone was so impoverished that he would sell things very cheaply out of a deep need to buy necessities.

The disguised Volpone continued, "Also, don't believe that the calumnious reports of that impudent detractor, and shame to our profession — Alessandro Buttone, I mean — who stated in public that I had been condemned a *sforzato*, aka slave, to the galleys, for poisoning the Cardinal Pietro Bembo's ... shall we say 'cook' ... have at all taken possession of me as would a serious illness or an officer of the law, much less merely dejected me.

"No, no, worthy gentlemen; to tell you the truth, I cannot endure to see the rabble of these ground *ciarlitani*, aka charlatans, who spread their cloaks on the pavement and stand on them rather than on a stage, as if they meant to do feats of acrobatics, and then come in lamely, with their moldy tales out of Giovanni Boccaccio's *Decameron*, like the stale Tabarine the storyteller did. Some of these ground *ciarlitani* talk about their travels and about their tedious captivity in the Turks' galleys, when, indeed, if the truth were known, they were the Christians' galleys, where very temperately they ate bread and drank water, as a wholesome penance, prescribed them by their confessors, for base pilferies."

According to the disguised Volpone, the ground *ciarlitani* were lucky to be the slaves of Christians, who helped them to be temperate — a virtue — by giving them only bread and water for nourishment.

Sir Politic Would-be said, "Observe closely the mountebank's bearing and his contempt for his rivals."

The disguised Volpone continued, "These turdy-facey-nasty-patey-lousy-fartical rogues, with one poor groat's-worth of unprepared antimony, finely wrapped up in several individual *scartoccios*, are able, very well, to kill their twenty patients a week, and then these rogues play and have fun with the money they made."

A groat was worth four-pence.

The disguised Volpone was using "antimony" to baffle his hearers with bullshit. Unprepared antimony is the silvery ore; antimony is a chemical element that is a grey metalloid. The antimony is poisonous and kills people. Volpone may have wanted his hearers to think of anti-mony as anti-monk or monks' bane. Antimony was used effectively in chemical purification, but any monk foolish enough to swallow the poisonous antimony as a purgative would probably die.

A *scartoccio* was a piece of paper. A dose of medicine was placed in the piece of paper and sold.

The disguised Volpone was saying that his mountebank rivals took a little medicine — oops, I meant poison — divided it into a large number of individual doses, and then sold it to enough people that it would kill twenty people a week. This gave the rivals enough money to play for a week.

The disguised Volpone continued, "Yet, these meager, starved spirits, who have half stopped the organs of their minds with earthy oppilations that cause mental constipation, do not lack their favorers among your shriveled salad-eating artisans, who are overjoyed that they may have their half-pennyworth of medicine. Even though the medicine may purge them into another world, it doesn't matter."

The disguised Volpone was making fun of the salad-eating Italians. At least one of the English members of Volpone's audience — the English were meat eaters — approved.

"Excellent!" Sir Politic Would-be said to Peregrine. "Have you ever heard better language, sir?"

"Well, let them go," the disguised Volpone said. "And, gentlemen, honorable gentlemen, know that for this time our stage, being thus removed from the clamors of the *canaglia* — the riff-raff — shall be the scene of pleasure and delight, for I have nothing to sell, little or nothing to sell."

"I told you, sir, his purpose," Sir Politic Would-be said.

He believed that the mountebank's purpose was to serve and improve Humankind, not to make money.

"You did so, sir," Peregrine said.

The disguised Volpone continued, "I protest that I and my six servants are not able to make enough of this precious liquor" — he held up a glass vial of the "medicine" he was selling — "so fast is it fetched away from my lodging by gentlemen of your city, foreigners from Venice's mainland holdings, honorable merchants, and yes, senators, too. These people, ever since my arrival here in Venice, have detained me to serve them by giving me their splendidous — most splendid — liberalities.

"And this has been to their great benefit, for what avails a rich man to have his storehouses stuffed with muscatel wine, or with wine of the purest grape, when his physicians prescribe him, on pain of death, to drink nothing but water boiled and flavored with aniseeds?

"Oh, health! Health! The blessing of the rich! The riches of the poor! Who can buy you at too dear a rate, since there is no enjoying this world without you?

"Be not then so sparing of your purses, honorable gentlemen, as to abridge and shorten the natural course of life."

Peregrine said, "You see his purpose in being here."

He meant that the purpose was to make money.

Sir Politic Would-be replied, "Yes, isn't it good?"

He meant that the purpose was to make people healthy.

The disguised Volpone continued, "For, when a humid discharge of catarrh, aka mucous, by the mutability of air, falls from your head into an arm or shoulder, or any other part, take a ducat, or a gold chequin, and apply it to the place affected, and see what good effect it can work."

In other words, money and gold won't cure a disease such as rheumatism, which people at this time thought was caused by a change in the weather making mucous descend from the head into another part of the body.

The disguised Volpone continued, "No, no, money and gold won't cure the disguise. It is this blessed *unguento*, aka unguent, aka ointment, this rare extraction, that has the only power to disperse all malignant humors that proceed either of hot, cold, moist, or windy causes."

Peregrine said, "I wish that he had mentioned dry, too."

The disguised Volpone had mentioned "hot, cold, moist, or windy causes" of illnesses. According to the medical theory of humors, the causes of illnesses were hot, cold, moist, or dry.

Sir Politic Would-be said, "Please observe him closely."

The disguised Volpone said, "This blessed ointment has the power to fortify the sourest stomach suffering from indigestion, yes, even if it were one that, through extreme weakness, vomited blood, by applying only a warm napkin to the place, after the application of the ointment and massage.

"This blessed ointment has the power to cure dizziness in the head if you put only a drop in your nostrils and likewise behind your ears. It is a most sovereign and approved remedy.

"This blessed ointment can also cure these ailments:

"The *mal caduco*, aka the falling sickness, aka epilepsy.

"Cramps.

"Convulsions.

"Paralyses.

"Epilepsies.

"*Tremor cordia*, aka palpitations of the heart.

"Retired nerves, aka shrunken sinews.

"Ill vapors of the spleen, aka hysteria.

"Stoppings of the liver.

"The stone, aka kidney stones.

"The strangury, aka difficult urination.

"*Hernia ventosa*, aka a windy hernia.

"*Iliaca passio*, aka painful obstruction of the small intestine.

"It also immediately stops dysentery.

"It eases the torsion of the small guts, aka colic.

"It also cures *melancholia hypocondriaca*, aka depression.

"This medicine cures all of these diseases as long as it is taken and applied according to my printed instructions."

The disguised Volpone held high first the instructions and then the vial of medicine as he said these things:

"For this is the physician, and this is the medicine.

"This counsels, and this cures.

"This gives the direction, and this works the effect."

He then said, "And, in sum, both together may be termed an abstract of the theory and practice in the Aesculapian art."

Aesculapius is the god of medicine.

The disguised Volpone continued, "It will cost you eight crowns. And —"

He pointed to Nano the dwarf and said, "Zan Fritada, please sing a verse extempore in honor of it."

"Zan Fritada" means "Jack Pancake." He was a zany who was famous for his skills in providing entertainments such as storytelling, singing, and ad-libbing.

Sir Politic Would-be asked, "How do you like him, sir?"

Peregrine replied, "Most strangely, I do!"

"Strangely" meant "unfavorably," and it meant "exceptionally." Peregrine meant "unfavorably," but Sir Politic Would-be understood him to mean "exceptionally well."

Sir Politic Would-be asked, "Is not his language rare?"

Peregrine replied, "I never heard the like except for alchemy or Broughton's books."

Alchemical texts were very difficult to understand, as were the theological texts of the Puritan Hugh Broughton.

The disguised Nano the dwarf and the disguised Mosca played musical instruments and sang this song:

"*Had old Hippocrates, or Galen,*

"*That to their books put med'cines all in,*

"*But known this secret, they had never*

"*(Of which they will be guilty ever)*

"*Been murderers of so much paper,*

"*Or wasted many a hurtless [harmless] taper [candle];*

"*No Indian drug had e'er been famed,*

"Tobacco, sassafras not named;

"Ne [Nor] yet, of guacum one small stick, sir,

"Nor Raymond Lully's great elixir.

"Ne [Nor] had been known the Danish Gonswart,

"Or Paracelsus, with his long sword."

Hippocrates and Galen were ancient physicians, each of whom had written many books, thereby murdering paper and candles.

Tobacco, sassafras, and guacum were used as medicines. Guacum came from the guacium tree.

Raymond Lully was thought to be an alchemist who had discovered the Elixir of Life, which would greatly lengthen one's life, possibly even making the person immortal.

The Danish Gonswart kept his secrets so closely hidden that no one today knows who he was. Or, possibly, "Danish Gonswart" is a portmanteau word combing "Danewort" (an herb also known as Dwarf Elder) and Goutwort (an herb used to cure gout). A "wort" is an herb used in medicine.

Paracelsus was an early Renaissance physician who combined medicine with magic. He was believed to keep his most important medicine and magics in the hollow pommel of his long sword. He was believed to have made the Philosopher's Stone, which would turn base metals into gold and silver. Powdered Philosopher's Stone was believed, if consumed, to cure all illnesses and greatly extend life.

Peregrine said, "All this, yet, will not do. Eight crowns is too high a price to pay."

The disguised Volpone said to Nona the dwarf, "No more."

He then said to his audience, "Gentlemen, I wish I had time to discourse to you the miraculous effects of this my oil, surnamed *Oglio del Scoto*, aka Scoto's Oil, with the countless catalogue of those whom I have cured of the illnesses I have mentioned, and of many more diseases.

"Gentlemen, I wish I had time to discourse to you the patents and privileges of all the princes and commonwealths of Christendom."

Patents are official certificates that confer certain rights, such as the right and the privilege to sell something. Of course, the disguised Volpone wanted his audience to think that all the princes and commonwealths of Christendom had given this right and privilege to him.

The disguised Volpone continued, "Gentlemen, I wish I had time to discourse to you just the depositions of those who appeared on my behalf before the Signiory of the Sanita, which licenses mountebanks, and the most learned College of Physicians, where I was authorized, after notice was taken of the admirable virtues of my medicaments, and my own excellency in the matter of rare and unknown secrets, not only to disperse them publicly in this famous city, but also in all the territories that happily experience joy under the government of the most pious and magnificent states of Italy.

"But some gallant fellow may say, 'Oh, there are many people who claim to have as good, and as proven-by-experiments medicinal formulas as yours.'

"Indeed, very many people have attempted, like apes, in imitation of that which is really and essentially in me, to make this oil. They have bestowed great cost in such alchemical equipment as furnaces, stills, and alembecks, as well as continual fires and preparation of the ingredients (as indeed there goes into it six hundred different herbs, besides some quantity of human fat, for the conglutination, aka gluing together — we buy the human fat from the anatomists), but when these practitioners come to the last decoction, aka boiling down, they blow, blow, puff, puff to make the fire hotter, and all flies *in fumo* — everything goes up in smoke! Ha! Ha! Ha!"

Anybody who consumes the "medicine" is consuming human fat and so is a cannibal.

In fumo is Latin for "in smoke."

"Poor wretches! I pity their folly and indiscretion rather than their loss of time and money because time and money may be recovered by industry, but to be born a fool is an incurable disease.

"As for myself, I always from my youth have endeavored to get the rarest secrets, and learn them, either in exchange for my own secret knowledge or for money. I have spared neither cost nor labor, where anything was worthy to be learned.

"And gentlemen, honorable gentlemen, I will undertake, by virtue of chemical art, out of the honorable hat that covers your head, to extract the four elements — that is to say, the fire, air, water, and earth — and return to you your felt hat without burn or stain."

The secret knowledge that the disguised Volpone said he had labored so hard for so long and so expensively to acquire allows him to remove burn marks and stains from felt hats.

The disguised Volpone continued, "For, while others have been playing the ball game known as the Balloo, I have been at my books and I am now past the craggy paths of study and have come to the flowery plains of honor and reputation."

Sir Politic Would-be said, "I do assure you, sir, that is his aim."

According to Sir Politic Would-be, the mountebank's aim was to acquire honor and reputation.

The disguised Volpone continued, "But, about our price —"

Peregrine said, "And that is another of his aims, Sir Pol."

According to Peregrine, the mountebank's aim was to acquire money.

The disguised Volpone continued, "You all know, honorable gentlemen, I have never valued this ampulla, or vial, at less than eight crowns, but for this time, I am content to be deprived of it for six. Six crowns is the price, and less, I know you cannot offer me out of courtesy.

"Take it, or leave it; in either case, both it is and I am at your service. I ask you not for the price that the value of the thing would demand, for then I should demand from you a thousand crowns.

"That is the price that the Cardinals Montalto and Fernese, the great Duke of Tuscany, the godfather of my child, and several other princes, have given me, but I despise money.

"Only to show my affection to you, honorable gentlemen, and your illustrious State here, I have neglected the messages of these princes, neglected my own duties, made my journey here, just to present you with the fruits of my travels."

He then turned to the disguised Nano the dwarf and the disguised Mosca and said, "Tune your voices once more to the touch of your instruments, and give the honorable assembly some delightful recreation."

Peregrine said, "What monstrous and most painful circumstance — unnecessary ado — is being made here just to get some three or four small coins, some three-pence in the whole! For that is what the profits will come to."

The disguised Nano the dwarf and the disguised Mosca sang this song:

"You that [who] would last long, list [listen] to my song,

"Make no more coil [fuss], but buy of this oil.
"Would you be ever fair [always beautiful] and young?
"Stout of teeth, and strong of tongue?
"Tart [Keen] of palate? Quick of ear?
"Sharp of sight? Of nostril clear?
"Moist of hand? [Horny.] And light of foot?
"Or, I will come nearer to't [state what I mean more clearly],
"Would you live free from all diseases?
"Do the act your mistress pleases;
"Yet fright [frighten] all aches from your bones?
"Here's a med'cine for the nones."

The song stated that the medicine would do such things as give the taker a keen appetite and clear his or her sinuses. It was also very good at helping clear up sexual troubles. It would make the taker moist of hand — a sign of amorousness. You can guess the act that pleases your mistress. The medicine would also make the taker light of foot — promiscuous. It would also frighten the ache from the taker's bones — it would cure the venereal disease that made the bones ache.

It is a medicine for the nones — it will cure none, aka no one person, and it will cure none, aka no one disease, and it will cure at none, aka no one time or occasion. That is the reason for the plural: nones. Volpone, however, wanted the audience to think that "nones" was "nonces." "Nonce" means "particular purpose" and "particular occasion." This medicine would cure no one particular purpose at no one particular occasion.

The disguised Volpone said, "Well, I am in a humor — the mood — at this time to make a present of the small quantity my coffer contains; to the rich, in courtesy, and to the poor for God's sake.

"Therefore, now listen carefully: I asked you to pay six crowns, and six crowns, at other times, you have paid me, but you shall not now give me six crowns, nor five, nor four, nor three, nor two, nor one; nor half a ducat; no, nor a moccinigo. Six—"

Crowns, ducats, and moccinigos are all pieces of money.

The disguised Volpone paused to make the audience wait for the medicine's true price, and then he continued, "— pence it will cost you, or else it will cost you six hundred pounds, for I won't go any lower — expect no lower price, for I swear by the banner displayed in front of my stage that I will not abate a bagatine, or knock off a farthing."

He continued, "I will have only a small amount of money that is a pledge of your loves, so that I can carry something from among you away to show I am not despised by you.

"Therefore, now, toss your handkerchiefs, cheerfully, cheerfully, and be advised that the first heroic spirit who deigns to grace me with a handkerchief, I will give him or her a little remembrance of something, in addition to the medicine, that shall please that heroic spirit better than if I had presented it with a double pistolet."

The disguised Volpone was promising to give the first buyer an extra gift that would be valued at more than a double pistolet, which is a valuable coin.

Buyers of the medicine would tie the money in a handkerchief and toss it to the mountebank, who would take the money, tie the medicine in the handkerchief, and toss it back to the buyer. The first buyer would receive an additional gift in the handkerchief. At this time, handkerchiefs were used for ornamental rather than hygienic purposes.

Peregrine asked, "Will you be that heroic spark, Sir Pol? Will you be the first buyer?"

Celia, Corvino's wife, had been watching from the window. She now threw down her handkerchief — in which was tied six pence — to the disguised Volpone.

Peregrine said, "Oh, look! The lady at the window has beaten you and got there first."

The disguised Volpone said, "Lady, I kiss your bounty, and for this timely grace you have done your poor Scoto of Mantua, I will return you, over and above my oil, a secret of such high and inestimable nature that it shall make you forever enamored of that minute wherein your eye first descended on so mean, yet not altogether to be despised, an object.

"Here is a powder concealed in this paper, about which, if I would state its true worth, nine thousand volumes were but as one page, that page as a line, that line as a word — so short is this pilgrimage of man (which some call life) to the expressing of it."

The disguised Volpone had been speaking volumes of words about Scoto's oil — and now this powder — but if he were to state their true worth, he could do it in one word: crap.

He continued, "Would I reflect on the price? Why, the whole world is but as an empire, that empire as a province, that province as a bank, that bank as a private purse to the purchase of it."

The price of his medicine had gone from eight crowns to six pence. At this time, one crown was worth five shillings. A shilling was worth twelve pence. Therefore, one crown was worth 60 pence. The original price was eight crowns, or 480 pence. The final price was six pence.

He continued, "I will only tell you; it is the powder that made Venus a goddess (Apollo gave the powder to her) and kept her perpetually young, cleared her wrinkles, firmed her gums, filled her skin and made it free of wrinkles, and colored her hair.

"From Venus the secret of the powder went to Helen of Troy, and at the sack of Troy it was unfortunately lost until now, in this our age, it was as happily recovered, by a studious antiquarian, out of some ruins of Asia, who sent a moiety of it (but much adulterated) to the court of France and the ladies there now color their hair with it.

"The rest, at this present time, remains with me; it has been refined to a quintessence, so that, wherever it simply touches, it perpetually preserves that part in youth, restores the complexion in age, and seats your teeth — even if they have danced like the strings of a piano — as firmly as a wall and makes your teeth as white as ivory, even if they were as black as —"

Corvino arrived. He saw and recognized Celia's handkerchief, and he was instantly jealous, although she had given him no reason for being jealous.

Corvino finished the disguised Volpone's sentence for him in his own way: "— blood of the devil, and black as my shame!"

He then ordered the disguised Volpone, "Come down here from the stage! Come down! Have you no house but mine to make your scene?"

Corvino recognized that what he was seeing was like a *commedia dell'arte* comedy skit that used stock characters. Flaminio was the name of the lover in many skits. Franciscina was the name of the saucy, sexually willing maidservant. Pantalone di Besogniosi (Pantaloon of the Paupers) was the name of the aging, miserly merchant who wore pantaloons (a kind of trouser) and whose young wife often cuckolded him.

Corvino said to the disguised Volpone, "Signior Flaminio, will you come down, sir? Down? What, is my wife your Franciscina, sir? Are there no windows on the whole Piazza here to make your theatrical properties, but mine? None but mine?"

He beat the disguised Volpone and drove him and the disguised Nano and Mosca away. They ran fast.

He then said, "By God's heart, before tomorrow I shall be newly christened and called the Pantalone di Besogniosi by everyone in town."

Peregrine asked, "What does this mean, Sir Pol?"

"It is some trick of state, believe it," Sir Politic Would-be said. "I will go home."

Peregrine said, "It may be some design on you. Someone may be wanting to trick you."

The only person wanting to trick Sir Politic Would-be was Peregrine, who wanted to trick him into making more of a fool of himself.

"I don't know," Sir Politic Would-be said, "but I'll be on my guard."

"It is your best option, sir," Peregrine said.

Sir Politic Would-be said, "For the past three weeks, all my pieces of intelligence and news — all my letters — have been intercepted."

Actually, he had recently said that last Wednesday he had received intelligence and news about the Mamuluchi.

"Indeed, sir!" Peregrine said. "You had best be careful."

"So I will," Sir Politic Would-be said.

He exited.

Peregrine said to himself, "This knight, I must not lose him — because I want to laugh at him — until night."

He followed Sir Politic Would-be.

Volpone and Mosca talked together in a room in Volpone's house.

"Oh, I am wounded!" Volpone said.

"Where, sir?" Mosca asked.

"Not on the outside," Volpone said. "Corvino's blows were nothing. I could bear them forever. But angry Cupid, shooting arrows like thunderbolts from Corvino's wife's eyes, has shot himself into me like a flame. There, now, he flings about his burning heat, just like an ambitious — rising — fire, whose vent is stopped in a furnace. The fight is all within me."

A closed vent would cause the fire to die down through lack of air, so Volpone was saying the opposite of what he meant.

"I cannot live, unless you help me, Mosca. My liver melts, and I, without the hope of some soft air from her refreshing breath am but a heap of cinders."

Giving a fire more air would reduce the material being burned to a heap of cinders more quickly, so Volpone was saying the opposite of what he meant.

"Alas, good sir," Mosca said. "I wish that you had never seen her!"

"I wish that you had never told me about her!" Volpone said.

"Sir, it is true," Mosca said. "I confess I was made unfortunate and you were made unhappy by my telling you about her, but I'm bound in conscience no less than in duty to do my best to bring about the release of your torment, and I will, sir."

One way to release Volpone's torment would be to find a way to have Corvino's wife sleep with him.

"Dear Mosca, shall I hope to have my torment relieved?" Volpone asked.

"Sir, you who are more than dear to me, I will not advise you to despair of being without anything that a human can bring about," Mosca said. "And what you want is something that I can bring about."

"Oh, there spoke my better angel," Volpone said.

This is ironic. Volpone's "better angel" is someone who is willing to help him commit adultery, a sin that is punished in the Inferno unless it is repented while the adulterer is still alive.

"Mosca" means "fly," and Beelzebub is the Lord of the Flies. Beelzebub is a winged demon and a fallen angel.

Volpone handed Mosca his keys and said, "Mosca, take my keys. My gold, plate, and jewels, all's at your devotion."

He meant "at your disposal." The word "devotion" has ironic religious overtones. "Devotion" is a word used to name how many people react to God. Of course, Volpone worshipped and was devoted to gold and other material possessions.

Volpone continued, "Employ them however you will; indeed, coin me and employ me, too, as long as you crown my longings and get them satisfied, Mosca. Use whatever you have to, to get Corvino's wife to sleep with me."

"Use your patience," Mosca said.

He meant that it would take some time.

"So I have," Volpone replied.

He had not.

"I have no doubt that I will bring success to your desires," Mosca said. "I will get you what you want."

"In that case, I don't repent me being in my recent disguise as a mountebank," Volpone said.

"If you can horn Corvino, sir, you need not repent being disguised as a mountebank," Mosca said.

By "horn," he meant make a cuckold out of Corvino by sleeping with his wife. This society joked that cuckolds had invisible horns growing on their foreheads.

"That is true," Volpone said. "Besides, I have never meant Corvino to be my heir."

He meant that since he had never meant Corvino to be his heir, it was OK to make Corvino a cuckold. Actually, if he had meant Corvino to be his heir, it would make some (but not moral) sense to sleep with Corvino's wife. If she gave birth to a son for Volpone, eventually Volpone's son would inherit Volpone's wealth. The word "cuckold" comes from the cuckoo bird, which lays its eggs in other birds' nests; the other birds raise the cuckoo's nestlings.

Thinking about "heir" led Volpone to think about "hair," and he asked, "Won't the color of my beard and eyebrows make my identity known? Won't Corvino recognize that the mountebank is me because of the color of our hair?"

Foxes are known for red fur, and Volpone's hair and beard were red.

"Not a chance," Mosca said.

"I did my performance as the mountebank well," Volpone said.

Mosca replied, "So well that I wish I could follow you in my performance, with half the happiness and success!"

Mosca would put on a performance to manipulate Corvino to allow Volpone to sleep with his wife.

He thought, *And yet I would escape your epilogue — the beating that Corvino gave you!*

Volpone asked, "But were they gulled — fooled — with the belief that I was Scoto the mountebank?"

"Sir, Scoto himself could hardly have distinguished you from himself!" Mosca said. "But I don't have the time to flatter you now. We'll part, and as I prosper, so applaud my art. I will get you what you want."

A very angry and jealous Corvino dragged his innocent wife, Celia, into a room of their house. He had a sword in his hand.

Corvino said, "Death of my honor, with the city's fool! A juggling, tooth-pulling, prating mountebank!"

Mountebanks sometimes performed tooth extractions.

He continued, "And at a public window! Where, while he, with his strained overacting, and his mugging of faces, to his drug lecture draws your itching ears, a crew of old, unmarried, noted lechers stood leering up like satyrs, and you smiled most graciously and fanned your favors forth — that is, you flirted — to give your hot spectators satisfaction!

"Was your mountebank their call? Their whistle? Were the spectators using the mountebank to call and whistle to you like hunters calling and whistling to lure birds to be caught?

"Or were you enamored of his copper rings and his saffron jewelry with the toadstone in it?"

Copper rings were cheap rings that could fool fools into thinking they were made of gold. Saffron jewelry was jewelry that was stained to make it look like gold. Toads were thought to have a precious jewel with magical abilities located in their head.

He continued, "Or were you enamored of his embroidered suit with the cope-stitch, a suit that was made out of a hearse-cloth? Or were you enamored of his old tilt-feather? Or were you enamored of his starched beard?"

Hearse cloth was a drape for a coffin. According to Corvino, the mountebank had made a suit of the cloth and embroidered it to make it fancy, using a cope-stitch — a stitch used in making copes, aka ecclesiastical gowns. Some men at this time stiffened their beards with egg whites or gum so that they kept a fashionable shape.

Corvino continued, "Well, you shall have him, yes! He shall come home, and minister to you the fricace — massage — for the mother."

To treat a woman for hysteria, aka the mother, doctors would massage the woman's genitals until the woman had an orgasm. Actually, many doctors disliked doing this because it took so much time and so they trained midwives to do it.

Corvino continued, "Or, let me see, I think you'd rather mount; wouldn't you mount?"

He meant that his wife would like to mount the platform on which the mountebank performed — and he meant that his wife would like to sexually mount the mountebank.

He continued, "Why, if you'll mount, you may; yes, truly, you may. And so you may be seen, down to the foot."

If his wife climbed on the platform, people would get a good view of her and perhaps see more of her than this society thought was proper to be seen.

He continued, "Get yourself a cittern, Lady Vanity, and be a dealer with the manly man. Make one."

Prostitutes often played the musical instrument called a cittern. "To be a dealer" meant to be either a prostitute or a bawd. To "make one" meant to copulate and make one person out of two.

Corvino continued, "I'll just protest that I am a cuckold and save your dowry."

A wife who was convicted of committing adultery forfeited her dowry to her husband.

He continued, "I'm a Dutchman, I am! For, if you thought me to be an Italian, you would be damned before you did this, you whore!"

Dutchmen were thought to be calm, while Italians — such as Corvino — were thought to be hot-tempered and capable of great violence.

He continued, "You would tremble to imagine that the murder of your father, mother, brother, and the rest of your family would follow your adultery — that is the Italian way of justice."

His wife, Celia, pleaded, "Good sir, have patience."

Corvino replied, "What could you propose I do to yourself less than that in this heat of wrath and stung with my dishonor I should strike this steel sword into you with as many stabs as you were gazed on by goatish — lecherous — eyes? That is what you deserve!"

"Alas, sir, be at peace!" Celia said. "I could not think that my being at the window would move your impatience now more than at other times. I did no harm by being at the window."

"No!" Corvino said. "You didn't try to seek and entertain a parley — conversation — with a known knave, before a multitude of witnesses! You were an actor with your handkerchief, which he most sweetly kissed when he got it, and might, no doubt, return it with a letter, and appoint a place where you might meet — your sister's, your mother's, or your aunt's might serve the turn."

In this society, the word "aunt" sometimes meant "bawd." "Serve the term" meant both "serve the purpose" and "provide the sexual service."

Celia said, "Why, dear sir, when do I make these excuses, or ever stir out of doors, except to go to the church? And that I do so seldom —"

"Well, it shall be less in the future," Corvino said. "And your restraint before was liberty compared to what I now decree, and therefore pay close attention to what I now say.

"First, I will have this bawdy light — this window — dammed up, aka boarded up. And until that is done, some two or three yards away from the window, I'll chalk a line. If you happen to set your desperate, reckless, violent foot over that line, more Hell, more horror, and more wild remorseless rage shall seize on you than shall seize on a conjurer who has heedlessly left his circle's safety before his devil was sent back to Hell."

Conjurors were reputed to be able to call devils from out of Hell, but devils were dangerous, and so conjurors made a magic circle to keep themselves safe while the devil was present. If a conjuror stepped out of the magic circle, he was at the nonexistent mercy of the devil.

Corvino held up a chastity belt and said, "And then here's a lock that I will hang upon you."

The chastity belt prevented a woman from having sex.

He continued, "And, now I think about it, I will keep you backwards. Your lodging shall be backwards, at the back of the house. You will walk backwards. What you see — your prospect — all shall be backwards, and the only sexual pleasure that you shall know will be backwards — the back hole rather than the front hole.

"Indeed, since you force my honest nature, know that it is your own fault. Your being too open makes me treat you thus because you will not contain your subtle and cunning nostrils — used for smelling out lust — in a sweet room, but they must snuff the air of rank and sweaty passersby."

Knocking sounded at the door.

Corvino said, "Someone is knocking."

He said to his wife, "Leave, and don't be seen, on pain of your life. Don't look toward the window. If you do — wait and hear this — then let me not prosper, whore, unless I will make you an anatomy by dissecting you myself, and read a lecture about you to the city, and in public."

To make her an anatomy meant to make her a skeleton through dissecting her. It also meant to dissect her moral character in a lecture. Of course, Corvino now thought because of his jealousy that her moral character is bad.

He said, "Go away! Leave!"

A servant entered the room.

Corvino asked, "Who's there at the door?"

"It is Signior Mosca, sir."

"Let him come in."

The servant exited.

Corvino, assuming that Volpone had died and that Mosca had come to tell him that news, said to himself, "His master's dead. There's yet some good to counteract the bad."

Mosca entered the room.

"My Mosca, welcome!" Corvino said. "I guess your news."

"I fear you cannot, sir," Mosca said.

"Isn't your news that Volpone is dead?"

"Rather the contrary."

"Not his recovery?"

"Yes, sir," Mosca said.

"I am cursed, I am bewitched, my crosses meet to vex me," Corvino said.

To Corvino, the cross that he bore in Volpone's not dying was similar to the cross that Christ endured.

Corvino asked, "How? How? How? How?"

"Why, sir, with the mountebank Scoto's oil," Mosca replied. "Corbaccio and Voltore brought some of it to Volpone, while I was busy in an inner room."

"God's death!" Corvino said, "That damned mountebank! If not for the law, I could now kill the rascal! It cannot be that his oil should have the virtue of restoring Volpone's health. Haven't I known the mountebank Scoto to be a common rogue? He comes fiddling into the *osteria*, aka inn, with a tumbling whore, aka female acrobat or whore, whose work is tumbling in the hay, and when he has done all his forced tricks — tricks he is forced to perform to survive — hasn't he been glad to get a poor spoonful of stale wine with flies in it?

"It cannot be that his oil is effective. All his ingredients consist of a sheep's gall, a roasted bitch's marrow, some few boiled insects, pounded caterpillars, a little capon's grease, and fasting spittle. I know his ingredients to the smallest portion."

"Fasting spittle" is a starving man's spit. No doubt Corvino thought that Scoto was often a starving man.

"I don't know, sir," Mosca said, "but some of it they there poured into his ears, and some in his nostrils, and the medicine made him recover. All they did in addition was to massage the oil into his skin."

"A pox on that massage!" Corvino said.

"And since then, to seem the more zealous and flattering of — giving him high hopes concerning — his health, there, they have had, at extremely high fees, the college of physicians consulting about him and trying to determine how they might restore him to complete health.

"One doctor wants Volpone to have a poultice of spices. Another doctor wants a flayed ape clapped to Volpone's breast. A third doctor would have it be a dog, and a fourth doctor would have it be an oil, with wild cats' skins.

"At last, they all resolved that to preserve him there was no other means but that some young woman who is lusty and full of juice must be immediately sought out to sleep by him."

"Lusty" means "healthy and energetic" and "horny." "Full of juice" means "energetic" and "wet between the legs."

In 1 Kings 1:1-4, a young woman is brought to sleep with the very old King David to keep him warm, but he does not have sex with her:

1 Now king David was old and stricken in years; and they covered him with clothes, but he gat no heat.

2 Wherefore his servants said unto him, Let there be sought for my lord the king a young virgin: and let her stand before the king, and let her cherish him, and let her lie in thy bosom, that my lord the king may get heat.

3 So they sought for a fair damsel throughout all the coasts of Israel, and found Abishag a Shunammite, and brought her to the king.

4 And the damsel was very fair, and cherished the king, and ministered to him: but the king knew her not. (King James Version)

Mosca continued, "And in this service, most unhappily and most unwillingly I am now employed: I have been sent to find a young woman to sleep with Volpone. I thought to pre-acquaint you with that here, in order to get your advice, since it concerns you most and because I would not do anything that might cross your ends. I don't want to do anything that might prevent you from inheriting Volpone's wealth. On you I am wholly dependent, sir. After Volpone dies, I will need a new position.

"Yet, if I do not find a young woman to sleep with Volpone, Corbaccio and Voltore and the physicians may report my slackness to Volpone and work me out of his good opinion, and then all your hopes, ventures, or whatsoever will all be frustrated!

"I do but tell you, sir; I am simply reporting news you need to know. Besides, they are all now competing to determine who shall first present him with a young woman to sleep with. Therefore ... I entreat you to quickly decide what you will do, and I entreat you to act first and forestall them, if you can."

"This is death to my hopes!" Corvino said. "This is my villainous fortune! It is best to hire some common courtesan — some common prostitute."

"Yes, I thought about that, sir," Mosca said. "But whores are all so cunning, so full of artifice, and men of old age on the other hand are doting and gullible, so that — I cannot tell for sure — but we may, perhaps, light on a whore who may cheat us all. *She* may inherit Volpone's wealth!"

"That is true," Corvino said.

"So no, no to using a prostitute," Mosca said. "The young woman must be one who has no tricks, sir. Some simple thing, a creature who can be made to do it, some wench you may command. Have you no kinswoman you can order to do it? God's so —"

This expletive meant "By God's soul" and sounded like "*cazzo*," which is Italian for "cock."

Mosca continued, "Think, think, think, think, think, think, think, sir."

He hesitated and then added, "One of the doctors there offered his daughter."

"What!" Corvino said.

"Yes, Signior Lupo, the physician."

Lupo is Italian for "Wolf."

"His daughter!" Corvino said.

"And she is a virgin, sir," Mosca said. "Why? Alas, the physician knows the state of Volpone's body, what it is. The physician knows that nothing can warm Volpone's blood, sir, but a fever. The physician knows that no incantation can raise Volpone's spirit. A long forgetfulness has seized that part."

In other words, Mosca is saying nothing can raise Volpone's penis; he has been impotent for a long time.

Mosca added, "Besides, sir, who shall know it? Some one or two —"

Corvino interrupted, "Please let me think for a moment."

He walked a short distance away to think.

He said to himself, "If any man but I had had this luck. ... The thing in itself, I know, is nothing. ... Why shouldn't I command my blood and my affections just like this dull doctor does? In the point of honor, the cases are all one of wife and daughter."

"Command my blood and my affections" meant both "control my passions and feelings" and "order my relative, who is one with me and who is the object of my affections" to do something. In Corvino's case, the relative was his wife; in the doctor's case, the relative was his daughter. (Of course, Mosca had simply made up the doctor and daughter.)

Mosca said to himself, "I hear him coming."

The "coming" was "coming around to the way Mosca was persuading him" and "Corvino beginning to move toward Mosca."

Corvino said to himself, "She is my wife — she shall do it. It is done: I have made my decision. By God's light! If this doctor, who is not engaged, unless it be for his counsel, which is nothing, offers Volpone his daughter, what should I, who am so deeply in, do? The doctor stands to make a fee, but I stand to inherit all of Volpone's wealth. I will forestall the doctor.

"Wretch! Covetous wretch!"

Was he thinking that perhaps the doctor was making an attempt at inheriting Volpone's wealth and was therefore a covetous wretch? Or was Corvino referring to himself?

Corvino said out loud, "I have determined what I shall do."

"What is that, sir?" Mosca asked.

"We'll make all sure," Corvino said. "We'll make me sure of inheriting Volpone's wealth. Mosca, the party you know of shall be my own wife."

He used the euphemism "party you know of" because he was unwilling to say "young woman who shall sleep with Volpone."

Mosca said, "Sir, that is the thing — except that I would not seem to advise you — I would have proposed to you at the first. And now you make your count and inventory all of Volpone's possessions, which you are sure to inherit, because with this decision you have cut all your competitors' throats in this cutthroat competition.

"Why, this decision is directly taking a legal possession of Volpone's wealth!

"And when Volpone suffers his next fit, we may let him go and die. All we need to do is only to pull the pillow from under his head, and he is throttled to death. It would have been done previously, except for your moral scruples and doubts."

When people in this society were dying, their pillows were taken away from under their heads to make it easier to die. Mosca was making a joke: Removing Volpone's pillow would make it easier for Volpone to die because Mosca would use the pillow to smother Volpone to death.

"Yes, a plague on it," Corvino said. "My conscience fools my wit! My conscience won't allow me to do what my intelligence tells me I need to do to inherit Volpone's wealth.

"Well, I'll be quick, and so you should be, lest they should be before us and find a young woman to sleep with Volpone.

"Go home, prepare Volpone, tell him with what zeal and willingness I am doing it. Swear that it was on my first hearing about it (as you may do truly) that I made my own freely made proposal."

"Sir, I promise you that I'll so possess him with your generosity that the rest of his starved clients shall all be banished from his house and only you shall be allowed to visit him. But do not come, sir, until I send the OK to you because I have something else to ripen for your good — but you must not know what it is."

Mosca did not want Corvino and Celia to arrive early.

Corvino said, "Be careful not to forget to send the OK to me."

"You don't need to worry about that," Mosca said.

Mosca exited.

Corvino called, "Where are you, wife? My Celia? Wife?"

Corvino's wife, Celia, entered the room. She was crying.

Corvino said to her, "What, blubbering? Come, dry those tears. I think you thought that I was in earnest when I pretended to be jealous. Ha! By this light I swear that I talked like that only in order to test you. I think that the lightness of the occasion — the lack of any real reason for me to be jealous — should have assured you that I was only pretending to be jealous. Come, I am not jealous."

"No?" Celia asked.

"Indeed, I am not jealous, and I have never been jealous," Corvino said. "Jealousy is a poor and unprofitable emotion."

He was hoping to make considerable profit by not being jealous and by prostituting his wife to Volpone.

He continued, "Don't I know that if women have a will and the desire to engage in adulterous sex, they'll do it despite all the watchmen in the world, and don't I know that the fiercest spies are tamed with gold? Guards can be bribed.

"Tut, I am confident in you. You shall see it, and you'll see that I'll give you reason, too, to believe that I am confident in you."

Celia thought that he meant that he was confident that she was honest and chaste, but he meant that he was confident that she would do what he ordered her to do.

Corvino said, "Come kiss me. Go and make yourself ready, immediately. Wear all your best attire and your choicest jewelry. Put them all on, and with them, put on your best looks. We are invited to a formal banquet, at old Volpone's, where it shall appear how far I am free from jealousy or fear."

Corvino was lying to Celia about the formal banquet. He simply wanted her to dress extremely nicely as if she were going to a formal banquet.

Corvino also had no intention of waiting for Mosca's OK. He wanted to do this immediately.

CHAPTER 3
— 3.1 —

Mosca stood alone in the Piazza, aka public square.

He said to himself, "I fear that I shall begin to grow in love with my dear self, and my most prosperous parts, aka flourishing talents, because they so spring and burgeon and grow big that I can feel a whimsy in my blood. I don't know how, but success has made me wanton. I could skip out of my skin, now, like a cunning snake, I am so limber."

Mosca was in a good mood because his manipulation of Corvino had gone so well, and his good mood was such that it was like a sexual excitement. It was like the excitement that made a penis grow and come out from under its foreskin.

Now he began to reflect on parasites, people who live by flattering and serving other people. Some parasites are more capable than other parasites.

He said to himself, "Oh, your parasite is a very precious thing, dropped from above and God-given. Parasitism is not bred among clods and blockheads here on earth.

"I wonder why the mystery of parasitism has not been made a science because it is so liberally professed!"

In this society, a "mystery" is a craft such as being a carpenter or a blacksmith; it is skilled labor. In contrast is "science," aka liberal arts, which is what gentlemen study in higher education. The liberal arts consist of knowledge that is worthy for a free man. *Liber* is Latin for "free" and for "book."

"Liberally professed" meant both that parasitism is widely practiced and that even gentlemen practice it.

Mosca continued, "Almost all the wise world is little else, in nature, but parasites, or sub-parasites.

"And yet, by a true parasite, I don't mean parasites who have only a bare town-art, which is enough to know who's able to feed them. They have no house, no family, and no care, and therefore they mold tales — devise scandals — for men's ears, to tempt their hearing.

"Or they get kitchen-invention, and some stale receipts to please the belly and the groin."

Kitchen-invention is both gossip and food — both are cooked up in the kitchen. The stale receipts are stale recipes — uninteresting food. But the word "stale" also means "prostitute," and so stale receipts are the tricks of whores. Food that pleases the groin is aphrodisiacal.

To Mosca, a true parasite does more than simply serve his master by telling the master gossip and providing the master with whores.

Mosca continued, "Nor by 'parasite' do I mean those with their court dog-tricks, who can fawn and fleer, and make their revenue out of legs and faces, echo my lord, and lick away a mote."

To Mosca, a true parasite does more than simply serve his master by fawning like a dog. To "fleer" is to "smile obsequiously." Such poor parasites make legs, aka bows, and faces, aka smirks. They echo their master's opinions back to him, and they are sycophants who will remove lint from their master's coat or shirt. Mosca emphasized these parasites' servility by saying that they would lick away such items.

Mosca now described what he considered a true parasite:

"But a true parasite is your fine elegant rascal, who can rise and stoop, almost at the same time, and like an arrow shoot through the air as nimbly as a falling star, aka meteor, and who can turn as quickly as a swallow does, and be here, and there, and here, and yonder, all at once, and who can be present to any humor and all occasions, and change a visor, aka mask, aka his personality, swifter than a thought!"

According to Mosca, a true parasite is very changeable. He will change to fit his master's every mood, and he will change to fit any occasion. A true parasite can adapt.

Mosca himself was a master of adapting. He was able to think of ways to manipulate other people to serve his master, Volpone. He had certainly shown that in his dealings with Voltore, Corbaccio, and Corvino.

Mosca continued, "This is the creature who has had the art of parasitism born with him. He doesn't toil to learn it, but he practices it out of most excellent nature, and such sparks are the true parasites. Other parasites are only their zanis — their comic servants."

And yet Mosca was doing the same things that he criticized lesser parasites of doing. He had certainly flattered Volpone for his performance as a mountebank, and he was acting as a pander when he was manipulating Corvino into allowing Volpone to sleep with Celia. He also had invented gossip and scandal: Signior Lupus is offering his virgin daughter to Volpone to sleep with! A parasite is a flatterer; Mosca had flattered Volpone and his victims, and in this conversation with himself, Mosca was flattering himself.

The difference between a true parasite and other parasites may be enjoyment and competence. A true parasite enjoys being a parasite. A true parasite is at ease when adapting to every mood and every occasion, and a true parasite is at ease while manipulating other people. A true parasite enjoys using his wits and is competent at manipulating other people.

Bonario walked onto the scene.

Mosca said, "Who's this? Bonario, old Corbaccio's son? The exact person I was going to seek!"

He said to Bonario, "Fair sir, you are happily met."

"I cannot be happily met by you," Bonario replied.

"Why not, sir?" Mosca asked.

"Please know your path and go on your way and leave me," Bonario said. "I would be loath to engage in conversation with such a contemptible fellow as you are."

"Courteous sir, don't scorn me because of my poverty," Mosca said.

"I don't, by Heaven," Bonario said, "but you shall give me leave to hate you because of your baseness."

"My baseness!" Mosca said.

"Yes," Bonario said. "Answer me this: Isn't your sloth sufficient reason for me to hate you? And your flattery? And your means of getting food to eat?"

The charge of sloth may seem unfair. Mosca certainly acted quickly to serve his master. But one meaning of sloth — found in Dante's *Divine Comedy* — is slackness in pursuing the things that ought to be pursued. Mosca worked hard to serve Volpone, but he did not work hard to save his own soul.

"May Heaven be good to me!" Mosca said. "Sir, these imputations are too commonly made and easily stuck on virtue when she's poor. Poor people are often undeservedly called base.

"You are unequal — unjust to, and of higher social standing than — me, and even if what you say about me were righteous, yet you are not righteous when you — before you know me — proceed to censure me. May St. Mark, patron saint of Venice, bear witness against you because what you are doing is inhuman."

Mosca pretended to cry.

Bonario said to himself, "What! Is he crying? The crying is a soft and good sign; it indicates a gentle nature. I am sorry that I was so harsh to him."

Mosca said, "It is true that because I am swayed by strong necessity, I am forced to eat my gotten-with-much-trouble bread with too much obsequiousness. It is true, besides, that I am fain to spin my own poor raiment — obtain my own clothing — out of my service as a servant alone, being not born to a free fortune ...”

The word “fain” means both “obliged” and “eager.” Mosca wanted Bonario to think that he (Mosca) was forced to be a parasite in order to get clothing, but actually Mosca enjoyed being a parasite — it gave him an opportunity to use his wits to manipulate other people and attempt to improve his situation in life.

Matthew 6:28 asks, *“And why take ye thought for raiment? Consider the lilies of the field, how they grow; they toil not, neither do they spin”* (King James Version).

Mosca continued, “... but that I have done base offices, in rending friends asunder, dividing families, betraying counsels, whispering false lies, or undermining men with praises, enticed their credulity with perjuries, corrupted chastity, or that I am in love with my own tender ease, but would not rather undergo as a test the most rugged and laborious course that might redeem my present estimation and lift my reputation from bad to good, let me here perish in all hope of goodness.”

This is ambiguous. Does “It is true” apply to these words?

If “It is true” applies to these words, then Mosca was saying the truth: It is true that he has done these evil deeds and it is true that he would rather not do the rugged and laborious deeds that would give him a good reputation, and it is true that Bonario ought to allow him to die here and now so that Mosca would not be able to do these evil deeds and so that goodness would exist.

If “It is true” does not apply to these words, then Mosca was lying to Bonario: He (Mosca) has not done these evil things, and he would prefer to do the rugged and laborious deeds that would give him a good reputation, and if what he just claimed is not true, then let him (Mosca) perish in all hope of goodness — let him give up all hope of eternal life in Heaven.

By being ambiguous, Mosca was able to lie to Bonario yet tell the truth to himself.

Bonario was convinced by Mosca’s crying and by his words. He thought, *This cannot be an impersonated passion. This cannot be false emotion.*

He said to Mosca, “I am to blame. I was mistaken about your nature and character. Please forgive me and tell me your business.”

"Sir, it concerns you," Mosca said, "and although I may seem at first to make a grievous offence in my manners, and in my gratitude to my master, yet out of the pure love that I bear all right, and out of my hatred of the wrong, I must reveal it.

"At this very hour, your father is carrying out his intention to disinherit you —"

"What!" Bonario said.

Mosca continued, "— and thrust you forth into the world, as a complete stranger to his blood. It is true, sir. The work in no way concerns me personally, except as I claim an interest in the general state of goodness and true virtue, which I hear abounds in you, and only for that reason and without a second, ulterior motive, sir, I have done it."

"This tale has lost you much of the recent trust I had in you," Bonario said. "What you say is impossible. I don't know how to believe that my father should be so unnatural as to disinherit me, his flesh and blood."

"You have a confidence in your father that well becomes your filial piety," Mosca said, "and it is formed, no doubt, from your own simple innocence, which makes the wrong done to you all the more monstrous and abhorred."

"Simple" can mean "straightforward," but Mosca was thinking of "simple-minded."

Mosca continued, "But, sir, I now will tell you more. This very minute, the act of disinheriting you is now or soon will be happening, and if you shall only be pleased to go with me, I'll bring you, I dare not say where you shall *see*, but where your *ear* shall be a witness of the deed. You will hear yourself written off as a bastard, and you will hear yourself proclaimed to be the common issue of the earth."

"The common issue of the earth" means "of unknown parentage."

"I am amazed!" Bonario said. "I am bewildered!"

"Sir, if I don't do what I said I would do, draw your just sword, and mark your vengeance on my forehead and face — mark me up as your villain. You are having too much wrong done to you, and I suffer for you, sir. My heart weeps blood in anguish —"

Bonario interrupted, "Lead. I will follow you."

In a room in Volpone's house stood Volpone, Nano the dwarf, Androgyno the hermaphrodite, and Castrone the eunuch.

Volpone said, "Mosca has stayed away for a long time, I think. Bring forth your skills in entertainment, and help to make the wretched time sweet. I am bored; entertain me."

Volpone had sent Mosca to persuade Corvino to allow his wife to sleep with him. Volpone did not know about Mosca's conversation with Bonario.

Nano the dwarf, Androgyno the hermaphrodite, and Castrone the eunuch performed a skit in which they competed to be Volpone's favorite. In doing so, they were mocking the greedy legacy-hunters: Voltore, Corbaccio, and Corvino.

Nano the dwarf recited:

"Dwarf, fool, and eunuch, well met here we be.

"A question it were now, whether [which] of us three,

"Being all the known delicates [acknowledged darlings/favorites] of a rich man,

"In pleasing him, claim the precedency can?"

Castrone the eunuch recited:

"I claim for myself."

Androgyno the hermaphrodite, who was the professional Fool of the group, recited:

"And so does the Fool."

Nano the dwarf recited:

"It is foolish indeed. Let me set you both to school [instruct you both].

"First for your dwarf, he's little and witty,

"And everything, as it is little, is pretty [the littler it is, the prettier it is];

"Else why do men say to a creature of my shape,

"So [As] soon as they see him, 'It's a pretty little ape'?

"And why a pretty 'ape,' but for pleasing imitation

"Of greater men's actions, in a ridiculous fashion?"

Some dwarves made a living by imitating and mocking VIPs.

Nano the dwarf continued:

"Besides, this feat [dainty] body of mine does not crave

"Half the meat, drink, and cloth, one of your bulks [large bodies] will have."

Nano the dwarf now began to talk about Androgyno the hermaphrodite, who was the professional Fool of the group:

"Admit [that] your Fool's face be [is] the mother of laughter,

"Yet, [as] for his brain, it must always come after [be less important]:

"And though that [a funny face that causes laughter] do feed him, it is a pitiful case,

"His body is beholding [beholden] to such a bad face."

Knocking sounded at the door.

"Who's there?" Volpone said.

He then said, "I must go to my couch and appear to be ill."

He then said to Androgyno the hermaphrodite and Castrone the eunuch, "Leave!"

Androgyno the hermaphrodite and Castrone the eunuch exited.

Volpone then said, "Go and look, Nano. See who it is. But give me my caps, first."

Nano the dwarf handed him his two caps.

Volpone then said to him, "Go and enquire who it is."

Nano the dwarf exited.

Volpone prayed to the god of love, "Now, may Cupid let the knocker be Mosca, and may Cupid let Mosca come with good news!"

The good news would be that Volpone could sleep with Corvino's wife.

Nano the dwarf returned and said, "It is the beauteous madam —"

"Lady Would-be? Is it she?" Volpone asked.

Lady Would-be was not beauteous, but that was how she required people to announce her presence.

"The same," Nano the dwarf replied.

"Now torment has come to me!" Volpone said.

He did not want to talk to her, but he had earlier told Mosca to tell her squire to tell her to come back later and visit him.

He said, "Escort her in because she will enter my room or dwell forever in the outer room. Bring her in quickly. The quicker she is here, the quicker she will leave."

Nano the dwarf exited.

Volpone lay on the sleeping couch and said, "I wish that this hardship — her visit — were over. This is one Hell, and I fear a second Hell, too — I fear that my loathing this woman, Lady Would-be, will quite expel my appetite for the other woman, Celia. I wish that the tedious Lady Would-be were now taking her leave. Lord, what I am about to suffer threatens me!"

Nano the dwarf escorted Lady Would-be into the room. She resembled a parrot. Her dress was green with a red collar, and her nose was red from makeup.

"I thank you, good sir," Lady Would-be said to Nano the dwarf. "Please signify to your patron that I am here."

She looked at herself in a mirror and said, "The top of my dress does not show enough of my neck."

The current Italian fashion was to wear a low-cut dress that displayed the breasts more than the English considered proper.

She said to Nano the dwarf, "I need to trouble you, sir. Let me request that you tell one of my women to come here to me."

Nano the dwarf exited to carry out the request.

Looking at herself in the mirror again, Lady Would-be said sarcastically, "Truly, I am dressed most favorably, today! It doesn't matter; it is good enough."

In part, she meant that her waiting-women had not dressed her well, including dressing her hair.

The first waiting-woman and Nano the dwarf entered the room.

Looking in the mirror, Lady Would-be had noticed that the curls on the top of her head were uneven. One curl on the side of her head was higher than all the others.

She said to her waiting-woman about the uneven curls, "Look, and see these insolent, petulant things."

She then said, "How could they have done this?"

"They" referred to both the waiting-women and the curls.

Volpone, unnoticed by Lady Would-be, said to himself, "I feel the fever entering my body at my ears."

Unfortunately for him, it was not a sexual fever.

He added quietly, "Oh, for a charm to frighten it away."

Lady Would-be said to the waiting-woman, "Come nearer. Is this curl in its right place, or is it in this place that you see? Why is this curl higher than all the rest? You have not yet washed your eyes! You can't see because you still have sleep-gum in your eyes! Or are your eyes uneven in your head? Where is your fellow waiting-woman? Bring her to me."

The first waiting-woman exited.

Nano the dwarf said to himself, "May St. Mark deliver us now! Soon, she will beat her serving-women because her nose is red."

The first serving-woman returned with the second serving-woman.

Lady Would-be said, "Please look at my headdress and my hair, forsooth. Are all things apt, or no? Is everything in its right place?"

Pointing, the first serving-woman said, "One hair a little, here, sticks out, forsooth."

Lady Would-be said, "Does it, forsooth? And where was your dear sight, when it did so, forsooth! What! Are you bird-eyed?"

She said to the second serving-woman, "And are you bird-eyed, too?"

"Bird-eyed" meant "round-eyed." The serving-women were surprised and frightened at how seriously Lady Would-be was treating such a small thing.

Lady Would-be said to the two serving-women, "Please, both of you come to me and fix my hair."

They did.

Lady Would-be scolded them as if she were a professor and they were her pupils: "Now, by that light, I muse that you are not ashamed! I, who have preached these things so often to you, read you the principles, argued all the grounds and fundamentals, disputed the pros and cons of every fitness and every grace, called you to meetings to discuss my frequent hairdressing sessions —"

Nano the dwarf thought, *She protects her hair more carefully than she does her reputation or honor.*

Lady Would-be continued, "I have made you acquainted with what an ample dowry the knowledge of these things would be to you. With this knowledge of hairdressing, you would be able, alone, to get yourselves noble husbands at your return to England, and still you neglect to acquire that knowledge like this!

"Besides, you know what a curious and particular nation of people the Italians are. What will they say about me? They will say, 'The English lady cannot dress herself.' Here's a fine imputation for our country of England to be charged with.

"Well, go your ways, and stay in the next room.

"This fucus — skin makeup — I am wearing is too coarse, too, but it doesn't matter."

She asked Nano the dwarf, "Good sir, will you entertain them?"

Nano the dwarf and the two waiting-women exited.

Lady Would-be had been so busy looking in the mirror and complaining to her serving-women that she had not noticed Volpone, who now said to himself, "The storm comes toward me."

Seeing Volpone, Lady Would-be went over to him and asked, "How is my Volpone doing?"

"Troubled with noise, I cannot sleep," Volpone replied. "I dreamt that a strange Fury entered, just now, my house, and with the dreadful tempest of her voice, she split my roof in two."

A Fury is an avenging goddess. They especially take vengeance on people who tear families apart. When Orestes murdered his mother, the Furies pursued and tormented him. Volpone was very willing to tear Corvino's marriage apart by sleeping with his wife, Celia.

Volpone was comparing Lady Would-be in part to the Fury. Furies keep their victims from finding any rest, and Lady Would-be was doing that to him.

Lady Would-be was oblivious to the hint that she was disturbing Volpone. Rather than listen to him, she immediately came up with something to say.

Believing that the topic of conversation was dreams, she said, "Believe me, I had the most fearful dream, if I could remember it."

Volpone thought, *Damn my fate! I have given her the opportunity to torment me. Now she will tell me her dream.*

Lady Would-be said, "I thought that the golden mediocrity is polite and delicate —"

The "golden mediocrity" is the golden mean. Horace used the phrase "*aurea mediocritas*" in his *Odes* Book 2, Poem 10, line 5. The golden mean is the ideal moderate position that lies between two immoderate extremes. For example: Too little courage is cowardice. Too much courage is foolhardiness and rashness. The golden mean is true courage.

In this case, the "golden mediocrity" is a telling phrase. Most of the characters in *Volpone* are immoderately pursuing gold, and that leads to them being golden mediocrities. For example, rather than doing anything important with his life, Volpone spends much of his time pretending to be a very ill man even though this leads to a lack of freedom for him. Because he is supposed to be close to dying, he cannot leave his home unless he is in disguise.

Volpone said to Lady Would-be, "Oh, if you respect and love me, say no more. I sweat and I suffer at the mention of any dream. You can feel me to see how I am still trembling."

Unfortunately, Volpone's mention of his trembling gave Lady Would-be the opportunity to diagnose the "illness" and to prescribe "cures."

"Alas, good soul!" she said. "You suffer from the passion — the suffering — of the heart."

This referred to heartburn and illnesses other than lovesickness affecting the heart.

She instantly began making recommendations of what she considered to be cures: "Seed-pearl would be good now, boiled with syrup of apples, tincture of gold, and coral, citron-pills, elicampane root, myrobalanes —"

Volpone thought, "Damn, I have taken a grasshopper by the wings!"

Grasshoppers make noise with their legs. Holding a grasshopper by the wings does not prevent it from making noise.

Although Volpone wanted Lady Would-be to leave, it seemed as if every word he said was making her stay.

Lady Would-be continued, "— burnt silk, and ambergris. You have good muscatel in the house —"

Ingredients for a cure were often crushed and mixed with muscatel wine for the ill person to drink.

Volpone asked, "Won't you have a drink, and then depart?"

It was customary for visitors ending their visit to be offered a drink before they left.

Lady Would-be said, "No, don't worry that I will do that."

She continued her list of cures: "I'm afraid that we won't be able to get some English saffron — half a dram would be enough. We also need sixteen cloves, a little musk, dried mints, bugloss, and barley-meal —"

Her "cures" were indiscriminate; they were used for a wide range of illnesses, including smallpox and depression, not just for heartburn and other heart ailments.

Volpone thought, *She's set off again! Before, I faked illnesses. Now, I feel as if I really have one!*

Lady Would-be said, "And these ingredients need to be made into a poultice and applied with a true-scarlet cloth."

Volpone thought, *Another flood of words! A complete torrent!*

Lady Would-be asked, "Shall I, sir, make you a poultice?"

"No, no, no," Volpone said. "I am very well. You need prescribe no more medicines."

"I have studied medicine a little," Lady Politic said, "but now, I'm all for music, except I have an hour or two for painting in the mornings.

"I want ladies, indeed, to know all arts and letters, aka fine arts and the literary arts. She should be able to discourse, to write, and to paint, but principal in importance, as Plato holds, is music — and wise Pythagoras, I take it, believes the same thing. Music is the true rapture and harmony.

"When there is harmony in face, in voice, and clothes, that is, indeed, the female sex's chiefest ornament."

Harmony in face apparently includes even — not lopsided — curls, harmony in voice apparently includes talk, talk, talk, and harmony in clothes apparently includes low-cut dresses.

Volpone said, "The poet as old in time as Plato, and as knowing, says that the highest female grace is silence."

In Sophocles' *Ajax*, as translated by R. C. Trevelyan, Tecmessa, Ajax' spear-bride, states that Ajax once told her, "Woman, silence is the grace of woman."

Lady Would-be asked, "Which of your poets? Petrarch, or Tasso, or Dante? Guarini? Ariosto? Aretine? Cieco d'Adria? I have read them all."

She was ignorant of exactly when Plato and these Italian writers lived. None of the writers she mentioned is "as old in time as Plato."

Plato (died 348-347 BCE) is famous for his *Dialogues,* many of which have Socrates as a main speaker. "Plato" means "broad." If you are not cynical, you can think of "broad-shouldered." If you are cynical, you can think of "fatso."

Francesco Petrarch (1304-1374) is a great Italian writer of love poetry.

Torquato Tasso (1544-1595) wrote the epic poem *Gerusalemme Liberata* about the First Crusade. In English, the title is *Jerusalem Delivered.*

Dante Alighieri (1265-1321), one of the greatest poets who ever lived, wrote *The Divine Comedy*, which consists of the *Inferno*, *Purgatory*, and *Paradise*. It describes his imaginative trip to the three destinations of the afterlife.

Battista Guarini (1537-1612) wrote the pastoral tragicomedy *Il Pastor Fido*. In 1602, it was translated into English as *The Faithful Shepherd*. Although Lady Would-be thought Guarini to be a contemporary of Plato, he was still alive at the time she was speaking.

Ludovico Ariosto (1474-1533) wrote *Orlando Furioso* about Charlemagne, Orlando (aka Roland), and the Franks, a collection of Germanic peoples.

Pietro Aretine (1492-1556), a satirist, wrote his "Sonnets of Lust" to accompany sixteen pornographic images by the artist Giulio Romano. The Italian title is *Sonetti Lussuriosi*.

Cieco d'Adria (1541-1585) was a playwright who also translated the first book of Homer's *Iliad*. He is much less well known as an author than the other literary figures mentioned. *Cieco d'Adria* means "the blind man of Adria." His real name is Luigi Groto. Adria is a town in the Veneto region of Northern Italy.

Volpone said to himself, "Is everything a cause to my destruction? Does everything I say cause her to talk and talk and talk?"

Lady Would-be said, "I think I have two or three of their books with me."

Volpone said to himself, "The Sun and the sea will both stand still sooner than her eternal tongue; nothing can escape it."

Lady Would-be found a book and said, "Here's Battista Guarini's *Pastor Fido* —"

Volpone said to himself, "Maintain an obstinate silence. That's now my safest course of action."

Lady Would-be said, "All our English writers, I mean such as are happy enough to be proficient in the Italian language, will deign to steal out of this author, Battista Guarini, mainly. They will steal from him almost as much as from Montagnié's *Essays*."

She pronounced the name Montaigne with too many syllables.

She continued, "Battista Guarini has so modern and facile a vein, befitting the time, and catching the court-ear!

"Petrarch is more passionate, yet he, in the days when writing sonnets was popular, entrusted English writers with much for them to imitate.

"Dante is hard, and few can understand him.

"For an outrageous wit, there's Aretine, but his pictures are a little obscene."

The pictures were actually by the artist Giulio Romano, and they were definitely pornographic.

Lady Would-be said to Volpone, who was maintaining an obstinate silence, "You aren't listening to me."

Volpone replied, "Alas, my mind is perturbed."

Lady Would-be said, "Why, in such cases, we must cure ourselves. We must make use of our philosophy —"

"Oh, me!" Volpone groaned.

Lady Would-be continued, "— and as we find that our emotions strongly rebel, we must encounter them with reason, or divert them, by giving scope to some other emotion of lesser danger."

If we are overcome by one emotion, we may be able to overcome it by reason, or by making an effort to feel another emotion. A person who feels too much melancholy may be able to realize rationally that things are better than they seem or to realize rationally that a certain plan of action will improve things, or may be able to perform some action — listen to music or take a walk, perhaps — that will relieve the melancholy.

Lady Would-be continued, "Just as, in political bodies, there's nothing more that overwhelms the judgment, and clouds the understanding, than too much settling and fixing, and, as it were, subsiding upon one object."

She was using alchemical terms. "Settling" refers to dregs settling in a liquid. "Fixing" refers to making a volatile substance not volatile. "Subsiding" refers to the precipitation of sediment. A political body can spend too much time on one issue. It can expend all its effort on the one issue and then subside into inaction. A more effective political body may work on more than one issue at a time and make incremental improvements on each issue.

Lady Would-be continued, "For the incorporating of these same outward things — these things that compete for our attention — into that part, which we call mental, leaves some certain dregs that stop the organs, and as Plato says, assassinate our knowledge."

Plato wrote about the Theory of the Forms in his books, including *The Republic*. True reality is found in the Forms, such as the Form of Justice. What most people call reality, according to Plato, is only a reflection of true reality.

Lady Would-be's meaning is unclear. Perhaps she meant that people need to take time on think about more important matters. Concentrating on trivial things can be intellectually debilitating, and concentrating on the doing of immoral actions can be very spiritually debilitating. If so, she has made an important point. Concentrating on amassing wealth through immoral means is very debilitating; less debilitating is concentrating on whether one's hairstyle has exactly even curls. Concentrating on achieving something of lasting positive importance can be intellectually and spiritually uplifting.

Volpone said to himself, "May the spirit of patience help me now!"

Lady Would-be said, "Come, truly I must visit you on more days and make you well. I need to make you laugh and be lusty."

One meaning of "lusty" is "to be in vigorous good health."

Volpone said to himself, "May my good angel save me!"

Lady Would-be said, "There was but one sole man in all the world with whom I ever could sympathize, and he would lie, often, three, four hours together to hear me speak, and he would be sometimes so rapt, that he would answer me quite from the purpose, with a non sequitur, like you, and you are like him, exactly."

Apparently, the man either wasn't paying attention to her conversation or wanted to get rid of her.

She continued, "I'll tell you, if only for the purpose, sir, to make you fall asleep, how that man and I spent our time and loves together, for some six years."

Volpone moaned one time for each of the six years: "Oh! Oh! Oh! Oh! Oh! Oh!"

Lady Would-be said, "For we were *coaetanei* — the same age — and brought up —"

Volpone said to himself, "May some power, some fate, some fortune rescue me!"

Mosca entered the room and said, "May God save you, madam!"

"Good sir," Lady Would-be said.

"Mosca?" Volpone said. "Welcome. Welcome to my redemption."

Mosca went over to Volpone and asked, "What do you mean, sir?"

Volpone said quietly so that Lady Would-be would not hear, "Oh, rid me of this my torture, quickly. There she is: my madam, with the everlasting voice. The church bells, in times of pestilence, when they ring constantly to announce each new death from the plague, never made a noise like hers or were in perpetual motion like her tongue! The noise made in cockpits when cocks fight and men gamble is not close to the noise she makes. My entire house, just now, steamed like a bath because of her thick breath. A lawyer could not have been heard, nor scarcely another woman, such a hail of words she has let fall. For Hell's sake, make her leave my home."

Mosca asked, "Has she given you a present?"

Visitors, and especially visiting legacy-hunters, often gave Volpone presents.

"Oh, I do not care about a present from her," Volpone said. "I'll pay any price and suffer any loss for her absence."

Mosca said, "Madam —"

Lady Would-be now gave her present: "I have brought your patron a trifle, a cap here, with my own embroidery."

"That is good," Mosca said.

He added, "I forgot to tell you that I saw your husband the knight at a place where you would little think he would be."

"Where?" Lady Would-be asked.

"Indeed, where yet, if you make haste, you may find him," Mosca said. "He is rowing on the water in a gondola with the most skillful courtesan of Venice."

"Is that true?" Lady Would-be asked.

"Pursue them, and believe your own eyes," Mosca said. "Leave, and I will give your gift to my patron."

Lady Would-be exited hastily.

Mosca said to Volpone, "I knew that trick would work because it is common knowledge that those who give themselves the greatest freedom to flirt are always the most jealous."

Many Italian men were surprised at how much freedom Englishwomen had.

Volpone said, "Mosca, I give you hearty thanks for your quick lie to Lady Would-be and for your delivery of me.

"Now, about my hope to sleep with Celia, Corvino's wife, what news do you have?"

Lady Would-be reentered the room and said, "Listen to me, sir."

Volpone said to himself, "Again! I fear a paroxysm. Any more of this, and I will have a stroke."

Lady Would-be asked Mosca, "Which way did they row together? In which direction were they headed?"

"Toward the Rialto Bridge," Mosca replied.

"Please lend me your dwarf," Lady Would-be requested.

"Please take him," Mosca replied.

Lady Would-be exited.

Mosca said to Volpone, "Your hopes, sir, are like happy blossoms. They are fair, and they promise timely fruit, if you will wait for the ripening. Keep lying on your couch. Corbaccio will arrive quickly with the will. When he has gone, I'll tell you more."

Mosca exited.

Volpone said to himself, "My blood and my spirits are returned. I am alive, and like your reckless gamester, at the game of primero, whose thought had whispered to him, do not go less, I think that I lie, and draw, for an encounter."

The terms he used were from the game of primero. "Not go less" meant either "not make a smaller bet" or "make the highest bet." "Lie" meant "place the bet." "Draw" meant "draw a card." "Encounter" meant "have the cards for a winning hand."

Volpone intended to go through with the seduction. He would lie on the couch and draw Celia toward him for a sexual encounter. He would not go for less than that.

— 3.6 —

Mosca and Bonario talked; they were within hearing distance of Volpone's room.

Mosca showed Bonario a closet and said, "Sir, here you may be entirely concealed, but please have some patience, sir."

Knocking sounded at the door.

Mosca said, "That is the way that your father knocks. I have to leave you."

"Do so," Bonario said.

Mosca exited.

Bonario said to himself, "Yet, I cannot imagine that this is true. I can't believe that I am doing this, and I can't believe that my father would disinherit me."

He went into the closet.

Mosca answered the door and discovered that he had been mistaken. He had expected Bonario's father, Corbaccio, to come, and so he had thought that Corbaccio had knocked. Instead, Corvino and his wife, Celia, were at the door. This was contrary to Mosca's plan. He wanted Bonario to witness his father disinheriting him; he did not want Bonario to witness Volpone sleeping with Celia.

"Death on me!" Mosca said. "You have come too soon. Why did you? Didn't I say that I would send word to you about when to come?"

"Yes, but I feared that you might forget," Corvino said, "and then my rivals might strike first."

Mosca thought, *They might strike first! Has a man ever been so eager to be given the horns of a cuckold! A courtier would not work this eagerly even for a sinecure — a position with much money but little work — at court!*

He said, "Well, now there's no helping it. Stay here. I'll be right back."

He exited.

Corvino looked behind him and said, "Where are you, Celia? Do you know why I have brought you here?"

Celia replied, "Not well, except what you have told me."

Corvino said, "Now I will tell you in more detail. Come here and listen."

They talked together.

Mosca went to the closet in which Bonario was concealed and knocked.

Bonario opened the closet door, and Mosca said to him, "Sir, your father has sent word that it will be half an hour before he comes, and therefore, if you please to walk to that gallery at the upper end, there are some books to entertain you and pass the time, and I'll take care that no man shall come and see you, sir."

Bonario replied, "Yes, I will stay there."

He thought, *I don't trust this fellow.*

He exited.

Mosca watched him go and said to himself, "He is far enough away there that he can hear nothing. And, as for his father, I can keep him away until the right time."

Mosca then went to Volpone's room, where Volpone was lying on a couch, pretending to be ill. Mosca entered the room and went to him.

Meanwhile, Bonario returned and reentered the closet because he did not trust Mosca. Bonario could hear whatever happened in Volpone's room.

Corvino and Celia argued as he forced her into Volpone's room. Volpone and Mosca were able to overhear them.

Corvino said, "Now, there is no going back, and therefore, resolve upon doing what I tell you to do. I have so decreed: It must be done. Nor would I tell you before this because I wanted to avoid all shifts and tricks that might deny me what I want."

Celia said, "Sir, let me beg you not to continue to make these strange trials of my chastity."

Earlier, Corvino had said that he was testing her when he "pretended" to be jealous of her and the mountebank. Celia was hoping that this was another test.

She continued, "If you doubt my chastity, why, lock me up forever: Make me the heir of darkness. Let me live where I may set your jealous fears to rest, even if I don't have your trust."

"Believe it, I have no such jealousy," her husband said. "All that I speak I mean, yet I'm not mad. Nor am I horn-mad, do you see?"

A horn-mad man was afraid of being cuckolded, or he was angry at being cuckolded. Corvino was acting in such a way that it seemed he wanted his wife to cuckold him, and so he was not horn-mad.

He said, "Show me that you are an obedient wife."

"Oh, Heaven!" Celia said.

"I say to you that I want you to do this," Corvino said.

"Is this a trap you have set for me?" Celia asked.

"I've told you the reasons for doing this," her husband said. "The physicians have determined that Volpone is impotent and is dying."

So Corvino had been led to believe.

He continued, "Volpone's death and his will concern me very much. I have made commitments in this business venture: I have given many expensive gifts to Volpone, and it is a necessity for me to regain those gifts and a profit in the form of a legacy. Therefore, if you are my loyal wife, be won over to my side and respect my venture by doing what I tell you to do."

"Should I respect your venture more than I respect your honor?" Celia asked. "Is your financial venture more important than your honor?"

"What is 'honor'?" Corvino asked. "Tut, it is only a breath. There's no such thing in nature. 'Honor' is a mere term invented to awe fools. What! Is my gold the worse because other people have touched it? Are my clothes the worse because other people have looked at them? Why, this is no more."

No more? He meant that his wife would be no worse should Volpone touch her and see her in bed. She would also be no worse if she slept with Volpone.

Corvino continued, "Volpone is an old decrepit wretch, and he has lost the use of his senses. He has no strength. He has to be fed his food with other people's fingers. All he knows is to open his mouth when his gums are scalded with hot food. Volpone is only a voice, a shadow. How can this man hurt you?"

Celia prayed, "Lord, what evil spirit has entered my husband?"

Corvino said, "And as for being worried about your reputation, that's such a laughable excuse. As if I would go and tell what you will have done, and shout it out loud on the Piazza! Who shall know what you will have done, except Volpone, who cannot speak and tell anyone about it, and this fellow Mosca, whose lips are in my pocket? He serves me, and so he will be quiet about this. Unless you yourself proclaim what you will have done, I know no other way that others shall come to know about it."

Celia asked, "Are Heaven and saints then nothing? Will they be too blind to see this, or too stupid to understand what they see?"

"What!" Corvino said.

"Good sir," Celia said, "continue to be jealous about me. Emulate Heaven and the saints. Think about what hate they burn with toward every sin."

"I grant that if I thought this were a sin, I would not urge you to commit it," Corvino said. "If I would offer this to some young Frenchman, or some hot Tuscan blood who had read Aretine, conned all his pornographic prints, knew every twist and turn within lust's labyrinth, and were a professed expert in lechery, and if I would look upon him and applaud him, then this would be a sin.

"But this here is the contrary of a sin. It is a pious work, a good deed, and complete charity that will help an ill man, and it is an honorable course of action to assure that I will get my own."

What he considered "his own" were the gifts he had given to Volpone and the legacy he expected to receive when Volpone died.

"Oh, Heaven!" Celia said. "Can you, Heaven, endure such a change as this that has occurred in my husband?"

Corvino had gone from being overly jealous of his wife to being overly eager to place her in a position in which she could willingly commit adultery — or be raped.

Volpone said quietly, "You are my honor, Mosca, and my pride, my joy, my tickling, my delight! Go and bring them near."

Mosca went to Corvino and said, "Please come near, sir."

Corvino said to Celia, "Come on."

She stood still, and he said, "What! I won't allow you to be rebellious! By that light —"

Mosca said to Volpone, "Sir, Signior Corvino has come here to see you."

"Oh!" Volpone said weakly.

Mosca said, "And hearing about the medical consultation held so recently about your health, he has come to offer, or rather, sir, to prostitute —"

One meaning, now obsolete, of "to prostitute" was "to offer selflessly with complete devotion."

"Thanks, sweet Mosca," Corvino said.

Mosca continued, "— freely, unasked, and unentreated —"

"That is well said," Corvino said.

Mosca continued, "— as the true fervent instance of his love for you, his own most fair and proper wife, the beauty only of price in Venice —"

Celia was Corvino's fair and proper wife. She was beautiful, she was his legally married wife, and she was proper in her behavior. She was seemly, decorous, and respectable. To Corvino, however, she was "only of price." What he valued was only the wealth she could bring him by sleeping with Volpone.

"Only of price" also means "unique in value."

Corvino said to Mosca, "You have stated that well."

Mosca continued, "— to be your female comforter, and to preserve and save you."

Volpone said weakly, "Alas, I am already past being saved!"

Some readers may agree.

He continued, "Please thank him for his good care and promptness, but despite his good care and promptness, it is a vain labor even to fight against Heaven, and to apply fire to stone —"

He broke out in a fit of coughing: "Uh! Uh! Uh! Uh!"

"To apply fire to stone" was an expression denoting uselessness. It is useless to apply fire to stone in an attempt to make the stone catch on fire.

However, "stone" was also a slang word meaning "testicle," and bringing Celia to Volpone was applying sexual fire to Volpone's testicles.

Volpone had started coughing in order to keep himself from laughing at his own pun.

Volpone continued, "— or to make a dead leaf grow again."

A part of Volpone's body that was supposed to be dead would start to grow again if Volpone were left alone with Celia, if Volpone had his way, and his way with her.

Volpone continued, "I take his wishes kindly, though, and you may tell him what I have done for him."

Corvino listened closely, thinking that Volpone had definitely made him his heir.

Volpone continued, "Indeed, my state is hopeless. I wish for him to pray for me, and to use his fortune with reverence, when he comes to have it."

"Reverence" means "deep respect." Corvino's actions showed that he had no reverence for Volpone, Celia, or God.

Mosca said to Corvino, "Did you hear that, sir? Go to him with your wife."

Corvino tried to make Celia go over to Volpone's bed, but she resisted.

He swore, "Heart of my father! Will you persist in being thus obstinate? Come, please, come. You can see that it is nothing, Celia."

He meant that she could see that Volpone was too ill to be able to engage in sex.

Corvino continued, "By this hand—"

He raised his hand in the air and threatened her with it.

He continued, "— I swear that I shall grow violent. Come, do it, I say."

"Sir, kill me, instead," Celia said. "I will swallow poison, eat burning coals, do anything —"

Corvino interrupted, "Be damned! Sweetheart, I'll drag you away from here to home, by the hair. I will cry out in the streets that you are a strumpet. I will rip your face from your mouth to your ears, and I will slit your nose like I would slit the nose of a raw rotchet!"

A rotchet is a fish that is now called the red gurnard. Its head is bony, and to cut it requires much force.

He continued, "Do not provoke me. Come, yield to me, I am loath —"

He was loathsome.

Corvino continued, "By God's death I swear I will buy some slave whom I will kill, and I will bind you — alive — to him, and I will hang you outside my window. I will imagine some monstrous crime that I, in capital letters, will use acid and burning corrosives to eat into the flesh of your stubborn breast. Now, by the blood you have incensed in me, I'll do it!"

"Sir, what you please, you may do," Celia replied. "I am your martyr."

"Don't be obstinate like this," her husband said. "I have not deserved it. Think who it is who is entreating you to do this. Please, sweetheart, you shall indeed have jewels, gowns, clothing and headdresses. Think of what you want, and ask for it. Only go and kiss him, or just touch him ... for my sake ... at my request ... just this once. You won't! No! You will not! I shall remember this. Will you disgrace me thus? Do you crave — thirst for — my undoing, my ruination?"

Mosca said to Celia, "Gentle lady, be persuaded."

"No, no," Corvino said. "She has watched for the right time she can strike and ruin me. By God's precious blood, this action of hers is scurvy, it is very scurvy, and you, Celia, are —"

"Be calm, good sir," Mosca said.

Corvino continued, "—an arrant locust, by Heaven, a locust! A plague of locusts! Whore, crocodile, you who have prepared your tears in advance, anticipating the best time that you can let them flow —"

Crocodiles were thought to cry tears in order to draw their prey toward them. Earlier, Mosca had shed tears in order to manipulate Bonario.

"Please, sir," Mosca said. "She will consider your request."

Celia said, "I wish that the loss of my life would serve to satisfy —"

"By God's death!" Corvino swore. "If she would just speak to him, and save my reputation, it would be something, but she spitefully desires my utter ruination!"

Mosca said, "It is true that you have now put your fortune in her hands."

In other words, Celia *must* sleep with Volpone, or Corvino will be ruined.

Mosca continued, "Why, truly she is holding back because of her modesty. I must acquit her of having any other motivation. If you were absent, she would be more forthcoming."

He thought, *And she would be more cumming.*

He continued, "I know it, and I dare undertake to say that for her. What woman can before her husband?"

Can what? Commit adultery.

Mosca continued, "Please, let us depart, and leave her here."

Corvino said, "Sweet Celia, you may still redeem everything. I'll say no more. If you don't, consider yourself as lost."

Corvino and Mosca began to leave.

Celia tried to follow them, but her husband ordered her, "No, stay there."

Corvino and Mosca exited.

Celia said to herself, "Oh, God, and His good angels! To where, where, has shame fled from human breasts? How is it possible that with such ease men dare put off your — God's and the good angels' — honors, and their own? Is honorable marriage, which always was a cause of life — a reason to live, and an honorable way to bring children into the world — now placed beneath the basest circumstance? Is honorable marriage now valued less than the worst situation? And has modesty been made an exile because of money?"

Volpone said with vigorous good health, "Yes, in the case of Corvino, and other such earth-fed minds —"

He jumped off the couch and continued "— who have never tasted the true Heaven of love. Assure yourself, Celia, that he who would sell you only for the hope of gain — and that hope uncertain — would have sold his portion of Paradise for ready money, if he had met a merchant who would buy it."

Celia, of course, was amazed to see Volpone's vigorous good health.

Volpone asked, "Why are you amazed to see me thus revived? You should rather applaud the miracle that your beauty has made; my revival is your great work. Your beauty has, not just now, but many times raised me, in several shapes."

One shape was the form of an erect penis; the other shape was the disguise of a mountebank. He was lying that he had assumed additional shapes, aka figures, aka disguises, to see her.

He continued, "Just this morning, I assumed the disguise of a mountebank in order to see you at your window. Yes, before I would have stopped my scheming for your love, in varying figures, I would have contended with the blue Proteus, or the horned flood."

Proteus was a sea-god who was a shape-shifter. In Homer's *Odyssey*, Menelaus tells a story of sneaking up on Proteus and holding on to him as he changed shapes and tried to escape. After Proteus gave up trying to escape, he answered Menelaus' questions. As a sea-god, Proteus was sea-colored, aka blue.

In this culture, rivers were often called floods. The horned flood referred to was the shape-shifting river-god Achelous. Hercules and Achelous fought over the mortal woman Deianira. Achelous assumed three shapes — a bull, a snake, and a man with an ox-like face — but Hercules defeated each shape.

Volpone said, "Now you are welcome."

"Sir!" Celia said, backing away from him as he advanced toward her.

"No, don't flee from me," Volpone said. "And don't let your false imagination that I was bedridden make you think I am so. You shall not find that to be true. I am now as fresh, as hot, as high, and in as Jovian a situation as when, in that so celebrated scene, at the recitation of our comedy, for the entertainment of the great Valois, I acted the part of young Antinous and attracted the eyes and ears of all the ladies present — they admired each of my graceful gestures, notes, and movements."

A typical Jovian situation is one in which Jove, King of the gods, transforms himself into another shape in order to commit adultery — often consisting of rape — with a mortal woman. For example, he transformed into a swan in order to have sex with Leda, who gave birth to Castor and Pollux, and he transformed into a shower of gold in order to have sex with Semele, who became the mother of Bacchus.

The "great Valois" is Henry of Valois, who became King Henry III of France. When his brother King Charles IX of France died without leaving children in 1574, Henry returned to France. He traveled through Venice, where he was royally entertained, including with theatrical entertainments.

Antinous was a beautiful young man who was a favorite of the Roman Emperor Hadrian. Henry of Valois was thought to be a transvestite who would have enjoyed looking at — and perhaps more — the beautiful young man.

Volpone thought of Jove — and himself — as so good-looking that women found themselves attracted to them. But Jove often committed rape.

Volpone now sang this song:

"Come, my Celia, let us prove [try],

"While we can, the sports of love,

"Time will not be ours forever,

"He [Time], at length, our good [well-being] will sever;

"Spend not then his gifts in vain;

"Suns, that set, may rise again:

"But if once we lose this light,

"It is with us perpetual night [death].

"Why should we defer our joys?

"Fame [Reputation] and rumor [gossip] are but toys [trifles].

"Cannot we delude the eyes

"Of a few poor household spies?

"Or his [Corvino's] easier ears beguile,

"Thus removed [not present] by our wile [trick]? —

"It is no sin love's fruits to steal:

"But the sweet thefts to reveal;

"To be taken [caught in the act], to be seen,

"These have crimes accounted been."

This was a *carpe diem* — seize the day — song. Soon we will die, and therefore we ought to enjoy what pleasure we can. It was also a seduction song arguing that it is not the committing of adultery that is wrong — instead, getting caught committing adultery is wrong.

Celia prayed, "May some malignant mist blast me or some dire lightning strike this my offending face!"

Her face offended her because its beauty was causing Volpone to act like a beast.

"Why droops my Celia?" Volpone said. "You have, in place of a base husband, found a worthy lover. Use your fortune well, with secrecy and pleasure."

He opened his treasure chest and said, "Look and behold what you are Queen of, not merely in expectation, as I feed the hope of expectation to others; instead, you are definitely possessed of this treasure, and you are crowned as its Queen."

Volpone held a necklace and said, "Look! Here is a pearl necklace. Each pearl is more valuable than that pearl the brave Egyptian queen caroused with. Dissolve these pearls and drink them."

Cleopatra, Queen of Egypt, once dissolved a very valuable pearl in vinegar and drank it in order to impress Mark Antony. Things ended badly for them; both of them committed suicide.

Volpone held some jewels and said, "Look! Here is a ruby that may put out both the eyes of our St. Mark of Venice."

The ruby was so valuable that, according to Volpone, it could bribe even a saint to close his eyes and not see adultery being committed under his nose.

Volpone continued, "Here is a diamond that would have bought Lollia Paulina, when she came in like starlight, hidden under jewels that were the spoils of provinces."

Lollia Paulina, wife of the Roman Emperor Caligula, wore alternate layers of emeralds and pearls "upon her head, in her hair, in her wreaths, in her ears, upon her neck, in her bracelets, and on her fingers," according to the Roman historian Pliny. Her grandfather had taken the jewels from the provinces he ruled. Things ended badly for all of these people. Caligula was assassinated, and both Lollia and her grandfather committed suicide.

Volpone continued, "Take these jewels and wear and lose them. There still remains an earring valuable enough to purchase them again, and this whole state of Venice."

His words were ambiguous. They could have meant that there still remained an earring that was valuable enough to purchase again the lost jewels as well as the whole state of Venice (in which case, he was lying), or his words could have meant there still remains a valuable earring and there still remains the whole state of Venice.

He continued, "A gem that is worth only an individual person's entire estate is nothing: We will eat the value of such a gem at a single meal. The heads of parrots, the tongues of nightingales, and the brains of peacocks and ostriches shall be our food, and if we could get the phoenix, although the bird would become extinct, it would be our dish."

The phoenix is a mythical bird of Arabia. Only one exists at a time, and every five hundred years it sets itself on fire and is reborn from the ashes. Since only one phoenix exists, if Volpone and Celia were to eat it, it would become extinct.

Celia said, "Good sir, these things might move a mind affected by such delights, but I, whose innocence is all I can think is valuable, or worth the enjoying, and which, once lost, I have nothing to lose beyond it, cannot be captured with these sensual baits. If you have a conscience —"

Volpone interrupted, "A conscience is the beggar's virtue. If you have wisdom, listen to me, Celia. Your baths shall be the juice of July-flowers and of the spirit of roses and of violets, the milk of unicorns, and panthers' breath gathered in bags, and mixed with Cretan wines."

July-flowers are clove-scented pinks, unicorns are mythological beings associated with virgins, panthers were believed to have sweet breath that attracted prey, and wine from Crete was expensive.

He continued, "Our drink shall be prepared with gold and ambergris, which we will drink until my roof whirls round with the vertigo. And my dwarf shall dance, my eunuch shall sing, and my Fool shall make up the antic, aka grotesque dance, while we, in changed shapes, will enact Ovid's tales of changes and metamorphoses. Now you shall be like Europa, and I will be like Jove."

Europa was a Phoenician woman whom Jove, King of the gods, lusted after. He transformed himself into a white bull, Europa climbed onto his back, and he kidnapped her by running into the ocean and swimming to Crete, where he either seduced or raped her. She became the first Queen of Crete and the mother of Minos. Europe is named after her.

Volpone continued, "Then I will be like Mars, and you will be like Erycine."

Erycine is a name for Venus, goddess of sexual passion. A temple on Mount Eryx in Sicily was dedicated to her. In Homer's *Odyssey*, a blind bard sings a story of how the two immortals had an affair, which ended badly for them. Being immortal, Mars and Venus cannot die, but Venus' husband, Vulcan, discovered the affair and set a trap for them. While they were having sex, he threw fine chains over them, netting and trapping them. Then he called over the gods and goddesses to look at and laugh at the unhappy adulterers. The goddesses were embarrassed and stayed home, but the gods came to jeer and mock and laugh. By the way, the immortals' Greek names are Ares (Mars), Aphrodite (Venus), and Hephaestus (Vulcan).

Volpone continued, "We will change into the shapes of all the rest of the lovers in Ovid's *Metamorphoses* until we have quite run through them and wearied all the fables of the gods.

"Then I will have you sexually in more modern forms. You will be attired like some sprightly dame of France, a splendid Tuscan lady, or a proud Spanish beauty. Sometimes, you will seem to be the Persian Shah's wife, or the Grand Signior of Turkey's mistress, and for a change you will appear to be one of Venice's most skillful courtesans, or some sexually quick and lively Negro, or a cold Russian, and I will meet you sexually in as many shapes where we may so transfuse our wandering souls" — he kissed her, an act that in the case of spiritual love involved an interchange of souls — "out at our lips, and score up such sums of pleasures —"

He sang these lines:

"That the curious shall not know

"How to tell [count] them as they flow;

"And the envious, when they find

"What their number is, will be pined [pained]."

They would kiss so many times that curious onlookers would not be able to count them and envious people, once they found out the number of kisses, would feel pain.

As she tried to escape from Volpone's advances, Celia pleaded, "If you have ears that will be pierced — or eyes that can be opened — or a heart that may be touched — or any part that yet proclaims manhood about you —"

Volpone would think that his penis proclaims his manhood, but for Celia true manhood lay in spiritual strength.

She continued, "— if you have the slightest trace of the purity of the holy saints — or of Heaven — give me mercy and let me escape — if not, be bountiful and kill me. You know that I am a creature, here ill betrayed by one — my husband — whose shame I would like to forget it is.

"If you will deign to give me neither of these graces, yet feed your wrath, sir, rather than your lust — wrath is a vice that comes closer to manliness — and punish that unhappy crime of nature, that crime which you miscall my beauty. Skin my face, or poison it with ointments, as a punishment for its seducing your blood and passion to this rebellion against ethical conduct. Rub these hands of mine with something that may cause an eating leprosy all the way down to my bones and marrow. Do anything that will disfigure me, except when it comes to my honor — and I will kneel to you, I will pray for you, I will make a thousand hourly vows, sir, for your health, and I will report to everyone — and believe it, too — that you are virtuous —"

The thought of his being virtuous enraged Volpone, who considered it a charge of impotence.

He said, "Do you think that I am cold, frozen, and impotent, and so you will report that to everyone? You seem to think that I have Nestor's hernia."

Nestor was an old Greek advisor to Agamemnon, leader of the Greek troops during the Trojan War. The Roman satirist Juvenal wrote much later that Nestor had a hernia. Some hernias occur in the groin.

Volpone said, "I degenerate and abuse my nation by playing with opportunity thus long."

By "degenerate and abuse my nation," he meant that he had not been acting as macho as he felt Italian men should act.

He continued, "I should have done the act of sex with you, and then have conversed with you. Yield to me, or I'll force you — I'll rape you!"

He grabbed her.

Celia prayed, "Oh, just God!"

Volpone said, "You pray in vain."

Bonario had been listening. Now he rushed in and separated Volpone and Celia, saying, "Forbear, foul ravisher, libidinous swine! Free the forced lady, or you die, impostor. Except that I'm loath to snatch your punishment out of the hand of justice, you would yet be made the timely sacrifice of vengeance before this altar and this dross, your idol."

The altar was Volpone's treasure chest, and the dross was his gold.

Bonario said to Celia, "Lady, let's leave this place; it is the den of villainy. Fear nothing, you have a guard: me. And he, Volpone, before long, shall meet his just reward."

Bonario wanted a law court to justly punish Volpone.

Bonario and Celia exited.

Volpone cried, "Fall on me, roof, and bury me in ruin. Become my grave, you that were my shelter! Oh, I am unmasked, dispirited and flaccid, undone and ruined, betrayed to beggary, betrayed to infamy —"

Mosca entered the room. His face was bleeding where Bonario had wounded him.

He said, "Where shall I, the most wretched shame of men, run so I can beat out my unlucky brains?"

"Here, here," Volpone said, intending to comfort Mosca, but unintentionally answering his question. "What! Are you bleeding?"

"Oh, I wish that Bonario's well-driven sword had been so good as to have cleft me down to the navel before I lived to see my life, my hopes, my spirits, my patron, all thus desperately entangled as a result of my error!"

"Woe on your fortune!" Volpone said.

"And on my follies, sir," Mosca said.

"You have made me miserable," Volpone said.

Mosca had arranged for Celia to come to Volpone. Mosca would also claim to not know that Bonario had hidden himself and eavesdropped on Volpone and Celia.

"And I have made myself miserable, sir," Mosca said. "Who would have thought that Bonario would have eavesdropped, so?"

"What shall we do?" Volpone asked.

"I don't know," Mosca said. "If my heart could expiate — do penance for — this mischance, I'd pluck it out. Will you please hang me? Or cut my throat? And I'll requite you, sir; I'll do the same for you. Let us die like Romans, since we have lived like Grecians."

The Greeks had a reputation for extravagant and reckless living. The Romans had a reputation for dying with honor; some famous Romans had preferred to commit suicide rather than surrender. For example, Cato the Younger had committed suicide rather than surrender to Julius Caesar. Also, Brutus and Cassius committed suicide rather than surrender to Octavian Caesar.

Knocking sounded on the door.

"Listen," Volpone said to Mosca. "Who's there? I hear some footsteps. Venetian police officers have come to apprehend us! I feel the brand hissing already at my forehead; now, my ears are boring."

A Venetian punishment was to brand offenders, often on the forehead. A short while ago, Celia had asked Volpone if he had ears that could be pierced — by her words. Now, his ears were boring — making a hole in themselves. Now, he was wishing that he had listened to her.

Mosca said, "Go to your couch, sir. You must make that place good, whatever it takes. You must keep up the pretense of being an invalid."

Volpone lay down on the couch.

Mosca said, "Guilty men always dread and anticipate what they deserve."

Mosca opened the door and said, "Signior Corbaccio!"

Corbaccio, Bonario's elderly father, walked into the room.

Seeing Mosca's bloody face, Corbaccio said, "Why, what has happened, Mosca?"

The legacy-hunter Voltore arrived and stood in the doorway, unnoticed.

"Oh, I am ruined, amazed, and confused, sir," Mosca said. "Your son, I don't know how, became aware of your changing your will and changing it to make my patron and not him your heir. Bonario violently entered our house, and with his sword drawn he sought you, called you an unnatural wretch, and vowed that he would kill you."

In Mosca's story, Bonario regarded his father as unnatural because his father was disinheriting him. It's natural for parents to take care of their children and make them their heirs.

"Kill me!" Corbaccio said.

"Yes, and he said that he would kill my patron," Mosca said.

"This act shall disinherit him indeed," Corbaccio said.

He gave Mosca a paper and said, "Here is my will naming Volpone as my heir."

Originally, the will was supposed to be a ruse to get Volpone to reciprocate by naming Corbaccio as his heir, but now Corbaccio really intended to disinherit his own son.

"This is good, sir," Mosca said. "It is in the proper legal form."

"It is right and well," Corbaccio said. "Be you as careful now for me. Look after my interests."

"My life, sir, will not be treated with more tender concern than I will have for your interests," Mosca said. "I am only yours."

"How is Volpone?" Corbaccio asked. "Will he die shortly, do you think?"

"I fear that he'll outlast May," Mosca said.

The hard-of-hearing Corbaccio asked, "Today?"

"No, I fear that he will live through May, sir."

"Can't you give him a dram?" Corbaccio asked.

A dram is a measure of liquid medicine, but Mosca understood that Corbaccio meant liquid poison.

Mosca replied, "Oh, by no means, sir."

"I'll not beg you to," Corbaccio said.

Voltore stepped into the room and said, referring to Mosca, "This is a knave, I see."

Seeing Voltore for the first time, Mosca thought, *What! Signior Voltore! Did he overhear me?*

Voltore hissed, "Parasite!"

Mosca said, "Who's that? Oh, sir, you have come at a very good time."

He walked over to Voltore so that Corbaccio could see but not hear them.

"I am scarcely in time to discover your tricks, I fear," Voltore said. "You are only his? And you are only mine, also? Isn't that right?"

"Who?" Mosca said. "I, sir?"

"You, sir," Voltore said. "What plot is this about a will?"

"It is a plot to benefit you, sir," Mosca said.

"Come on," Voltore said. "Don't put your foists upon me; I shall scent them."

The word "foist" means both "trick" and "silent fart." The name "Voltore" means "vulture," and vultures have a keen sense of smell.

"Didn't you hear the plot?" Mosca asked.

"Yes, I heard that Corbaccio has made your patron there" — he pointed to Volpone — "his heir."

"That is true," Mosca said. "This happened as a result of my action. He was persuaded to make the will by my plot, with the hope —"

Voltore interrupted, "— that your patron should reciprocate and make Corbaccio his heir? And you have promised Corbaccio that that will happen?"

"Yes, I did that for your benefit, I did, sir," Mosca said. "Even more, I told his son and brought and hid him here, where he might hear his father give the deed to me. I was determined to do this course of action by the thought, sir, that the unnaturalness (it is unnatural for a father to disinherit a son), first, of the act, and then his father's often disclaiming Bonario as his biological son would surely enrage Bonario (a rage that I intended to inflame) and make him do some violence upon his parent. Because of that violence, the law would take sufficient hold on Bonario to deny him the inheritance, and you would be instated in a double hope."

Mosca was saying that Bonario would kill Corbaccio, his father. Volpone would then inherit Corbaccio's wealth, and after Volpone died, Voltore would inherit the wealth of both Corbaccio and Volpone.

Apparently, Mosca really did want Bonario to kill Corbaccio; this would allow Volpone to immediately inherit Corbaccio's wealth. Mosca was willing to be not only a pimp for Volpone but also an accessory to murder.

Mosca said, "With truth as my comfort and my conscience, I swear that my only aim was to dig you a fortune out of these two old rotten sepulchers —"

Mosca was comparing Corbaccio and Volpone to old rotten sepulchers that contained wealth — wealth that would be robbed from the sepulchers.

Voltore said, "I beg your pardon, Mosca."

Mosca continued, "— a fortune worth your patience, and your great merit, sir. But see the change that Bonario has created in my plan!"

"Why, what happened?" Voltore asked.

"Misfortune," Mosca said. "You must help, sir. While we were awaiting the old raven, Corbaccio, in comes Corvino's wife, sent here by her husband —"

"What, with a present?" Voltore asked.

"No, sir, she was visiting," Mosca said. "I'll tell you why, soon. Because she stayed a long time, the young Bonario grew impatient, rushed forth, seized the lady, wounded me, and made her swear — or he would murder her, that was his vow — to charge that my patron, Volpone, tried to rape her."

Mosca pointed to Volpone, who was lying on the couch, pretending to be a very ill old man, and said, "You can see how unlikely it is that he would attempt to rape her!"

He then continued, "And now with that pretext he's gone away from here to accuse his father, defame my patron, and defeat you in the matter of a legacy from Volpone."

"Where is her husband?" Voltore said. "Let him be sent for immediately."

"Sir, I'll go and fetch him," Mosca said.

"Bring him to the Scrutineo."

Voltore, a lawyer, was very familiar with the Scrutineo, the law court in the Senate House.

"Sir, I will," Mosca said.

"This must be stopped," Voltore said.

"Oh, you do nobly, sir," Mosca said. "Alas, all this was labored, sir, for your good, nor was there any lack of sagacity and planning in the plot. But fortune can, at any time, overthrow the projects of a hundred learned scholars, sir."

The hard-of-hearing Corbaccio asked, "What's that?"

Voltore asked him, "Will it please you, sir, to go along with me?"

Voltore and Corbaccio exited.

Mosca said to Volpone, "Patron, go in and pray for our success."

Volpone rose from the couch and said, "Need makes devotion: People pray most when they most need help. May Heaven bless your labor!"

CHAPTER 4

— 4.1. —

Sir Politic Would-be and Peregrine talked while standing on a street.

Sir Politic Would-be said, referring to the episode with the mountebank (but his words were appropriate to the just-finished episode of Volpone and Celia), "I told you, sir, it was a plot! You see what observation is! You see what keeping your eyes open can do for you!"

He added, "You mentioned to me that you had the need for some instructions about traveling. Since we have met here in this height, aka latitude, of Venice, I will tell you, sir, a few particulars I have set down that are relevant only for this meridian of Venice and are fit to be known by your inexperienced traveller, and they are these that I will tell you. I will not touch, sir, on your language or your clothes, for they are old."

Sir Politic Would-be was using the word "your" indefinitely — "your clothes" meant the clothing of travelers in general. This use of "your" was an affectation that then-travelers to Venice picked up, but in order to make a joke, Peregrine pretended that Sir Politic Would-be was criticizing his clothes.

"Sir, I have better clothes," Peregrine said.

Sir Politic Would-be said, "I meant, as they are themes, aka topics. Language and clothes are old themes that have been much talked about, and so travelers tend to know much about them.

"Oh, sir, proceed," Peregrine said. "I'll slander you no more of wit, good sir."

His last sentence was ambiguous. Sir Politic Would-be understood it to mean this: I won't misrepresent what you say in order to make a joke. Peregrine meant this: I won't slander you by saying that you have wit.

Sir Politic Would-be said, "First, as for your demeanor, you must be grave and serious, very reserved, and closed-mouthed. Do not tell a secret on any terms, not even to your father. You can just barely tell a fable, aka fictitious story, but use caution: Make sure choice both of your company and of your discourse. Be careful that you never speak a truth —"

"What!" Peregrine said.

Sir Politic Would-be continued, "Don't tell the truth to foreigners, for those are the people you must most converse with. Others — travelers from Britain — I would not know, sir, except at a distance, so that I still might be a saver in them. Otherwise, you shall have tricks passed upon you hourly."

A saver is a gambler who neither wins nor loses, but comes out even. By avoiding travelers from his own country — Sir Politic Would-be ignored his own advice when it came to Peregrine — he lost what could have been new friends, but he saved money that he could have lost if he had given them loans. (Sir Politic Would-be spent much time thinking about money; he had taken out loans from the Jewish moneylenders of Venice.)

He added, "And then, as for your religion, profess none, but wonder at the diversity of all religions, and, for your part state that if there were no other than simply the laws of the land, you could be happy. Nick Machiavelli and Monsieur Bodin were both of this mind."

Sir Politic Would-be advised professing to be an atheist as a way of keeping out of trouble while traveling in Venice. At the time, much anti-Catholic feeling was current in England, and Protestant English rulers worried that English travelers might acquire what the rulers considered to be bad religious thought in Catholic countries such as Italy.

Niccolo Machiavelli wrote in *The Prince* that political goals came before religious goals. Jean Bodin argued in *La Republique* that to avoid civic unrest political rulers ought to be religiously tolerant. It is wrong to say that these authors advocated atheism.

Of course, believers consider it a virtue not to hide their religion.

Sir Politic Would-be continued, "Then you must learn the use and handling of your silver fork at meals and the metal of your glass (these are important matters to your Italian) and to know the hour when you must eat your melons and your figs."

Forks were still not widely used in England at the time, but they would be in a few years. Venice was famous for its glassware, and the "metal" of the glass referred to the quality of the molten glass used to make the glassware.

"Is that a point of state, aka a point of diplomacy, too?" Peregrine asked.

"Here in Venice it is," Sir Politic Would-be said. "As for your Venetian, if he sees a man who is even a little bit preposterous and not behaving in the conventionally correct manner, he immediately makes a judgment about his character, and he strips him of his dignity by taunting him."

Actually, that is true of many people other than Venetians. It was true of Peregrine, for example, as events have already and would soon show.

Sir Politic Would-be continued, "I'll acquaint you, sir, with the knowledge that I now have lived here some fourteen months since the first week of my landing here. Everyone took me for a citizen of Venice because I knew the forms so well —"

Peregrine thought, — *the forms and nothing else.*

He meant that Sir Politic Would-be knew the outward appearance but nothing of any real substance.

Sir Politic Would-be said, "I had read Contarini."

Cardinal Gasparo Contarini's *De Magistratibus et Republica Venetorum*, was published in 1589. Sir Lewis Lewkenor's English translation *The Commonwealth and Government of Venice* was published in 1599.

He continued, "I leased a house, dealt with my Jewish moneylenders to furnish it with moveable property — well, if I could but find one man, one man after my own heart, whom I dared to trust, I would —"

"Would what, sir?" Peregrine asked.

"— make him rich," Sir Politic Would-be said. "Make him a fortune. He should not think again. I would command it."

The other man would not have to think; Sir Politic would do the thinking for both of them.

"How?" Peregrine asked.

"With certain projects that I have," Sir Politic Would-be said, "which I may not reveal."

Sir Politic Would-be seems to have been leery of lending money to other travelers. That is good advice for Peregrine. Many people have hare-minded projects that are certain or almost certain to lose money. That was true then, and it is true now.

Peregrine thought, *If I had even one person to wager with, I would lay odds now that Sir Politic will reveal his projects to me immediately.*

"One of my projects," Sir Politic Would-be said, "and it is one that I don't care greatly who knows about it, is to serve the state of Venice with smoked herrings for three years, and at a certain rate, from Rotterdam in the Netherlands, where I have correspondence."

Given that Venice is located on the Adriatic Sea, one wonders about the intelligence of importing fish all the way from the Netherlands.

Holding a paper, Sir Politic Would-be continued, "There's a letter, sent me from one of the States, and to that purpose."

The word "States" was deliberately ambiguous. By "one of the States," Sir Politic Would-be meant "one of the provinces"; Rotterdam is located in the province of South Holland. However, he was hoping that Peregrine would understand "one of the States" to mean "one of the members of the Dutch States-General," the bicameral legislature of the Netherlands.

Sir Politic Would-be continued, "He cannot write his name, but that's his mark."

He wanted Peregrine to think the correspondent could not write his name on the letter because of the confidential content of the letter, but Peregrine was likely to think, *Yes, Sir Politic Would-be is exactly the kind of man who would receive a letter from a man who is unable to write anything, including his own name.*

Peregrine called the bluff: "Is the writer of the letter a chandler?"

A chandler is either a retail grocer or a ship's provisioner.

Sir Politic Would-be replied, "No, a cheesemonger — a seller of cheeses and other dairy products. There are some others, too, with whom I treat about the same negotiation, and I will undertake it. For this is how it will work: I'll do it with ease because I have planned it all. Your hoy carries only three men in her, and a boy."

A hoy is a small Dutch sloop used for short hauls along the coast; it is too small for a voyage from the Netherlands to Venice, Italy.

He continued, "And she shall make me three round trips a year."

That means three cargoes of smoked herring.

He continued, "So, if there comes to fruition only one of three, I save."

He would break even if the hoy successfully made one voyage. However, this is true only if the first voyage is successful. If the hoy sinks on the first voyage, there will not be a second or a third voyage.

He continued, "If two voyages are successful, I can defalk."

The word "defalcation" means "diminution" or "reduction." Presumably, Sir Politic Would-be meant that if two voyages were successful, he would make a profit on the business venture and could pay back some of the money he owed to Jewish moneylenders. We should note that word "defalk" is very close to the spelling of the word "default," which is likely what Sir Politic Would-be would do with any loan gotten to finance the business venture.

Sir Politic Would-be continued, "But this is only if my main project fails."

"Then you have others?" Peregrine asked.

"I would be loath to draw the subtle and cunning air of such a place as Venice without coming up with a thousand schemes of my own," Sir Politic Would-be said. "I'll not lie, sir. Wherever I come to live, I love to be considerative: I love to analyze what is around me.

"And it is true that I have during my free hours thought upon some certain benefits for the state of Venice, which I call 'my Precautions,' and, sir, which I mean, in hopes of being granted a pension, to propound to the Great Council, then to the Forty, and so on up to the Ten."

The Great Council, the Forty, and the Ten were the most important governing bodies of Venice.

He continued, "My means are made already —"

The "means" were his means of access. He had to get access to the Great Council, the Forty, and the Ten in order to make his proposals to them. Normally, to do that you had to know someone important.

"By whom are they made?" Peregrine asked.

"Sir, by one whom, although his position is obscure and low, yet he can sway, and they will hear him. He's a police officer."

This is a minor court official who is in charge of arresting and summoning offenders.

"What!" Peregrine said. "A common sergeant?"

He was incredulous that such a minor court official could get Sir Politic Would-be access to the Great Council, the Forty, and the Ten.

"Sir, even minor court officials such as the police officer put into the mouths of the Great Council, the Forty, and the Ten what they should say, sometimes, just like greater men do. I think I have my notes to show you —"

He began to look through his pockets.

Peregrine began, "Good sir —"

Sir Politic Would-be interrupted, "But you shall swear to me, as you are a gentleman, not to steal my ideas —"

"I, sir!" Peregrine said.

"— nor to reveal any of the details of my plans."

He stopped searching his pockets and said, "My notes are not on me."

"Oh, but you can remember your ideas, sir," Peregrine said.

"My first idea concerns tinderboxes," Sir Politic Would-be said. "You must know that no family is here without its tinderbox. Now, sir, let's say that you or I were ill disposed toward the Venetian government. Tinderboxes are very portable, and with one in our pockets, might not you or I go into the Arsenal and come out again?"

The implication was that they could easily set fire to the Arsenal, which was the shipyard where ships and ordnance were located. In fact, in the 1560s, the Arsenal had exploded and burned.

Sir Politic Would-be continued, "And no one would be the wiser."

"Except yourself, sir," Peregrine said. Peregrine would definitely *not* set fire to the Arsenal, and he did not think the people of Venice would do so. Since the Arsenal was heavily guarded, it also seemed unlikely that the enemies of Venice would be able to use tinderboxes to set fire to the Arsenal.

"Very well, then," Sir Politic Would-be said. "I therefore would warn and advise the Venetian government how fitting it would be that none but such people as are known patriots, sound lovers of their country, should be allowed to enjoy tinderboxes in their houses. Also, those tinderboxes would be licensed at some government office, and they would be so big that they could not be hidden in pockets."

"Admirable!" Peregrine said.

Sir Politic Would-be said, "My next idea concerns how to find out by an immediate demonstration whether a ship, newly arrived from Syria or from any suspected part of all the Levant, aka the Eastern Mediterranean, is guilty of carrying the plague."

This would be useful, indeed, if it could be done accurately.

He continued, "Right now ships are quarantined for forty, fifty days, sometimes, around the two islands with a lazaretto, aka quarantine house, for their trial period. If no signs of plague show up after forty or fifty days, then the ships can come to Venice. I'll save that expense and loss for the merchant, and in an hour show whether or not the ship carries the plague —"

"Indeed, sir!" Peregrine said.

Sir Politic Would-be continued, "— or I will lose my labor."

If his test for determining whether a ship was or was not carrying the plague were implemented and failed, he could lose his life — and thousands of other people could lose their lives.

Peregrine said, "By my faith, that's much."

"Sir, understand me," Sir Politic Would-be said. "It will cost me in onions, some thirty *livres* —"

Livres are French pounds.

"Which is one pound sterling," Peregrine said.

"Beside my waterworks," Peregrine said, "for this is what I will do, sir. First, I will bring in your ship between two brick walls, but those the state shall invest in. On the one wall I will stretch a fair tarpaulin, and in that I will stick my onions, cut in halves. The other wall will be full of loop-holes, out at which I will thrust the noses of my bellows; and those bellows I will keep, using the waterworks, in perpetual motion, which is the easiest matter of a hundred. Now, sir, your onion, which does naturally attract the infection of plague, and your bellows blowing the air upon the onion, will show, instantly, by its changed color, that there is contagion, or if there is no contagion of the plague the onion will remain as fair as it was at the first."

His plan had a few faults:

1) The waterworks are powered by moving water, but Venice is unlikely to have a suitable source of moving water. Sir Politic Would-be seems to have gotten this part of his idea from a water-driven mill on a river.

2) People of the time believed that a cut onion would absorb plague particles from the air. This is wrong, but Sir Politic Would-be would look at the cut onion and see if its color had changed. In a short time, a cut onion will turn brown through exposure to even pure air. If Sir Peregrine were to look instantly at the onion, as he had said, the onion would not have changed color and so his test would conclude that every ship was free of the plague. If Sir Peregrine waited a short time to look at the onion, since it would take time for the test to be done, the onion would have changed color and so his test would conclude that every ship was infected with the plague.

Sir Politic Would-be said, "Now my idea is known, it is nothing."

He meant that once his idea was known, it seemed obvious.

"You are right, sir," Peregrine said.

He meant that the idea was worth nothing.

"I wish I had my notes," Sir Politic Would-be said as he looked through his pockets.

"Indeed, I wish the same thing," Peregrine said. "But you have done well for once, sir."

He had done well at amusing Peregrine.

"If I were traitorous, or would be made so," Sir Politic Would-be said, "I could show you ways that I could sell this state of Venice now, to the Turks, in spite of the Venetian galleys, or their —"

He was verging on getting himself — and Peregrine — in real trouble with the Venetian government, whose enemies were the Turks.

Peregrine began to caution him, "Please, Sir Pol —"

Sir Politic Would-be took the hint and said, "I don't have my notes on me."

"I feared that," Peregrine said, meaning both Sir Politic Would-be's treasonous ideas and his not having his notes on him.

Sir Politic Would-be found a notebook, and Peregrine said, "There are your notes, sir."

"No," Sir Politic Would-be said. "This is my diary, in which I note my actions of the day."

"Please let me see it, sir," Peregrine said.

Sir Politic Would-be handed him his diary, and Peregrine asked, "What is here?"

He read a part of Sir Politic Would-be's diary out loud:

"*Notandum, a rat had gnawn my spur-leathers; notwithstanding, I put on new spur-leathers, and did go forth, but first I threw three beans over the threshold.*"

Notandum is Latin for "It should be noted."

Sir Politic Would-be wore spurs to indicate his status as a knight, despite there being no practical reason for wearing spurs in Venice, a city without horses. Spur-leathers are laces that are used to tie spurs to boots.

His diary entry showed that he was superstitious. Throwing three beans over the threshold was supposed to ward off the evil foretold by the rat's gnawing the spur-leather.

Peregrine continued reading out loud:

"*I went and bought two toothpicks, of which I broke one immediately, in a discourse with a Dutch merchant about* ragion' del stato."

Ragion' del stato are "reasons of state," aka "political matters."

Peregrine continued to read Sir Politic Would-be's diary out loud:

"*From him I went and paid a* moccinigo, *aka small coin, for mending my silk stockings. Along my way, I bargained for herring, and at St. Mark's I peed.*"

Peregrine said, "Indeed, these are politic notes!"

Meanings of "politic" include "political, shrewd, cunning, and scheming." A better word to describe the contents of Sir Politic Would-be's diary is "trivial."

Sir Politic Would-be said, "Sir, I let pass no action of my life without making a note of it."

"Believe me, that is wise!" Peregrine said.

Sir Politic Would-be said, "Sir, continue to read."

Lady Would-be now arrived. With her were Nano the dwarf and her two waiting-women.

Lady Would-be said, "Where would this loose knight be, I wonder? I'm sure he's in a whorehouse and part of his body is housed in a whore's body."

"Why, then he's fast," Nano the dwarf said, punning on the con game known as fast and loose.

By "fast," he meant "fast-moving."

She replied, "Yes, he plays both — fast and loose — with me. By "loose," she meant that he was wanton and that he was now with a "loose" woman.

"Please stay here and rest for a moment. This heat will do more harm to my makeup than his heart is worth. I do not care to hinder and stop him, but instead to take him in the act."

She rubbed the side of her nose and said, "How my makeup is coming off!"

The first woman-servant saw Sir Politic Would-be and said, "My master's yonder."

"Where?" Lady Would-be asked.

The first woman-servant pointed and added, "He's with a young gentleman."

Lady Would-be said, "That person is the party we're after. She's dressed in male apparel!"

Venice was known for both its female courtesans and for its many homosexual transvestite prostitutes. Resenting the competition, some female courtesans began to wear men's clothing, apparently hoping to get business in sodomy. Lady Would-be thought that Peregrine, a young man, was a female courtesan who was wearing men's clothing.

Lady Would-be said to Nano the dwarf, "Please, sir, jostle my knight to get his attention. I'll be gentle out of concern for his reputation, however much he deserves blame."

Seeing her, Sir Politic Would-be said, "My lady!"

"Where?" Peregrine asked.

"It is she indeed, sir," he replied. "You shall know her. She is, I would say even if she were not mine, a lady of much merit as concerns fashion and behavior, and as for beauty I dare compare —"

"It seems you are not jealous," Peregrine said, "since you dare to praise her to another man."

"As for discourse and conversation —"

"Being your wife, she cannot miss that."

Peregrine meant that if she were Sir Politic Would-be's wife, she must be talkative.

Sir Politic Would-be tried to introduce Peregrine and his wife, "Madam, here is a gentleman. Please treat him well. He seems to be a youth, but he is —"

Lady Would-be finished the sentence: "— none."

She meant that Peregrine was a female prostitute dressed in men's clothing.

Sir Politic Would-be said, "Yes, he is a gentleman who has put his face so soon into the world —"

By "so soon," he meant "at so early an age."

Lady Would-be misunderstood him: "You mean, 'as early'? As early as today?"

She meant that Peregrine had begun to dress as a man only this day.

Sir Politic Would-be asked, "What do you mean?"

His wife replied, "Why, I mean in this suit of clothing, sir; you understand me, I am sure."

She believed that her husband definitely knew that Peregrine was a female courtesan dressed in men's clothing.

She continued, "Well, Master Would-be, this does not become you. I had thought the odor, sir, of your good name would have been more precious to you. I had thought that you would not have done this dire massacre on your honor, especially considering your gravity and rank! But knights, I see, care little for the oaths they make to ladies — chiefly, their own ladies."

One such oath is the oath they make in the marriage ceremony.

"Now by my spurs, the symbol of my knighthood —" Sir Politic Would-be began.

Peregrine thought, *Lord, how his brain is humbled for an oath!*

In thinking of an oath to make to his wife, Sir Politic Would-be's brain, aka thought, went down to his heels where his knight's spurs were. Also, Peregrine believed that Sir Politic Would-be had bought his knighthood rather than earned it. King James I of England made people knights in return for money.

Sir Politic Would-be finished his oath, "— I don't understand you."

His wife said, "Right, sir, your cunning may carry it off, thus. Go ahead. Pretend that you don't understand me."

She then said to Peregrine, "Sir, I want to have a word with you. I would be loath to argue publicly with any gentlewoman, or to seem perverse, or violent. I want to act as *The Courtier* advises."

The Courtier was a famous book of etiquette.

She continued, "Doing that comes too near rusticity, aka country vulgarity, in a lady, which I would shun by all means, and whatever I may deserve from Master Would-be, yet to have one fair gentlewoman thus be made the unnatural instrument to wrong another, and one she does not know, and to persevere in doing so ... well, in my poor judgment, that is not warranted because it is a solecism in our sex, if not in manners."

A "solecism" is an impropriety in grammar or in behavior.

In addressing Peregrine, she sometimes referred to him as male and sometimes as female. She believed him to be biologically female but dressed as male.

"What is this!" Peregrine said.

Sir Politic Would-be said to his wife, "Sweet madam, come nearer to your aim. Speak more plainly."

"Indeed, and I will, sir," Lady Would-be said, "since you provoke me with your impudence and laughter about your light, aka licentious, land-Siren here, your Sporus, your hermaphrodite —"

In Homer's epic poem *The Odyssey*, Sirens are dangerous creatures with beautiful voices that they use to lure sailors to sail their ships close to shore and wreck them on the rocks. Since her husband was on dry land, Lady Would-be called Peregrine a land-Siren.

Sporus was a young boy who was a favorite of the dissolute Roman Emperor Nero, who had him castrated and dressed in female clothing. Nero then "married" him.

"What do we have here?" Peregrine said. "Poetic fury, and historic storms?"

The Sirens came from poetry, and Sporus came from history.

Sir Politic Would-be said about Peregrine, "The gentleman, believe it, is a worthy man, and he is from our nation."

He meant that Peregrine was from England.

His wife said, "Yes, he is from your Whitefriars nation."

Whitefriars was a place in London where prostitutes flocked because it was a "liberty," a place where sanctuary was given.

Lady Would-be said, "Come, I blush for you, Master Would-be, and I am ashamed you should have no more forehead, aka sense of shame, than thus to play the patron, or St. George, to a lewd harlot, a base fricatrice, a female devil, wearing a male's appearance."

A "fricatrice" is a masseuse, or in this case, a prostitute.

Sir Politic Would-be now understood what his wife thought Peregrine was, and he thought that she might be right!

He said to Peregrine, "If you are such a person as my wife thinks you are, I must bid adieu to your delights. The case appears too liquid."

The word "liquid" meant "clear and transparent."

His wife said to him as he exited, "Yes, you may carry it clear and pretend not to know that this 'man' is a woman, with your state-face — your hypocritical demeanor!

"But as for this, your carnival concupiscence, who has fled here to Venice for liberty of conscience, from the furious persecution of the Marshal, I will discipline her."

The "carnival concupiscence" was Peregrine, whom she thought to have the lechery that was displayed by many people during carnivals.

Lady Would-be thought that Peregrine had fled to Venice for liberty of conscience. Puritans and Catholics and other people whose religion was persecuted used "liberty of conscience" to mean religious freedom, but she used it to mean "freedom from conscience" — the freedom to do whatever evil action one wishes to do without having to worry about being punished — often with a whipping — by the Marshal.

"This is fine, indeed!" Peregrine said. "And do you often act like this? Is this the way you exercise your wits in preparation for when you have the opportunity to use them? Madam —"

"Come off it, sir," Lady Would-be said sarcastically.

She grabbed his shirt and tried to pull it off in an attempt to show that Peregrine was in fact a woman.

"Do you hear me, lady?" Peregrine said. "Why, if your knight has made you beg for shirts, or to invite me home, you might have done it a nearer way, by far."

Peregrine was now thinking that Sir Politic Would-be had set a trap for him, a trap that perhaps included pimping his wife to Peregrine.

Lady Would-be said, "Your words won't get you out of my snare."

She held on tightly to his shirt.

"Why am I in your snare?" Peregrine said. "Tell me that. Indeed, your husband told me you were fair, and so you are, only your nose inclines, that side that's facing the Sun, to the queen-apple."

The queen-apple is red. Peregrine was saying that one side of her nose was red. The other side had lost its makeup when Lady Would-be had rubbed her nose.

"This cannot be endured by any patience," Lady Would-be said.

Mosca entered the scene.

Seeing Lady Would-be, he asked, "What is the matter, madam?"

She replied, "If the Venetian Senate doesn't do me justice in the suit I will make to them about this, I'll protest to all the world that they are no aristocracy."

Niccolo Machiavelli had stated in *The Prince* that Venetian aristocrats could not be real aristocrats because they were merchants.

"What is the injury he has done to you, lady?" Mosca asked.

"Why, the callet — the whore — you told me about, I have here taken disguised."

"Who?" Mosca said. "This person! What does your ladyship mean? The creature — the callet — I mentioned to you is apprehended now, and she is appearing before the Senate; you shall see her —"

"Where?" Lady Would-be asked.

"I'll take you to her," Mosca said. "As for this young gentleman, I saw him land this morning at the port."

"Is it possible!" Lady Would-be said. "How my judgment has wandered astray!"

She said to Peregrine, "Sir, I must, blushing, say to you that I have erred, and I beg your pardon."

A wary Peregrine said, "What, still more changes!"

Lady Would-be said, "I hope that you lack the malice to remember a gentlewoman's passion. If you stay in Venice here, please use me, sir —"

By "passion," she meant "anger," but the word is also used in the phrase "sexual passion."

By "use," she meant "allow me to help you" — she could help him socially. But the word is also used to mean "use sexually."

"Will you go now, madam?" Mosca asked.

Lady Would-be continued to speak to Peregrine, "Please, sir, use me. Indeed, the more you use me, the more I shall conceive ... that you have forgot our quarrel."

One meaning of the word "conceive" is "get pregnant."

Lady Would-be, Mosca, Nano the dwarf, and the two serving-women exited.

Peregrine was certain that Sir Politic Would-be was prostituting his wife to him.

Alone, Peregrine said to himself, "This is strange! Sir Politic Would-be? No, his name ought to be Sir Politic Bawd. To make me thus acquainted with his wife!

"Well, wise Sir Pol, since you have played this trick upon my innocent freshmanship, I'll test your salt-head to see how invulnerable it is against a counter-plot."

A salt-head is an experienced head. The word "salt" also means "wanton."

Voltore, Corbaccio, Corvino, and Mosca arrived at the Scrutineo.

Voltore, who was a lawyer and would be speaking for them in the court of law, said, "Well, now you know the management and conduct of the business. Your constancy is all that is required to the safety of it."

They had met and determined on the lying story they would tell the four Advocari, aka Judges. To get away with their lie, they had to stick to their story.

Mosca asked, "Is the lie safely and surely communicated among us? Is that definitely the case? Does every man know his burden?"

The "burden" is the refrain to a song. Mosca was asking whether each man knew his part of the lying story they would tell the Judges.

"Yes," Corvino said.

"Then shrink not," Mosca said, going over to Corvino.

"But does Voltore the advocate know the truth?" Corvino quietly asked Mosca.

The truth was that Corvino had tried to prostitute his wife, Celia, to Volpone.

"Oh, sir, by no means," Mosca quietly said. "I devised a tale that has completely saved your reputation. But be valiant, sir."

Corvino said quietly, "I fear no one but Voltore the lawyer. I fear that his pleading on our behalves could make him stand for a co-heir —"

"Co-halter!" Mosca quietly said. "Hang him."

A "halter" is a hangman's noose. Mosca wanted to put to rest Corvino's fear that anyone but him would be Volpone's heir.

Mosca quietly continued, "We will only use his tongue, his noise, as we do Croaker's here."

"Croaker" was a way of referring to Corbaccio, who as an old man spoke in a croaking voice.

"What shall he — Corbaccio — do?" Corvino said.

"When we have done, you mean?" Mosca asked.

"Yes."

"Why, we'll think about that," Mosca said. "We'll sell him for mummia; he's half dust already."

Mummia was a medicine that was made from mummies, or from dried corpses. As an old man, Corbaccio was already half-dried out.

Mosca went over to Voltore and said quietly, referring to Corvino, "Doesn't it make you smile to see this buffalo and how he playfully tosses his head?"

Buffalo and cuckolds have horns. Celia had not cuckolded Corvino, but that was not what these four men would testify in court.

Mosca thought, *I also will toss my head playfully if everything turns out well.*

Mosca said loudly to the hear-of-hearing Corbaccio, "Sir, only you are that man who shall enjoy the crop of all Volpone's wealth, and these other two men — Corvino and Voltore — don't know for whom they are toiling."

"True," Corbaccio said. "Peace. Be quiet."

He was worried that Corvino and Voltore would hear.

Mosca said to Corvino loudly enough for Voltore to hear, "But you shall eat the crop — you shall enjoy Volpone's wealth."

He then went to Voltore and quietly said, "Fat chance!"

He then said to Voltore loudly enough for all to hear, "Worshipful sir, may Mercury sit upon your thundering tongue, or the French Hercules."

Mercury is the god of eloquence, as well as the god of thieves and liars. The gods are much stronger than mortals.

After Hercules completed his Tenth Labor, stealing the cattle of Geryon, he passed through France and became the ancestor of the French people. According to the satirist Lucian, Hercules became a master of eloquence in his old age.

If Mercury were to sit upon Voltore's thundering tongue, he quite possibly could get it dirty or he could make it capable of telling eloquent lies.

If Mercury were to sit upon the French Hercules, it would be a case of might makes right. Hercules is strong, and the truth is strong, but both can be overcome by a greater strength and by guile.

Hercules killed the Centaur Nessus when Nessus tried to rape Hercules' wife, Deianira. As Nessus was dying, he told Deianira that his blood was charmed. She should soak one of Hercules' shirts with the blood and then give him the shirt if Hercules were ever attracted to another woman. Much later, Hercules was attracted to another woman, and Deianira gave him the shirt, but Nessus' blood was like acid, and Hercules killed himself to escape the torment.

Mosca loudly continued, "And may Hercules make your language as conquering as his club, to beat at full length flat, as with a tempest, our adversaries."

He then said quietly to Voltore, "But they are much more your adversaries, sir."

Voltore was going to argue to defeat his two adversaries in court: Celia and Bonario. In addition to defeating them, he was hoping to defeat his other two adversaries — Corvino and Corbaccio — and inherit all of Volpone's wealth.

"Here they come," Voltore said. "Be quiet now."

The four Judges and Celia, Bonario, the Notary, and the police officers were coming.

"I have another witness, if you need one, sir, whom I can produce," Mosca said.

"Who is it?" Voltore asked.

"Sir, I have her," Mosca said.

Events would reveal the other witness: Lady Would-be.

— 4.5 —

The four Judges, Celia, Bonario, the Notary, the police officers, and others arrived. The four Judges had already listened to the testimony of Bonario and Celia.

The four Judges sat and talked.

The First Judge said, "The like of this case the Venetian Senate has never heard of."

The Second Judge said, "It will sound most strange to them when we report it."

The Judges reviewed cases and could recommend them to go before the Venetian Senate. In this case, however, the Judges would decide to make the judgment themselves.

The Fourth Judge said, "Celia, the gentlewoman, has always been held to have an unreproved reputation. She has always been thought to be of good character."

The Third Judge said, "So has the youth Bonario."

The Fourth Judge said, "The more unnatural part is that of his father, Corbaccio."

Corbaccio had disinherited his son; this was unnatural — it was not something a biological father would do.

The Second Judge said, "Even more unnatural is the act of Celia's husband, Corvino."

Corvino had attempted to prostitute his wife, Celia, to Volpone.

The First Judge said, "I don't know what name to give his act because it is so monstrous!"

The Fourth Judge said, "But the impostor, Volpone, is a thing created to exceed precedent!"

Voltore was an imposter because he was pretending to be a seriously ill man although he was well enough to attempt to rape Celia.

The First Judge said, "And he was created to exceed all future possibilities!"

The Second Judge said, "I never heard a true voluptuary described, except for him."

A voluptuary is a sybarite, a person who is self-indulgent in the pursuit of luxury or gratification of the senses.

The Third Judge asked, "Has everyone who was subpoenaed arrived?"

The Notary replied, "All, except for the old *magnifico*, Volpone."

A *magnifico* is a great person in Venice.

The First Judge asked, "Why isn't he here?"

"If it please your Fatherhoods, here is Volpone's advocate," Mosca said. "Volpone himself is so weak, so feeble —"

"Fatherhoods" is in fact the correct way to address the Judges.

The Fourth Judge asked Mosca, "Who are you?"

"Volpone's parasite, his knave, his pandar," Bonario said. "I beseech the court to force Volpone to come to the court so that your grave eyes may bear strong witness of his strange impostures."

Voltore the lawyer said to the Judges, "Upon my faith and my credit with your virtues, I swear that Volpone is so ill that he is not able to endure the air."

The Second Judge said, "Bring him here, nevertheless."

The Third Judge said, "We will see him."

The Fourth Judge said, "Fetch him."

Voltore said, "May your Fatherhoods' fitting pleasures be obeyed."

Some officers of the law exited to get Volpone.

Voltore then said, "But surely, the sight of Volpone will rather move your pities than your indignation.

"May it please the court that in the meantime, he may be heard in me — I am his representative and can speak for him. I know that this place is most void of prejudice, and therefore I crave to be heard, since we have no reason to fear that our truth would hurt our case."

The Third Judge said, "Speak freely."

Voltore said, "Then know, most honored fathers, I must now reveal to your strangely imposed-upon ears the most prodigious and most shameless piece of downright impudence and treachery that vicious nature ever yet brought forth to shame the state of Venice."

He pointed to Celia and said, "This lewd woman, who lacks no artificial looks or tears to help the vizor — the mask — she has now put on, has long been known to be a secret adulteress with that lascivious youth there."

Celia was crying at being called "lewd." She was wearing the half-mask that many Venetian women wore while in public, but Voltore was saying that she wore a mask of innocence to hide her guilt.

He pointed to Bonario and then continued, "She has not just been suspected, I say, but definitely known, to be an adulteress, and she has been taken in the act with him."

He pointed to Corvino, her husband, and said, "She has been pardoned by this man, the too-easy, too-credulous husband, whose everlasting generosity makes him now stand here as the most unhappy, innocent person that man's own goodness ever made accused."

He then said, "Celia and Bonario received a gift of forgiveness of such very dear grace and mercy that they didn't know how to respond to it except with shame because it was such a very dear gift that they could never repay it. They began to hate the gift, and rather than to accept the gift with thanks, they tried to find a way to root out and eradicate the memory of the gift.

"I pray to your Fatherhoods to observe the malice of their reaction to the gift, yes, the rage of creatures discovered in their evils, and I pray to your Fatherhoods to observe the brazen insolence such people exhibit, even in their crimes — but that will become more apparent soon."

He pointed to Corbaccio and said, "This gentleman, the father, hearing of this foul crime, with many others, which daily struck at his too-tender ears, and grieved in nothing more than that he could not preserve himself as a parent — his son's ills growing to that strange flood and unnatural profusion of evil — at last decided to disinherit him."

The First Judge said, "These are strange turns of event!"

The First Judge said, "Bonario's reputation was always fair and honest."

Voltore said, "So much more full of danger is his vice, which can beguile so under the shade of virtue.

"But, as I said, my honored sires, his father had this settled purpose of disinheriting Bonario. We don't know by what means Bonario learned about this settled purpose, but after he learned that this day was appointed for the deed of disinheritance, that parricide — I cannot give Bonario a better title — he and Celia, his paramour, made a secret arrangement. She would be there when he entered Volpone's house. Volpone was the man, your Fatherhoods must understand, designated by Corbaccio to inherit his wealth.

"In Volpone's house, Bonario sought his father, Corbaccio. But for what purpose did Bonario seek his father, my lords? I tremble to pronounce it. I tremble to say that a son toward a father, and toward such a father, should have so foul, felonious intent! Bonario's intention was to murder him.

"Fortunately, he was unable to do that because of his father's lucky absence. But what did Bonario do then? He did not check his wicked thoughts; no, now he thought up new evil deeds.

"Evil always ends where it begins."

In other words, once evil is thought up, it will find an outlet. Evil thoughts always lead to evil deeds. Bonario had thought of committing an act of horror, and now he would commit an act of horror. The verb "ends" means "concludes" or "finishes."

Voltore continued, "Bonario committed an act of horror, Fathers! He dragged forth the aged gentleman Volpone — who had there lain bedridden three years and more — out of and off his innocent couch, naked in invalid's clothes upon the floor, and left him there.

"He also wounded Volpone's servant Mosca in the face.

"He also, along with this strumpet — Celia — who was the prostitute decoy to his invented, fraudulent plot and who was glad to be so sexually active — I shall here desire your Fatherhoods to note my conclusions as being most remarkable — thought at once to stop his father's intention to disinherit him.

"They attempted to discredit his father's free choice of the old gentleman, Volpone, as his heir. They also attempted to redeem themselves by laying infamy upon this man, Celia's husband, Corvino, to whom, with blushing, they should acknowledge as due their lives."

The First Judge asked, "What evidence do you have of this?"

Bonario interrupted, "Most honored fathers, I humbly beg that you give no credit to this man's mercenary tongue."

The First Judge said, "Stop interrupting. Be quiet."

Bonario said, "His soul lives in his fee. He cares more for money than he does for his soul."

Shocked, the Third Judge said, "Oh, sir!"

Bonario said, "This fellow, for six more small coins, would plead against his Maker."

The First Judge said, "You forget yourself. Remember where you are."

Voltore said, "Grave Fathers, let him have permission to speak. Can any man imagine that he will spare his accuser, me, when he would not have spared his parent? He was willing to murder his father, so he is certainly willing to insult and slander me."

The First Judge said to Voltore, "Well, produce your proofs. Show us your evidence."

Celia said, "I wish I could forget I were a creature."

One meaning of "creature" is "despicable person," but she meant a creature of God, Who created all human beings.

Voltone called a witness: "Signior Corbaccio."

Corbaccio came forward to testify.

The First Judge asked, "Who is he?"

Voltore replied, "He is Bonario's father."

The Second Judge asked, "Has he sworn under oath to tell the truth?"

The Notary answered, "Yes."

"What must I do now?" Corbaccio asked.

The Notary answered, "Your testimony's required. It is craved."

The hard-of-hearing Corbaccio asked, "Speak to the knave?"

By "knave," he meant his son, Bonario.

Corbaccio continued, "I'll have my mouth first stopped with earth — I'll die first. My heart hates knowing him. I disclaim any part of him. I am no kin of his."

The First Judge asked, "Why do you say that?"

Corbaccio said, "He is the mere portent of nature! He is a freak of nature! He is an utter stranger to my loins. I am not his biological father."

Bonario interrupted, "Have they forced you to say this?"

Corbaccio said, "I will not hear you — you monster of men, you swine, you goat, you wolf, you parricide! Speak not, you viper."

Because of Mosca's lies, he was convinced that Bonario had intended to murder him.

Bonario, an obedient son, said, "Sir, I will sit down, and rather wish my innocence should suffer than I resist the authority of a father."

Voltore called the next witness: "Signior Corvino!"

Corvino came forward to testify.

The Second Judge said, "This is strange."

The First Judge asked, "Who's this?"

The Notary replied, "Celia's husband."

The Fourth Judge asked, "Has he sworn under oath to tell the truth?"

The Notary answered, "Yes."

The Third Judge said to Corvino, "Speak, then."

Corvino said, "This woman, Celia, if it please your Fatherhoods, is a whore, of very hot sexual exercise, even more lecherous than a partridge, which is the most lecherous of creatures, according to Pliny's *Natural History* and Aelian's *On the Characteristics of Animals.* This is well known."

Shocked by Corvino's language and its content, the First Judge said, "No more."

Corvino said, "She neighs like a jennet — a horse — when it's in heat."

Shocked by Corvino's language and its content, the Notary ordered, "Preserve the honor of the court."

"I shall," Corvino said, "and I shall preserve the modesty of your most reverend ears. And yet I hope that I may say that these eyes of mine have seen her glued to that piece of cedar, that fine well-timbered gallant named Bonario."

"Well-timbered" meant "well-built" and hinted at "well-hung."

Corvino pointed to his forehead, where a cuckold's horns were said to grow, and said, "Here the letters may be read, through the horn, that make the story complete."

The cuckold's letter is V, and it is created by the cuckold's horns. Corvino used the plural "letters" because he was testifying that he had been cuckolded more than once.

He was also referring to a student's hornbook. Students would study a page that had the letters of the alphabet on it; a thin layer of horn protected the page. When it is very thin, horn is transparent, and when heated, horn is malleable.

Mosca said to Corvino, "Excellent testimony, sir!"

Corvino whispered to Mosca, "There's no shame in this now, is there?"

Corvino was worried that his testimony might not preserve the honor and the modesty of the court.

"None at all," Mosca replied.

Mosca meant that Corvino's testimony was shameless.

Corvino continued his testimony: "And I hope that I may say that I hope that Celia is well on her way to her damnation, if there is in fact a Hell that is greater than whore and woman — a good Catholic Christian may doubt that there is."

Corvino was not a good Catholic Christian.

The Third Judge said, "Corvino's grief has made him frantic."

The First Judge said, "Remove him from here."

Hearing that her husband hoped that she was well on her way to Hell, Celia fainted.

The Second Judge said, "Look after the woman."

"Splendid!" Corvino said. "Prettily feigned and acted, again!"

The Fourth Judge said, "Stand back from her."

The First Judge said, "Give her some air."

The Third Judge asked Mosca, "What can you say? What is your testimony?"

Mosca said, "My wound, may it please your wisdoms, speaks for me. I received it as I went to aid my good patron, Volpone, when Bonario missed his sought-for father and when that well-taught dame, Celia, had her cue given to her to cry out, 'Rape!'"

Bonario interrupted, "Oh, this is very carefully planned impudence! Fathers —"

The Third Judge interrupted, "Sir, be silent. You had your hearing free from interruption, and so must they."

The Second Judge said, "I begin to fear that there is some willful and fraudulent deception here."

He was beginning to believe that Bonario was at fault.

The Fourth Judge said, "This woman, Celia, has too many moods."

Voltore said, "Grave fathers, Celia is a creature of a most professed and prostituted lewdness."

By "creature," he meant "despicable person."

Corvino said, "Grave fathers, she is very impetuous and she is insatiable."

Voltore said, "I hope that her feignings will not deceive your wisdoms. Just this day she tempted a stranger, a grave knight, with her loose eyes, and more with her lascivious kisses."

He pointed to Mosca and said, "This man saw them together on the water in a gondola."

Mosca said, "Present is the lady herself who saw them, too. She is outside. When she saw them, she pursued them in the open streets in hopes of saving her knight's honor."

The First Judge said, "Produce that lady."

The Second Judge said, "Let her come."

Mosca exited to get Lady Would-be.

The Fourth Judge said, "These things strike me with wonder!"

The Fourth Judge said, "I am astonished. I have been turned into a stone."

Mosca returned with Lady Would-be.

He said to her, "Be resolute, madam."

He had coached her on what to say in the courtroom. Mosca had already told her that Peregrine was not a prostitute dressed as a woman. He, however, may have convinced her that Celia was a prostitute who had been with her husband on a gondola. Or he may have convinced her to deliberately commit perjury.

Lady Would-be pointed to Celia and said, "Yes, this same woman is she."

She was falsely testifying that her husband and Celia had been together on a gondola.

She said to Celia, "Get out, you chameleon harlot! Now your eyes vie with the tears of the hyena. Do you dare to look upon my wronged face?"

She called Celia a chameleon because she believed that although Celia was a prostitute, she could put on an innocent appearance.

Lady Would-be was mixing up the tears a crocodile sheds and the sound a hyena makes. A crocodile was believed to shed tears to lure its victims, while a hyena was believed to mimic a human voice to lure its victims.

Lady Would-be said to the Judges, "I beg your pardons, I fear I have forgettingly transgressed against the dignity of the court —"

The Second Judge said, "No, you haven't, madam."

Lady Would-be continued, "— and been exorbitant and immoderate in my speech."

The Second Judge said, "You haven't, lady."

The Fourth Judge said, "This evidence is strong."

Lady Would-be said, "Surely, I had no intention of scandalizing your honors, or my sex."

The Second Judge said, "We believe you."

Lady Would-be said, "Surely, you may believe it."

The Second Judge said, "Madam, we do."

Lady Would-be said, "Indeed, you may; my breeding is not so coarse —"

The First Judge said, "We know it."

Lady Would-be continued, "— as to offend with pertinacy —"

She was correct: She was not currently bringing up anything in court that was pertinent to the case.

The Third Judge said, "Lady —"

Lady Would-be continued, "— such a court! No, surely."

The First Judge said, "We well think it."

Lady Would-be continued, "You may think it."

The First Judge said, "Let her conquer us and have the last word."

He then asked Bonario, "What witnesses have you to make good your report?"

Bonario replied, "Our consciences."

Celia added, "And Heaven, which never fails the innocent."

The Fourth Judge said, "These are no testimonies."

Bonario said, "Not in your courts, where a greater number of, and louder, witnesses overcome."

The Fourth Judge said, "Now you grow insolent."

The officers who had gone after Volpone now returned, carrying Volpone on a couch. Volpone was acting as if he were very ill and utterly without the strength needed to engage in sex.

Voltore said, "Here comes the testimony that will convict and put to utter dumbness the bold tongues of Bonario and Celia."

He pointed to Volpone and said sarcastically, "See here, grave fathers, here's the ravisher, the rapist, the rider on other men's wives, the great impostor, the grand and horny voluptuary!

"Don't you think these limbs engage in sex? Don't you think these eyes covet a concubine? Please look at these hands — aren't they fit to stroke a lady's breasts?

"Or perhaps he is faking his illness!"

"So he is," Bonario said.

"Would you have him tortured?" Voltore asked.

"I would have him tested," Bonario said.

Voltore said, "Best test him then with spikes, or burning irons. Put him to the strappado."

The strappado is a form of torture in which the victim's hands are tied behind his or her back with a rope and then the victim is lifted high in the air. To increase the pain, weights can be tied to the victim's feet, or the victim can be raised and dropped partway, coming to a sudden stop. In this torture, the victim suffers dislocated shoulders.

Voltore sarcastically continued, "I have heard that the rack has cured the gout."

The rack is a form of torture in which ropes are tied to the victim's hands and other ropes are tied to the victim's feet, and the ropes are used to stretch the victim until their limbs are dislocated.

Being threatened with the rack is enough to make even a person suffering from gout try to run away.

Voltore sarcastically continued, "Indeed, put Volpone on the rack, and help rid him of a malady; be courteous.

"I say, before these honored Fathers, that Volpone is so ill that he shall still have as many diseases left as Celia has Biblically known adulterers, or as you, Bonario, have Biblically known strumpets."

He paused and then said to the Judges, "Oh, my just hearers, if these deeds, acts of this bold and most outrageous kind, may be done with impunity, can even one citizen escape losing his or her life and reputation to anyone who dares to slander him or her? Which of you are safe, my honored Fathers?

"I would ask, with the permission of your grave Fatherhoods, if their plot has any appearance of or resemblance to truth? With your permission, let me ask if, to the dullest nostril here, their plot does not smell like rank and most abhorred slander?

"I beg your care of this good gentleman, Volpone, whose life is much endangered by their lies, and as for them, I will conclude with this: Vicious persons, when they're hot and fleshed in — initiated in and eager for more — impious acts, their constancy abounds.

"Damned deeds are done with greatest confidence and boldness."

The First Judge said, "Take Bonario and Celia into custody, and separate them."

The Second Judge said, "It is a pity that two such monsters should live."

The First Judge said, "Let the old gentleman, Volpone, be returned to his home with care."

Some officers of the law carried Volpone away on his couch.

The First Judge added, "I'm sorry our credulity — our believing Bonario and Celia at first — has wronged him."

The Fourth Judge added, "Bonario and Celia are two creatures! They are thoroughly evil!"

The Third Judge said, "I feel as though I have an earthquake inside me."

The Second Judge added, "Their shame, even in their cradles, fled their faces. Even from infancy, Bonario and Celia have been shameless."

The Fourth Judge said to Voltore, "You have done a worthy service to the state, sir, by revealing their crimes."

The First Judge said, "You shall hear, before night, what punishment the court decrees upon them."

Voltore replied, "We thank your Fatherhoods."

The Judges, Notary, and officers of the law exited with Bonario and Celia.

Voltore asked Mosca, "How do you like the result of the trial?"

"It is splendid," Mosca replied. "I'd have your tongue, sir, tipped with gold for this. I'd have you be the heir to the whole city. I'd have the earth lack men before you lack a living: They're bound to erect your statue in St. Mark's."

He then said, "Signior Corvino, I want you to go and show yourself in public, so people know that you have conquered in this trial."

"Yes," Corvino replied.

Mosca and Corvino began to talk quietly together.

Mosca said, "It was much better that you should profess yourself a cuckold in public like this than that the other thing should have been proved."

The other thing was Corvino's attempt to prostitute his wife, Celia.

Corvino replied, "I considered that. Now it is her fault."

"It could have been yours," Mosca said.

"True," Corvino said, "but I still fear this lawyer: Voltore."

He still regarded Voltore as a rival who could inherit Volpone's wealth.

"Indeed, you need not fear him," Mosca said. "I dare to ease you of that fear."

"I trust you, Mosca," Corvino said.

Mosca replied, "You can trust me as you trust your own soul, sir."

Corvino's soul was rotten.

Corvino exited.

Corbaccio said, "Mosca!"

Mosca replied, "Now for your business, sir."

"What?" the hard-of-hearing Corbaccio asked. "Do you have business?"

"Yes, yours, sir," Mosca replied.

"Oh, none else?"

"None else, not I," Mosca said. "I have only your business."

"Be careful, then," Corbaccio said.

Voltore and Lady Would-be were listening. Because Corbaccio was hard of hearing, Mosca was speaking loudly.

"You can sleep with both your eyes shut," Mosca said. "Don't worry about anything."

"Dispatch my business," Corbaccio said.

He meant this: Get Volpone to make me his heir.

"Instantly," Mosca said. "Right away."

Corbaccio said, "And look that everything, whatever it is, is put in the inventory of his goods: jewels, plate, moneys, household stuff, bedding, curtains."

Mosca said, "Curtain-rings, sir."

The sarcasm went over Corbaccio's head.

Mosca added, "The advocate's fee must be deducted from the wealth you will gain."

"I'll pay him now," Corbaccio said. "You'll be too prodigal and generous."

Mosca said. "Sir, I must give Voltore his fee as advocate."

Corbaccio asked, "Two chequins is enough?"

"No, give him six chequins, sir," Mosca said.

"It is too much."

"He talked a long time. You must consider that, sir."

Corbaccio said, "Well, there's three," handing it over.

"I'll give it to him," Mosca said.

"Do so, and here's something for you."

Corbaccio handed Mosca a small coin.

Corbaccio exited.

Mosca said sarcastically, "Bountiful bones! What horrid and strange offence did he commit against nature in his youth to give him this old age?"

People who commit some horribly evil deed during their youth may be punished with suffering in their old age.

Mosca said to Voltore, who had heard everything, "You see, sir, how I work to help you accomplish your goals."

He gave Voltore the three chequins and added, "Take no notice of the smallness of this fee. It's not worth worrying about."

Voltore, whose eyes were on Volpone's wealth and whose mind was on making all of that wealth his, said, "I won't. I'll leave you now."

Mosca replied, "Good advocate!"

Voltore exited.

Mosca thought, *All is yours, the devil and all.*

This meant, *You think that everything is yours, including the devil and everything else.*

Mosca then said to Lady Would-be, "Madam, I'll escort you to your home."

"No, I'll go see your patron, Volpone," she replied.

"That you shall not," Mosca said, "and I'll tell you why. My intention is to urge my patron to rewrite his will and make you his heir because of the zeal you showed as you helped him with your testimony today. Before your testimony, you were only third or fourth in line to inherit his wealth, but you shall now be the first in line. But if you were present as I tried to persuade Volpone to rewrite his will, it would appear as if you were begging for his money. Therefore —"

Lady Would-be interrupted, "You shall sway me. I will go home."

Possibly, this is the exact time Lady Would-be became a legacy-hunter.

CHAPTER 5

— 5.1 —

Volpone was alone in his room.

He said to himself, "Well, I am here, and all this turmoil is in the past. I never disliked my disguise as a seriously ill person until this moment that just ended. Here in private my disguise is good, but out in public …

"Let me *cave* — take care — as I catch my breath."

Cave is Latin for "be wary" and "be on guard."

Volpone needed to be on his guard in case anyone — such as Lady Would-be — visited and caught him out of bed.

He continued, "By God, my left leg began to have the cramp, and I feared immediately that some power had struck me with a dead palsy."

A "dead palsy" is serious paralysis such as a stroke can cause.

He continued, "Well! I must be merry and shake it off. Too many of these fears would give me some villainous disease if they would come fast and thick upon me. I'll stop them. Give me a bowl of lusty wine to frighten away this sense of dread from my heart."

He poured himself some wine and drank deeply.

"Ah! The sense of dread is almost gone already; I shall conquer it completely. Any trick, now, of rare ingenious knavery that would possess me with a violent laughter, would make me a man again."

He drank deeply again.

"Ah! This heat is life; it is blood by this time."

This society believed that wine turned to blood after it was consumed. As blood, it conveyed heat and courage to the person who had consumed the wine.

Mosca entered the room.

"Mosca!" Volpone greeted him.

"How are you, sir?" Mosca asked.

He then asked rhetorically, "Does the day look clear again? Have we recovered from what could have been a disaster, and have we gotten off the path of error and gotten back to our correct path so that we can see our path before us? Is our path free from obstruction once more?"

He was mocking religious language about leaving the path of moral error and getting back on the path of moral behavior. Volpone and he were now free to continue their con games.

Volpone said, "Exquisite Mosca!"

Mosca was an exquisitely ingenious scoundrel.

"Was it not carried off learnedly?" Mosca asked.

"Yes, and stoutly and bravely," Volpone said. "Good wits are greatest in extreme crises."

"It would be a folly beyond thought to trust any grand act to a cowardly spirit," Mosca said. "You are not delighted with it enough, I think?"

Mosca knew Volpone well. Volpone was one to up the ante, to push things to an extreme that could break them. Mosca was usually satisfied with enough.

Volpone replied, "Oh, I was delighted more than if I had enjoyed the wench: Celia. The pleasure of sexually enjoying all womankind is not like the greater pleasure I got from deceiving the court."

"Why, now you're talking, sir," Mosca said. "That's exactly right."

He hesitated and then said, "We must here be fixed and stop while we're ahead. Here we must rest. This is our masterpiece: We cannot think to go beyond this."

"True," Volpone said, but soon he would seek to go beyond this. "You have played your prize part, my precious Mosca."

"Yes, sir," Mosca said, "To fool the court —"

Volpone interrupted, "And quite divert the torrent of the law upon the innocent."

"Yes," Mosca said, "and to make so splendid a music out of discords." The discords were the rival legacy-hunters who had come together and made splendid music to fool the court into finding innocent people guilty.

"Right," Volpone said. "That still to me is the strangest wonder: how you managed to do it! That these people, being so divided among themselves and not trusting each other, should not smell a rat either in me or in you, or doubt and fear the other members of their own side."

"True, they will not see it," Mosca said. "Too much light blinds them, I think. They ignore what should be obvious. Each of them is so possessed and stuffed with his own hopes of inheriting your money that anything to the contrary, no matter how true or apparent or palpable, they will resist it —"

Volpone sarcastically said, "— like a temptation of the devil."

Many people will strenuously resist a temptation of the devil, but the legacy-hunters were not such people. One temptation of the devil was the hope of inheriting Volpone's wealth.

"Right, sir," Mosca said. "Merchants may talk of trade, and your great signiors may talk of land that yields well, but if Italy has any glebe — plot of land — more fruitful than these fellows, I am deceived."

Volpone had gotten much wealth from the legacy-hunters.

Mosca asked, "Didn't your advocate, Voltore, perform splendidly?"

"Oh, he did," Volpone said.

He parodied Voltore's performance in the courtroom: "My most honored Fathers, my grave Fathers, under correction of your Fatherhoods, what face of truth is here? If these strange deeds may pass, most honored Fathers."

He added, "It took a lot of effort to keep from laughing."

Mosca said, "It seemed to me that you sweat, sir."

Volpone said, "True, I did a little."

Volpone had been afraid.

"Confess, sir," Mosca said. "Weren't you daunted?"

"Truly, I was a little in a mist — a little dazed — but I was not dejected and downcast. I was always my own self."

"I believe it, sir," Mosca said. "Now, so truth help me, I must necessarily say this, sir, and out of conscience for your advocate, Voltore. He has taken pains, truly, sir, and has very richly deserved, in my poor judgment — I speak it with goodwill and not to contradict you, sir — to be well cheated."

Mosca believed that Voltore deserved to be well cheated because he had lied in the courtroom. Applying the same logic to others, we have to conclude that Corbaccio, Corvino, Lady Would-be, Volpone, and Mosca also deserved to be well cheated.

"True," Volpone said, "I think so, too, judging by what I heard him say in the latter end of the trial."

Volpone had not been present for the first part of the trial.

"Oh, but what he said before you arrived, sir," Mosca said, "had you heard him first make the chief points of his argument and then aggravate and exaggerate the injuries he claimed Bonario and Celia had done, and then make his vehement figures — gestures and lawyerly figures of speech — I kept expecting him to change his shirt because of his sweating."

He added sarcastically, "And to think that he did this out of pure love, with no hope of gain."

"You are right," Volpone said. "He deserves to be cheated. I cannot repay him, Mosca, as I would like to, not yet; but for your sake, at your entreaty, I will begin, even now — to vex them all, this very instant."

Mosca had entreated him to cheat Voltore, and now Volpone was intending to vex all the legacy-hunters.

"Good sir —" Mosca said, wondering what Volpone was planning.

Volpone interrupted, "Call Nano the Dwarf and Castrone the Eunuch to come here."

Mosca called, "Castrone! Nano!"

Nano the dwarf and Castrone the eunuch entered the room.

"Here we are," Nano the dwarf said.

Volpone asked, "Shall we have a jig now?"

A jig or dance was often performed after a play was finished. Volpone and Mosca had just finished performing their parts in the trial. However, Volpone had in mind a con rather than a dance.

"Whatever you please, sir," Mosca said, wondering what Volpone was up to.

Volpone said to Nano the dwarf and Castrone the eunuch, "Go immediately into the streets, you two, and say that I am dead. Do it in character — do it seriously, do you hear? Say that I have died because of the grief caused me by being recently slandered as a would-be rapist."

Nano the dwarf and Castrone the eunuch exited.

"What do you have in mind, sir?" Mosca asked.

Volpone said, "My vulture, crow, and raven shall immediately come flying hither, on hearing the news, to peck for carrion. So will my she-wolf, and all will be greedy and full of expectation of inheriting my wealth."

The she-wolf was Lady Would-be, who usually was parrot-like.

"And then to have it ravished from their mouths!" Mosca said.

"That is true," Volpone said.

He elaborated on his plan: "I will have you put on more-respectable clothing, and you shall act as if you were my heir. You shall show them a will. Open that chest, and take out one of those wills that have the name of my beneficiary blank. I'll immediately write in your name."

Mosca gave him the will and said, "This is a splendid plot, sir."

"Yes," Volpone said. "When they just stand, open-mouthed, and find themselves deluded —"

"Yes," Mosca said.

"And you will treat them scurvily!" Volpone said. "Hurry. Put on better clothing, the clothing of an upper-class man!"

Mosca put on a fine shirt and asked, "But what about, sir, if they ask after the body?"

"Say that it was beginning to rot."

"I'll say it stank, sir," Mosca said, "and I was obliged to have it coffined up immediately, and sent away."

"Say anything that you want," Volpone said. "Wait, here's my will. Get yourself a cap, and have an account book, pen and ink, and papers in front of you. Sit as if you were taking an inventory of my property. I'll get up behind the curtain, on a stool, and listen. Occasionally, I'll peep over the curtain to see how they look, and with what degrees their blood leaves their faces. Oh, it will give me a rare meal of laughter!"

Mosca put on a cap, and put the required items on a table in front of him.

He said, "Your advocate, Voltore, will turn stark dull — completely insensible — upon hearing that I am your heir."

"It will take off his oratory's sharpness," Volpone said.

Mosca added, "But your *clarissimo*, Corbaccio, old round-back, he will crump — curl up — like a wood louse when it is touched."

A *clarissimo* is a grandee of Venice.

Corbaccio, an old man, was stooped-over.

"And what about Corvino?" Volpone asked.

"Oh, sir, look for him tomorrow morning to run around in the streets with a rope and dagger, thinking about committing suicide or violence," Mosca said. "When he learns that I am your heir, he must run mad. Lady Would-be, too, who came into the court to bear false witness for your worship —"

"Yes, and kissed me in front of the Fathers, although all my face flowed with oils," Volpone said.

"And with sweat, sir," Mosca said, saying the same thing that Volpone had said but using the less genteel term.

Mosca added, "Why, your gold is such medicine that it dries up all those offensive smells. It transforms people who are the most deformed, and it restores them and makes them lovely, as if it were the strange poetical girdle of Venus that makes anyone who wears it irresistible. Jove himself — the King of the gods — could not invent for himself clothing more cunning to pass by the guards of Acrisius."

Jove, aka Jupiter, had in fact worn gold when he visited Danaë, the daughter of Acrisius. He had appeared to her in a shower of gold after Acrisius had locked her in a tower after hearing a prophecy that she would give birth to a son who would kill him. Jove slept with Danaë, who gave birth to Perseus, who grew up and killed Acrisius.

Mosca continued, "Gold is the thing that gives all the world her grace, her youth, her beauty."

"I think she loves me," Volpone said, referring to gold.

"Who? The Lady Would-be, sir?" Mosca asked.

Realizing that Volpone was referring to gold, and knowing that Volpone would think he was referring to Lady Would-be, Mosca said, "She's jealous of you."

In addition to the meaning we know best, the word "jealous" had two meanings that are now obsolete: 1) devoted, and 2) doubtful and mistrustful.

Mosca meant that gold, like Lady Fortune, was a fickle mistress. Already Mosca was planning to make use of the will that Voltore had given to him.

"Do you think so?" Volpone said. "Do you think Lady Would-be is jealous of me?"

Knocking sounded at the door.

"Listen," Mosca said. "Someone is here already."

"Look and see who it is," Volpone ordered.

Mosca looked out a window and said, "It is the vulture: Voltore. He has the quickest scent."

Vultures are known for their ability to quickly sniff out dead bodies.

"I'll go to my place behind the curtain," Volpone said. "You be ready to act as though I am dead and you are my heir."

Volpone went behind the curtain.

Mosca said, "I am ready."

Volpone said, "Mosca, play the skilled torturer now. Torture them splendidly."

Voltore entered the room and asked, "How are you now, my Mosca?"

Mosca sat at the desk, writing as he inventoried Volpone's wealth. He said, "Turkish carpets, nine —"

Voltore said with approval, "Taking an inventory! That is good."

Mosca said, "Two suits of bedding, tissue —"

Voltore interrupted, "Where's the will? Let me read that while you take inventory."

Some servants entered, carrying Corbaccio in a chair.

Corbaccio said, "Set me down, and all of you go home."

The servants exited.

Voltore said, "Has he, Corbaccio, come now to trouble us!"

Mosca said, "— of cloth of gold, two more —"

Tissue of cloth of gold is high-quality cloth that has strands of gold and silver woven into it.

Corbaccio asked, "Is it done, Mosca?"

He was asking if Volpone's will had been changed to name him as heir.

Mosca said, "Of separate velvet hangings, eight —"

Voltore said, "I like the care Mosca is taking as he makes the inventory."

Corbaccio asked, "Didn't you hear me?"

Corvino entered the room and said, "Ha! Has the hour of Volpone's death come, Mosca?"

Volpone looked over the curtain and said, "Yes, now they muster."

Corvino asked, "What are the advocate Voltore and old Corbaccio doing here?

Corbaccio asked, "What are Voltore and Corvino doing here?"

Lady Would-be entered the room and said, "Mosca! Is Volpone's thread spun?"

She was referring to the Three Fates. Clotho spun the thread of a human's life, Lachesis measured it, and Atropos cut the thread at the time of the human's death.

Mosca said, "Eight chests of linen —"

Volpone looked over the curtain and said, "Oh, my fine Dame Would-be, too!"

Corvino said, "Mosca, give me the will so that I may show it to these people and get rid of them."

Mosca said, "Six chests of linen with a diamond-shaped pattern, four of damask."

He then picked up the will that named him as heir, and gave it to Corvino carelessly over his shoulder, saying, "There."

Corbaccio asked, "Is that the will?"

Mosca said, "Down-beds, and bolsters —"

A bolster is a long pillow placed under other pillows as support.

Volpone looked over the curtain and said, "Splendid! Continue to be busy. Now the legacy-hunters begin to flutter! They never think of me. Look! See! See! See! How their swift eyes run over the long deed, to the name, and to the legacies, seeking what is bequeathed to them there —"

Mosca said, "Ten sets of wall hangings —"

Volpone looked over the curtain and said, "Hangings, yes, in their garters, Mosca. Now their hopes are at the last gasp."

An insult of the time was, "Go hang yourself in your own garters!"

Voltore said, "Mosca is the heir?"

The hard-of-hearing Corbaccio asked, "What's that?"

Volpone looked over the curtain and said, "My advocate, Voltore, is struck dumb. Look at my merchant, Corvino; he has heard of some strange storm, a ship of his has been lost, and he faints. My lady will swoon. Old glass-eyes, aka Corbaccio with his eyeglasses, has not reached his despair yet."

Corbaccio took the will, saying, "All these others are out of hope. I am surely the man who has been named Volpone's heir."

Corvino asked, "But, Mosca —"

Still writing the inventory, Mosca said, "Two cabinets."

Corvino asked, "Is this in earnest? Is this for real?"

Mosca said, "One made of ebony —"

Corvino asked, "Or are you only deluding me?"

Mosca said, "The other, made of mother of pearl."

He looked at Corvino and said, "I am very busy. Indeed, this is a fortune that has been thrown upon me —"

He wrote as he said, "Item, one salt cellar made out of agate —"

He looked at Corvino and said, "— a fortune that has been thrown upon me without my seeking it."

This is something that would especially hurt the legacy-hunters. They had sought the legacy and not gotten it; Mosca had not sought the legacy and had gotten it.

Lady Would-be asked, "Do you hear me, sir?"

Mosca said, "A perfumed box —"

He said to Lady Would-be, "Please stop bothering me. You see I'm busy —"

He continued, "— made of an onyx —"

Lady Would-be said, "What!"

Mosca said to all the legacy-hunters, "Tomorrow or the next day, I shall be at leisure to talk with you all."

Corvino asked, "Is this the end result of my great expectations?"

Lady Would-be said to Mosca, "Sir, I must have a fairer answer."

"Madam!" Mosca said. "Indeed, and you shall. Please fairly leave my house."

She looked angry.

He added, "No, raise no tempest with your looks, but listen to me. Remember what your ladyship offered me to put you in Volpone's will as an heir."

Mosca was saying obliquely that she had offered him sex. Apparently, this had happened after the trial.

He added, "Go ahead, think on it. And think on what you said even the best madams did to provide for themselves, and why shouldn't you? Enough. Go home, and treat the poor Sir Pol, your knight, well, out of fear I tell some riddles — some secrets. Go and be melancholy."

Lady Would-be exited.

Volpone looked over the curtain and said, "Oh, my fine devil!"

Corvino said, "Mosca, I would like a word with you."

"Lord!" Mosca said. "Won't you take your leave from here yet? I think, of all the legacy-hunters here, you should have been the example for the others and left first. Why should you stay here? What are you thinking? What do you think you will get? Listen to me. Don't you know that I know you are an ass, and that you would most eagerly have been a willing cuckold, if fortune would have allowed you to be? Don't you know that I know you are declared to be a cuckold, and you are OK with it?"

He picked up various jewels as he said, "This pearl, you'll say, was yours? That is correct. This diamond, you'll say, was yours? I'll not deny it, but I will say 'Thank you.' Much here else, you'll say, was yours? It may be so. Why, think that these good deeds — your gifts — may help to hide your bad deeds."

He added, "I'll not betray you. Although you are extraordinary, and you are a cuckold only in title but not in deed, since Celia never committed adultery, it is enough. Go home. Be melancholy, too, or be insane."

Corvino exited.

Volpone looked over the curtain and said, "Splendid Mosca! How his villainy becomes him!"

Voltore said to himself, "Certainly Mosca is deluding all these other legacy-hunters for me."

Looking at the will, the eyeglasses-wearing Corbaccio said, "Mosca is the heir!"

Volpone looked over the curtain and said, "Oh, his four eyes have found it."

Corbaccio said, "I am tricked, cheated, by a parasite slave."

He said to Mosca, "Harlot, you have gulled me."

At this time, the word "harlot" meant "rascal" when applied to a man.

"Yes, sir," Mosca said. "I have cheated you. Stop your mouth, or I shall pull out the only tooth that is left.

"Aren't you he, that filthy covetous wretch, with the three legs — one of them a cane — who here, in hope of prey, have, any time these past three years, snuffed about, with your most groveling nose, and would have hired me to poison my patron, sir?

"Aren't you the man who has today in court professed the disinheriting of your son?

"Aren't you the man who has today in court perjured yourself?

"Go home, and die, and stink. If you but croak a syllable, all comes out. Go away, and call your porters to carry you home!"

Corbaccio exited.

Mosca said, "Go. Go and stink."

Volpone looked over the curtain and said, "Excellent varlet!"

Voltore said, "Now, my faithful Mosca, I find your loyalty —"

"Sir!" Mosca said.

"— to be sincere," Voltore finished.

Mosca wrote on the inventory and said, "A table made of porphyry."

He then said to Voltore, "I marvel that you'll be thus troublesome to me."

Volpone said, "Stop your act now. The others are gone. We are alone."

"Why? Who are you?" Mosca said. "What! Who sent for you?"

He began to imitate Voltore: "Oh, I beg your mercy, reverend sir! In good faith, I am grieved for you that any good luck of mine should thus defeat your — I must necessarily say — most deserving travails."

Voltore had worked very hard and suffered travails in his attempts to inherit Volpone's wealth.

Mosca continued, "But I protest, sir, Volpone's fortune was cast upon me, and I could almost wish to be without it except that the will of the dead must be observed.

"Indeed, my joy is that you don't need it. You have a gift, sir — thank your education — that will never let you go without while there are men and malice to breed lawsuits. I wish I had only half the means of making a living like yours. For that, I would give all my fortune, sir!

"If I should have any lawsuits — but I hope, since things are so easy and direct and the will is so clear, I shall not — I will make bold with your obstreperous, aka noisy, aid. Please understand, sir, that I will pay your usual fee, sir.

"In the meantime, I know that you who know so much law will also have the conscience not to be covetous of what is mine.

"Good sir, I thank you for my plate — the gold plate you gave to Volpone that is now mine. It will help to set up in life a young man — me.

"Indeed, you look as if you were constipated. You had best go home and take a laxative, sir."

Voltore exited.

Volpone came out from behind the curtain and said, "Tell him to eat a lot of lettuce; I hear it acts as a laxative.

"My witty mischief, let me embrace you. Oh, I wish that I could now transform you to a Venus!"

To Volpone, cheating people was an aphrodisiac; it made him horny.

He added, "Mosca, go, immediately get my outdoors clothing of a *clarissimo* — a Venetian gentleman. Now that everyone thinks that you are rich, you can wear it. Put it on, and walk on the public streets. Be seen by the legacy-hunters, and torment them some more. We must pursue, as well as plot. Who would have lost this feast? Who would have missed out on all this fun?"

"I fear doing that will lose them," Mosca said.

He feared that any more mockery would kill the geese that had been laying golden eggs — the legacy-hunters would never again give gifts.

"Oh, my recovery shall recover all," Volpone said optimistically. "They will find that I am still alive, and they will be as greedy as ever for my wealth.

"I wish that I could now think of some disguise that I could wear and meet them and ask them questions. How I would vex them always at every turn!"

"Sir, I can fit you," Mosca said. "I can give you what you need."

He was ambiguous when he said "what you need." Volpone needed a disguise — and a comeuppance.

"Can you?" Volpone asked.

"Yes," Mosca said. "I know one of the Commandatori, one of the police officers, sir, a man who greatly resembles you. I will immediately make him drunk and bring you his uniform."

Volpone, who had been drinking, said, "This will be a splendid disguise, and one that is worthy of your brain! Oh, I will be a sharp pain to the legacy-hunters."

"Sir, while in disguise, you must look for curses — the legacy-hunters will definitely curse you."

Volpone said, "They will curse me until they burst. The fox always fares best when he is cursed."

That is true. When the fox escapes the hunters, they curse it.

Outside Sir Politic Would-be's house, Peregrine, who was in disguise, and three merchants talked.

Peregrine asked, "Am I well enough disguised?"

The First Merchant said, "I promise that you are."

"All my ambition is only to frighten him," Peregrine said. "That is the extent of my goal."

The Second Merchant said, "If you could ship him away, it would be excellent."

The Third Merchant said, "To Zant, or to Aleppo?"

Zant was a Greek island under the control of Venice, and Aleppo was a Syrian city. The merchants were talking about kidnapping Sir Politic Would-be and sending him far, far away.

"Yes, we could do that," Peregrine said, "and then he would have his adventures put in the *Book of Voyages* and his gulled story registered for the truth."

He was against kidnapping Sir Politic Would-be, although they could if they wanted. If they were to kidnap Sir Politic Would-be and ship him away, he would make up a fantastic tale — a tale to fool other people by making his part in it much more heroic than the reality — and it would appear in popular travel books of extraordinary tales. One such travel book was Richard Hakluyt's three-volume *The Principal Navigations, Voiages, Traffiques and Discoueries of the English Nation.*

Peregrine said, "Well, gentlemen, when I have been inside for a while, and you think that Sir Politic Would-be and I are warm in our conversation, know your war-like approaches. Show up at the right time."

The First Merchant said, "Trust it to our care. We will do it right."

The merchants hid themselves.

Peregrine knocked, and a waiting-woman arrived.

He said, "May God save you, fair lady! Is Sir Pol inside?"

"I do not know, sir," the waiting-woman replied.

"Please say to him that I am a merchant, on serious business, and I want to speak with him."

"I will see, sir."

She allowed him to go inside into a waiting room.

"Thank you."

The waiting-woman exited.

Peregrine said to himself, "I see the servants of the household are all female here."

He had recently referred to Sir Pol as "Sir Bawd." He thought that Sir Pol's house was a brothel.

The waiting-woman returned and said, "He says, sir, that he has weighty affairs of state that now require his whole attention. At some other time you may possess his time."

Peregrine said, "Please go to him again and say that if those weighty affairs of state require his whole attention, these weighty affairs of state that I will talk to him about will forcibly compel him to pay attention. Those are the kinds of weighty affairs of state that I am bringing him tidings of."

The waiting-woman exited.

Peregrine said to himself, "What might be his grave affair of state now! How to make Bolognian sausages here in Venice, leaving out one of the ingredients in order to reduce the cost of making them?"

The waiting-woman returned and said, "Sir, he says that he knows by your word 'tidings' that you are no statesman, and therefore he wills you to wait."

Sir Politic Would-be believed that a statesman would use the word "intelligence" instead of "tidings."

The waiting-woman's words about willing Peregrine to wait were not clear. Peregrine thought that Sir Pol regarded him as being no statesman and therefore of no importance, and so Sir Pol was telling him to wait until Sir Pol deigned to meet him.

An angry Peregrine said, "Sweetheart, please return to him. I have not read as many proclamations and studied them for words to use, as he has done, but —"

He saw Sir Politic Would-be coming and said, "But — here he deigns to come."

The waiting-woman's words about willing Peregrine to wait really meant that since Peregrine was no statesman he was not dangerous to Sir Politic

Would-be and so Sir Politic Would-be in fact would be out quickly to meet him. Sir Politic believed, or pretended to believe, that spies were watching him.

The waiting-woman exited.

Sir Politic Would-be said to the disguised Peregrine, "Sir, I must crave your courteous pardon. There has chanced today an unkind disaster between my lady and me, and I was penning my apology, to give her satisfaction, just as you came now."

Sir Politic Would-be's "weighty affairs of state" had been writing a letter of apology to his wife.

The disguised Peregrine said, "Sir, I am grieved that I bring you a worse disaster. The gentleman you met at the port today who told you that he was newly arrived —"

He was referring to himself.

Sir Politic Would-be asked, "Yes, was he a fugitive prostitute?"

He still believed that Peregrine had been a female prostitute dressed in men's clothing.

"No, sir," Peregrine said. "He was a spy set on you, and he related to the Venetian Senate that you professed to him to have a plot to sell the State of Venice to the Turks."

"Oh!" Sir Politic Would-be said.

That crime was punishable by torture and death.

The disguised Peregrine said, "For which crime, warrants have been signed by this time to arrest you, and to search your study for papers —"

Sir Politic Would-be said, "Alas, sir, I have none, except notes drawn out of play-books —"

Many of his political ideas came out of books of plays.

"All the better to convict you, sir," the disguised Peregrine said.

In fact, political authorities read and watched plays to ascertain if they were guilty of sedition. Political authorities sometimes arrested and tortured or threatened to torture playwrights.

Sir Politic Would-be continued, "— and some essays."

Ben Jonson disliked many essays because he believed that the authors made too great use of quotations, thus making the essay's information second-hand. Since Sir Politic Would-be got some of his political ideas from essays, any of that information he would impart would be third-hand.

Sir Politic Would-be asked, "What shall I do?"

The disguised Peregrine said, "Sir, it would be best to hide yourself in a chest for holding sugar. Or, if you could lie curled up, a frail would be splendid. In either case, I could send you onboard a ship."

A frail is a rush basket used to ship figs and raisins.

Sir Politic Would-be said, "Sir, I just talked about the plot merely for the sake of conversation."

Knocking sounded at the door.

The disguised Peregrine said, "Listen! They are here!"

"I am a wretch! A wretch!" Sir Politic Would-be said.

"What will you do, sir?" the disguised Peregrine said. "Haven't you a cask or barrel to leap into? They'll torture you on the rack; you must be quick to avoid being arrested."

Sir Politic Would-be said, "Sir, I have a stratagem —"

The Third Merchant yelled from outside, "Sir Politic Would-be!"

The Second Merchant yelled from outside, "Where is he?"

Sir Politic Would-be continued, "— that I have thought up before this time in case it was needed."

"What is it?" the disguised Peregrine asked.

"I shall never endure the torture," Sir Politic Would-be said to himself.

He then said to the disguised Peregrine, "Indeed, it is, sir, a tortoise shell that is fit for this emergency. Please, sir, help me."

He lifted a cover to reveal the shell of a large sea turtle and said, "Here I've got a place, sir, to put my legs. Please lay the shell on me, sir."

He lay down while the disguised Peregrine placed the shell on top of him.

Sir Politic Would-be said, "With this cap, and my black gloves, I'll lie, sir, like a tortoise, until they are gone."

The disguised Peregrine thought, *And you call this a stratagem?*

"It's my own idea," Sir Politic Would-be said. "Good sir, tell my wife's waiting-women to burn my papers."

The disguised Peregrine exited.

The three merchants now rushed into the room.

The First Merchant asked, "Where has he hidden?"

The Third Merchant said, "We must and surely will find him."

The Second Merchant asked, "Which is his study?"

The disguised Peregrine returned.

The First Merchant asked, "Who are you, sir?"

The disguised Peregrine said, "I am a merchant who came here to look at this tortoise."

The Third Merchant said, "What!"

The First Merchant said, "By St. Mark, what beast is this!"

The disguised Peregrine said, "It is a fish."

The Second Merchant said to the "tortoise," "Come out here!"

The disguised Peregrine said, "You may strike the tortoise, sir, and walk on him. He's strong enough to bear a cart."

The First Merchant said, "What? Strong enough to bear a cart running over him?"

The disguised Peregrine said, "Yes, sir."

The Third Merchant said, "Let's jump on him."

The Second Merchant said, "Can't he move?"

"He creeps, sir," the disguised Peregrine said.

The First Merchant said, "Let's see him creep."

"No, good sir," the disguised Peregrine said. "You will hurt him."

The Second Merchant said, "By God's heart, I will see him creep, or I will prick his guts."

The Third Merchant said to the "tortoise," "Come out here!"

"Please, sir!" the disguised Peregrine said.

He whispered to Sir Politic Would-be, "Creep a little."

The First Merchant said, "Come forth."

The "tortoise" moved a little.

The Second Merchant said, "Come farther still."

"Good sir!" the disguised Peregrine said.

He whispered to Sir Politic Would-be, "Creep."

The Second Merchant said, "We'll see his legs."

The three merchants pulled the shell off Sir Politic Would-be.

The Third Merchant said, "By God's soul, the tortoise is wearing garters!"

The First Merchant said, "Yes, and gloves!"

The Second Merchant said, "Is this your fearful tortoise!"

The tortoise at one time had made its prey fearful, but now the "tortoise" was full of fear.

Peregrine removed his disguise and said, "Now, Sir Pol, we are even. I shall be prepared for your next project. I am sorry for the funeral — on a burning pier — of your notes, sir."

Peregrine thought that Sir Politic Would-be had tried to set a trap for him with the help of Lady Would-be. Peregrine was wrong.

The First Merchant said, "This would make a splendid puppet show to be seen in Fleet Street."

The Second Merchant said, "Yes, in the Term, when the law courts are in session and lots of people are in town."

The First Merchant said, "Or at Smithfield, when Bartholomew Fair is being held."

Because the three merchants had a good knowledge of England and were apparently good friends with Peregrine, they may have sailed together on the same ship to Venice and disembarked earlier this day.

The Third Merchant said, "I think this is just a melancholy sight."

Peregrine said, "Farewell, most politic tortoise!"

Peregrine and the three merchants exited.

Sir Politic Would-be said to the waiting-woman, "Where's my lady? Does she know about this?"

He thought that she might have known about the trick.

The waiting-woman replied, "I don't know, sir."

Sir Politic Would-be said, "Find out."

The waiting-woman exited.

He lamented, "Oh, I shall be the fable told at all feasts, the freight of the newspapers, the tale of the ship-boys, and which is worst, even the main topic of gossip at the taverns."

The waiting-woman returned and said, "My lady's come home. She is very melancholy and says, sir, she will immediately go to sea for her health."

Sir Politic Would-be said, "And I will go to sea in order to shun this place and climate forever. I will creep with my house on my back and think it well to shrink my poor head in my politic shell."

Sir Politic Would-be and his wife would most likely return home to England. Apparently, he had learned something: not to pretend to be a statesman or a spy. A tortoise is a symbol of positive qualities: It does not pretend to be what it is not. Its house, which it carries on its back, is exactly what it needs. No tortoise has a grander or a lesser house than it needs. The tortoise is known for its slow but steady movement, and its ability to steadily move toward a goal often allows it to achieve the goal when faster, flashier, overconfident animals cannot; this is the moral of the Aesop fable "The Tortoise and the Hare." Whether or not Sir Politic Would-be had come to Venice to gain knowledge, he had gained knowledge.

Erasmus wrote that "the mind fortified with virtue and philosophy fears the assaults of Fortune no more than a tortoise fears flies." Many characters in this book need to learn this.

Just outside Volpone's house, Volpone and Mosca were talking. Mosca was wearing the clothing of a *clarissimo*, aka Venetian gentleman. Volpone was wearing the uniform of a police officer.

Volpone asked, "Do I look like the police officer?"

"Oh, sir, you are he," Mosca said. "No man can tell the difference between you."

"Good," Volpone said.

"But what do I look like?" Mosca asked.

"Before Heaven, I say that you look like a brave *clarissimo*. You finely suit that suit of fine clothing! It's a pity that you weren't born a *clarissimo*."

Mosca thought, *If I can hold on to my artificial position of* clarissimo, *it will go well for me.*

Volpone said, "I'll go and see first what the news is at the court."

Mosca said, "Do so."

Volpone exited.

Alone, Mosca said, "My fox is out of his hole, and before he shall re-enter it, I'll make him languish in his borrowed disguise until he comes to terms with me."

He called, "Androgyno, Castrone, Nano!"

The three servants entered and said, "Here!"

Mosca said, "Go and entertain yourselves outside; go and have fun."

They exited.

Alone, Mosca said, "So, now I have the keys, and I am possessed."

He meant that he was in possession of the house. Readers may be forgiven if they thought he was possessed by a demon of Hell.

He continued, "Since Volpone wants to be dead before his time, I'll bury him or gain by him. I am his heir, and so I will continue to be, until he at least shares his wealth with me. To cheat him out of everything he has would be only a well-deserved con: No man would call it a sin. Let the entertainment he gets out of conning others pay for his being conned; this is called the Fox-trap."

Let's think about this.

According to Mosca, to cheat Corbaccio and Corvino out of everything they have would be only a well-deserved con: No man would call it a sin.

It's not true. By cheating Corbaccio, Volpone is also cheating Bonario, Corbaccio's innocent son. By cheating Corvino, Volpone is also cheating Celia, Corvino's innocent wife.

Even in the case of Mosca's cheating Voltore, cheating him is still a sin and a crime.

Corbaccio and Corvino talked on a Venetian street.

Corbaccio said, "They say that the court is set. It is ready to begin."

Corvino said, "We must continue to maintain the tale we told at the first court session, for both our reputations."

He meant that they needed to continue to tell the falsehoods they had earlier told. In Corvino's case, he needed to continue to lie that his wife had cuckolded him.

Corbaccio said, "Why, mine's no tale: My son would there have killed me."

He was telling only part of the truth — or at least part of what he believed to be the truth. When he had made Volpone his heir, his son had not even been suspected of anything evil. Of course, his son had had no intention of murdering him.

"That's true, I had forgotten —" Corvino said.

He thought, *My testimony is a tale — a lie — I am sure.*

He continued, "But as for your will, sir."

"Yes, I'll make a demand upon Mosca for that hereafter, now that his patron, Volpone, is dead."

Mosca still had the will that Corbaccio had made that listed Volpone as his heir.

Volpone, disguised as a police officer, entered the scene. His purpose was to torment the two legacy-hunters with their failure to inherit his wealth.

"Signior Corvino! And Corbaccio!" he called.

He said to Corbaccio, "Sir, much joy to you."

Corvino asked, "Much joy from what?"

"The sudden good that has dropped down upon you," the disguised Volpone answered.

"Where?" Corbaccio asked.

"None knows how, but it came from old Volpone, sir," the disguised Volpone said.

"Go away, arrant knave!" Corbaccio said.

"Don't allow your too much wealth, sir, to make you furious," the disguised Volpone said.

"Go away, you varlet!" Corbaccio said.

"Why, sir?" the disguised Volpone asked.

"Do you mock me?" Corbaccio asked.

"You mock everyone in the entire world, sir," the disguised Volpone said. "Didn't you and Volpone make each other your heir?"

Corbaccio said, "Out, harlot!"

The disguised Volpone said, "Oh, if Corbaccio didn't inherit Volpone's wealth, then probably you are the man, Signior Corvino. Indeed, you carry your new wealth well; you haven't grown insane because of your new riches. I love your spirit: You haven't swollen up like bread with too much yeast because of your fortune. Some people would swell now like a wine-vat with such an autumn harvest of grapes, which is a metaphor for your new riches. Did he give you everything, sir?"

"Get lost, you rascal!" Corvino said.

"Truly, your wife has shown that she is every inch a woman by committing adultery, but you are well and you need not care because you have a good estate to bear the burden of being a cuckold, sir, and your estate is made much, much better by Volpone's death — unless Corbaccio has a share."

"Go away, varlet," Corbaccio said.

"You will not acknowledge that you are the heir, sir," the disguised Volpone said. "Why, that is wise. Thus do all gamblers, at all games, mislead other people. No man wants to appear as if he has won."

Corvino and Corbaccio exited.

Seeing Voltore coming toward him, the disguised Volpone said, "Here comes my vulture, heaving his beak up in the air, and snuffing."

Voltore complained to himself, "Outstripped thus, by a parasite — a man dependent upon another for the necessities of life! A slave who used to run errands, and make bows for crumbs! Well, what I'll do —"

The disguised Volpone said, "The court waits for your worship. I even rejoice, sir, at your worship's happiness, and I rejoice that it fell into so learned hands, which understand the fingering —"

Clever cheaters make clever use of their fingers.

"What do you mean?" Voltore interrupted.

"I mean to be a suitor to your worship, for the small tenement, which needs repairs and is at the end of your long row of houses by the Piscaria, aka the fish market. It was, in the time of Volpone, your predecessor, before he grew diseased, as handsome, pretty, and well patronized a bawdy-house as any was in Venice, with no dispraise intended toward any of them. But it fell into disrepair along with him; his body and that house decayed, together."

The disguised Volpone was pretending that Voltore had inherited the tenement from Volpone, who may have received income from the bawdy-house before making money from legacy-hunters.

"Come sir, stop your prating," Voltore said.

"Why, if your worship will just give me your hand in a handshake to acknowledge that I may have the first refusal, I will have finished. That house is a mere toy, aka trifle, to you, sir; it is candle-rents."

"Candle-rents" are the rents that come from a house that is dilapidated and growing worse. The house is wearing out and soon will bring in no more rent. Similarly, candles give off light, but they consume themselves in the process.

The disguised Volpone continued, "As your learned worship knows —"

Voltore interrupted, "What do I know?"

"Indeed, you know no end of your wealth, sir," the disguised Volpone said. "May God decrease it!"

He deliberately said "decrease" rather than "increase." A stereotype of police officers was they made many malapropisms — they misused words.

"Mistaking knave!" Voltore said. "Are you mocking my misfortune?"

"God's blessing on your heart, sir," the disguised Volpone said. "I wish it were more!"

The "more" could be God's blessing on Voltore's heart or God's decreasing Voltore's wealth.

Voltore exited.

The disguised Volpone said, "Now I will go to and mock my first victims — Corbaccio and Corvino — again, at the next corner."

Corbaccio and Corvino stood on another part of the street as Mosca appeared and walked by them.

"Look at him," Corbaccio said. "He is wearing our clothing — the clothing of a Venetian gentleman! Look at the impudent varlet!"

"I wish that I could shoot my eyes at him like stone cannonballs," Corvino said.

The disguised Volpone walked over to them and asked, "But is this true, sir, about Mosca the parasite?"

Corbaccio said, "You again! Here to afflict us! Monster!"

"In good faith, sir," the disguised Volpone said, "I'm heartily grieved that a man with a beard of your grave length should be so overreached. I never could endure that parasite's hair; I thought that even his nose looked like that of a con man. There always was something in his look that promised the bane of a *clarissimo*."

Corbaccio, Corvino, Voltore, and Volpone himself all had the title of *clarissimo*.

Corbaccio began, "Knave —"

The disguised Volpone interrupted, "I still think that you, who are so experienced in the world, a witty merchant, the fine bird, Corvino, who have such moral emblems on your name, should not have sung your shame, and dropped your cheese, to let the fox laugh at your emptiness."

A moral emblem is an illustration with a printed explanation that points out the moral. Many moral emblems come from animal fables.

Volpone was referring to Aesop's fable about the Fox, the Cheese, and the Crow. Corvino, whose name means "crow," had sung about his shame — the shame of being cuckolded — in open court. Now the fox — Volpone — was laughing at Corvino's emptiness. The crow's belly was empty in the fable, but Corvino's head was empty. He lacked intelligence and moral insight.

Corvino said, "Sirrah, you think the privilege of the place, and your red saucy cap, that seems to me nailed to your blockhead with those two chequins, can warrant and officially sanction your abuses."

They stood on a public street, and in particular a public street just outside the courtroom. No violence would be tolerated there. In addition, Volpone was wearing the uniform of a police officer, which included a cap with two medallions of St. Mark — the medallions resembled the gold coins known as chequins.

He continued, "If you come hither, you shall perceive, sir, that I dare to beat you; approach."

"There is no haste, sir," the disguised Volpone said. "I know your valor well, since you dare to publish what you are, sir."

Volpone did know Corvino's valor well; Corvino had beaten Volpone when he was disguised as a mountebank; however, Volpone's "compliment" was actually an insult: Corvino must be a brave man in order to announce publicly in court that he is a cuckold.

Corvino said, "Wait, I want to speak with you."

"Sir, sir, another time," the disguised Volpone said.

"No, now," Corvino insisted.

"Oh lord, sir!" the disguised Volpone said, adding sarcastically, "I would be a wise man if I would stand and face the fury of a distracted cuckold."

He began to run away just as Mosca returned.

Corbaccio said, "What! Mosca has come again!"

Volpone said as he neared Mosca, "Face them, Mosca! Save me!"

Corbaccio said, "The air's infected where Mosca breathes."

Corvino said, "Let's flee from him."

Corbaccio and Corvino exited.

Volpone said to Mosca, "Excellent basilisk! Voltore is coming. Turn upon the vulture."

A basilisk is a mythical serpent that can kill anyone with its look.

Voltore walked over to Mosca and said, "Well, flesh-fly, it is summer with you now."

A flesh-fly is a fly that lays its eggs in dead bodies. The Italian word *mosca* means "flesh-fly."

Voltore continued, "Your winter will come on."

Flies die in the winter in the Northern Hemisphere.

Mosca replied, "Good advocate, please don't rail, nor threaten out of place like this. You will make a solecism, as madam — Lady Would-be — says."

A solecism is a breach of propriety.

Mosca continued, "Get yourself another lawyer's cap; your brain is breaking loose and falling out of the one you are now wearing."

Voltore said, "Well, sir."

Mosca exited.

The disguised Volpone asked Voltore, "Do you want me to beat the insolent slave and throw dirt upon his first good clothes?"

Voltore, who knew he was being mocked, looked at the disguised Volpone and said to himself, "This man is doubtless some familiar."

He meant that the disguised Volpone was a familiar friend of Mosca, or a member of Mosca's household, or a familiar spirit of a witch.

The disguised Volpone said, "Sir, the court truly is waiting for you. I am mad that a mule that never read Justinian should get up and ride an advocate."

Lawyers often rode mules to the court. Volpone meant that Mosca, who never had read the codified law that the Roman Emperor Justinian had ordered to be made, had gotten the better of Voltore. It was as if a mule were riding the lawyer, rather than the lawyer riding the mule.

The disguised Volpone continued, "Had you no lawyerly trick to avoid being made a fool, sir, by such a creature? I hope that you are only jesting; he has not done it. It is just a confederacy between you and Mosca so that you can blind the rest to the true fact that you are the heir."

Voltore said, "You are a strange, officious, troublesome knave! You torment me."

The disguised Volpone said, "I know ... that it cannot be, sir, that you should be cheated. It is not within the wit of man to do it. You are so wise and so prudent, and it is fit that wealth and wisdom should always go together."

Voltore exited with the disguised Volpone following and tormenting him.

— 5.10 —

The Judges, the Notary, Bonario, Celia, Corbaccio, Corvino, police officers, etc. were in the Scrutineo.

The First Judge asked, "Are all the parties here?"

The Notary answered, "All except the advocate Voltore."

The Second Judge said, "And here he comes."

Voltore and the disguised Volpone arrived.

The First Judge ordered, "Now bring Bonario and Celia forth to be sentenced."

Putting on an act of suffering great emotional turmoil, Voltore said, "Oh, my most honored fathers, let your mercy for once win out over your justice, to forgive — I am distracted, greatly troubled, divided —"

The disguised Volpone thought, *What is he doing?*

What Voltore was doing was trying to get revenge on Mosca, who had been tormenting him.

Voltore said, "Oh, I don't know who to address myself to first — whether your Fatherhoods, or these innocents, Bonario and Celia —"

Will he betray himself? Corvino thought.

Voltore continued, "— whom equally I have abused, out of most covetous motivations —"

Corvino said out loud, "The man is insane!"

Corbaccio asked, "What's that? What did you say?"

"Voltore is possessed by the devil," Corvino said.

Voltore continued, "— for which, now struck in conscience, here I prostrate myself at your offended feet, and I ask for pardon."

He knelt.

The First and Second Judges said, "Arise."

Voltore stood up.

Celia said, "Oh, Heaven, how just you are!"

Volpone thought, *I am caught in my own noose.*

By pretending to be dead and to have made Mosca his heir, and by having Mosca torment Voltore, he had given Voltore a reason to speak up in court.

Corvino said to Corbaccio, "Be constant, sir. Don't change the story you told in court earlier. Nothing now can help, except for impudence."

He wanted Corbaccio and himself to continue to maintain as true the lies they had testified to in court earlier that day.

The First Judge said, "Continue speaking."

A police officer ordered the people in the courtroom, "Silence!"

Voltore said, "It is not madness in me, reverend fathers, but only conscience, conscience, my good sires, that makes me now tell the truth. That parasite, that knave, has been the instrument of all. He is the party responsible for what is wrong."

The First Judge said, "Where is that knave? Fetch him."

Volpone, still disguised as a police officer, said, "I will go and fetch him."

He exited.

Worried about being found guilty of committing perjury in the earlier trial, Corvino said, "Grave fathers, this man — Voltore — is distracted and out of his wits. He confessed it just now. For, hoping to be the heir of old Volpone, who now is dead —"

"What!" the Third Judge said.

"Is Volpone dead?" the Second Judge asked.

Corvino answered, "He has died since you last saw him, grave Fathers —"

Bonario said, "Oh, this is surely vengeance!"

He believed that God had punished Volpone because Volpone had tried to rape Celia.

The First Judge said, "Wait, then Volpone was no deceiver?"

If Volpone had been a deceiver, he would have been in good health and only pretending to be sick. His death showed that he was no deceiver.

Voltore replied, "Oh, no, he was not a deceiver."

As far as Voltore knew, Volpone was not a deceiver. Volpone believed that Volpone had really been ill for three years and had really just died, and therefore he must have been too ill to attempt to rape Celia.

Voltore continued, "But as for the parasite, grave Fathers —"

Corvino said, "Voltore is speaking only out of complete envy because Volpone's servant has gotten the thing Voltore hoped to swallow. If it please your Fatherhoods, this is the truth, though I'll not exonerate the parasite, for he may be somewhat at fault."

Corvino would be happy to get Mosca in trouble.

Voltore said, "Yes, the parasite is responsible for dashing your hopes, as well as mine, Corvino, but I'll use modesty, moderation, and restraint as I talk."

Voltore was trying to tell Corvino that Corvino's perjury need not come out. Voltore wanted to get Mosca in trouble, and if he could do that without getting Corvino in trouble, that would be OK. But that was a deliberate deception. His papers would inform the Judges that Celia had been forcibly brought to Volpone's house by Corvino, her husband, and left there. Voltore's papers would also say that Mosca had lied about Bonario and about Celia. Mosca had said that Bonario had wanted to kill Corbaccio, his own father. He had also testified that Celia had come to Volpone's house of her own free will.

Voltore gave the Judges some papers and said, "If it pleases your wisdoms to view these certain, reliable notes, and simply confer about them, as I hope you will favor me, they shall speak the clear truth."

Still worried, Corvino said, "The devil has entered him!"

Bonario said, "Or bides in you."

The Fourth Judge said, "We have done ill by sending a public police officer for him, if he really is the heir."

The Second Judge asked, "For whom?"

The Fourth Judge said, "The man whom they call the parasite; he is apparently Volpone's heir and a rich man now."

So far, Mosca's name had not been mentioned during the trials; he had always been referred to as a parasite and a knave.

The Third Judge said, "That is true. He is a man of great estate now that he is Volpone's heir and Volpone has died."

The Fourth Judge said to the Notary, "Go and learn his name, and say to him that the court requests his presence here only for the clearing up of a few questions."

Because Mosca was thought to be a rich man now, the Judges wanted to treat him with respect and definitely not call him a parasite.

The Notary exited.

The Second Judge, who had been reading Volpone's notes, said, "This is a labyrinth!"

Volpone's notes contradicted some of what had been said at the previous trial.

The First Judge asked Corvino, "Do you stand by your testimony in the first trial? Is that testimony true?"

Corvino said, "My estate, my life, my reputation —"

Bonario said sarcastically, "What reputation!"

Corvino continued, "— are at the stake."

His words were ambiguous. One meaning was that he was staking his estate, life, and reputation on the truth of his earlier testimony. Another meaning was that his estate, life, and reputation were tied to a stake like a bear at a bear-baiting. In the "sport" of bear-baiting, a bear would be tied to a stake and then dogs would be set to torment it.

The First Judge asked Corbaccio, "Do you also stand by your testimony in the first trial? Is that testimony true?"

Corbaccio answered, "The advocate — Voltore — is a knave, and he has a forked tongue —"

The Second Judge said, "Speak to the point. Answer the question."

Corbaccio saying that Voltore is a knave is not the same thing as Corbaccio saying that his earlier testimony had been true.

Corbaccio added, "So is the parasite. He is a knave, too."

The First Judge said, "This is all confusion."

Voltore said, "I beseech your Fatherhoods just to read those papers I gave you."

Corvino said to the Judges, "Give no credit to anything that the false spirit has written. Nothing else is possible except that Voltore is possessed by a devil, grave fathers."

Volpone walked on a street, alone.

He said to himself, "I have made a snare — a noose — for my own neck by pretending to have died! I have run my head into the snare and noose of my own free will! And I did it while I was laughing at and tormenting the legacy-hunters! Plus, I did it when I had just escaped from the first trial and was free and clear. I did it — got myself into new trouble — out of mere wantonness! Oh, the dull devil of stupidity and alcohol was in this brain of mine when I devised my plan, and Mosca seconded it. He must now help me to sear up — cauterize — this vein, or we will bleed out and die."

Nano the dwarf, Androgyno the hermaphrodite, and Castrone the eunuch came walking down the street and met Volpone.

Volpone asked, "What is going on? Who let you loose out of the house? Where are you going now? To buy gingerbread? Or to drown kittens?"

Nano the dwarf said, "Sir, master Mosca called us out of doors and told us all to go and have a day off, and he took the keys."

Androgyno the hermaphrodite said, "Yes, what Nano said is the truth."

Volpone said, "Did master Mosca take the keys? Well! I'm in deeper trouble than I thought."

He was immediately suspicious of Mosca. If Mosca had the keys, he could prevent Volpone from entering his own house.

He continued, "These are my fine schemes! I must be merry, and the result is evil to me! What a vile wretch was I, who could not bear my fortune soberly! I had to have my fancies and my whims!

"Well, all of you go and seek Mosca. His reason for taking my keys may be more loyal to me than I fear it is. Tell him that he must immediately come to me in the court. Thither I will go, and if it is possible, I will unscrew my advocate, Voltore, who is wound tight, by giving him new hopes of inheriting my property. When I provoked him, then I lost myself."

In the Scrutineo, the Judges had been examining Voltore's papers.

The First Judge said, "Voltore here in these papers states that the gentleman Bonario was wronged and that the gentlewoman Celia was forcibly brought to Volpone's house by her husband, and left there."

Voltore said, "That is very true."

Celia said, "How ready is Heaven to help those who pray!"

The First Judge said, "But that Volpone attempted to rape her, he holds to be utterly false. He says that he knows that Volpone was impotent."

Voltore certainly believed that to have been the truth.

Corvino, desperate to stay out of trouble, said, "Grave Fathers, Voltore is possessed. Again, I say that a devil has possessed his body. Indeed, if it is possible for possession and obsession to exist together, he has both."

In possession, a devil enters the person's body and controls it. If lust for gold is a demon, Voltore was possessed. In obsession, a devil controls the person from outside the body. The disguised Volpone would show up almost immediately and would control Voltore.

The Third Judge said, "Here comes our police officer."

Volpone, still disguised as a police officer, entered the courtroom.

He said, "The parasite will immediately be here, grave Fathers."

The Fourth Judge said severely, "You might invent some name other than 'parasite' for him, Sir Varlet."

The use of "Sir" was sarcastic.

The Third Judge asked, "Didn't the Notary meet him?"

"Him" referred to Mosca.

"Not that I know," the disguised Volpone said.

The Fourth Judge said, "His [Mosca's] testimony will clear up everything."

"So far," the Second Judge said, "everything is misty."

Voltore said, "May it please your Fatherhoods —"

The disguised Volpone whispered to him, "Sir, the parasite wanted me to tell you that his master is still alive, you are still the heir, your hopes are the same as they were before his supposed death, and this was only a jest —"

"How is this possible?" Voltore asked.

The disguised Volpone said, "Sir, he wanted to test if you were loyal to him, and how you were disposed toward him."

"Are you sure he is alive?" Voltore asked.

"Do I live, sir?" the disguised Volpone asked. "I am as sure he is alive as I am sure I am alive."

"Oh, me!" Voltore said. "I have been too violent, aggressive, and bold."

"Sir, you may redeem it," the disguised Volpone said. "They said you were possessed by a devil. Fall down, and seem to be possessed. I'll help you to pull this trick off."

Voltore fell to the floor as if he were having a fit.

The disguised Volpone said loudly, "God bless the man!"

He whispered to Voltore, "Breathe deeply, hold your breath, and swell your cheeks."

He said loudly, "Look! Look! Look! Look! He vomits crooked pins! His eyes are staring like a dead hare's hung in a poulterer's shop! His mouth's awry!"

He said to Corvino, "Do you see, signior?"

Voltore pretended that a devil was moving around in his body. He moved different muscles to simulate the devil's movements.

The disguised Volpone said, "Now it is in his belly!"

Corvino, recognizing an opportunity to discount Voltore's previous testimony, said, "Yes, it's the devil!"

Voltore made swallowing movements.

The disguised Volpone said, "Now it's in his throat!"

Corvino said, "Yes, I perceive it plainly."

The disguised Volpone said, "The devil is coming out! It's leaving the body! Stand clear. See, where it flies, in the shape of a blue toad, with a bat's wings!"

This society believed in demonic possessions and in exorcisms. Demonic possessions and exorcisms were sometimes faked.

Sulphur, which is associated with devils, burns with a blue color. In this society, toads and bats were also associated with devils.

The disguised Volpone asked, "Corbaccio, don't you also see it, sir?"

"What?" Corbaccio said. "I think I do."

Corvino said, "It is very evident. I definitely saw it."

The disguised Volpone said, "Look! Voltore is coming to himself! He is regaining consciousness!"

"Where am I?" Voltore asked.

"Take good heart, the worst is past, sir," the disguised Volpone said. "You are dispossessed."

"What a strange turn of events this is!" the First Judge said.

"It is sudden, and full of wonder!" the Second Judge said.

"If Voltore were possessed, as it appears he was, all this he has said is nothing," the Third Judge said. "We can't believe his papers or his testimony."

"He has been often subject to these fits," Corvino said.

The First Judge said, "Show him that writing."

Voltore's papers were handed to him.

The First Judge asked, "Do you know these papers, sir?"

Volpone whispered to Voltore, "Deny them, sir. Forswear them. Don't admit you know them."

"Yes, I know them well," Voltore said to the Judges. "This is my handwriting, but everything written in these papers is false."

"Oh, this is deceit!" Bonario said.

"What a maze this is!" the Second Judge said.

"Is he not guilty then?" the First Judge said. "I mean the man you call the parasite in your papers."

"Grave fathers," Voltore said, "He is no more guilty than his good patron, old Volpone."

"Why, he is dead," the Fourth Judge said.

"Oh no, my honored fathers," Voltore said. "Volpone still lives."

"What!" the First Judge said. "Is he still alive?"

"Yes," Voltore said. "He is still alive."

"This is getting even more complicated!" the Second Judge said.

"You said he was dead," the Third Judge said.

"Never," Voltore said.

"You said so," the Third Judge said.

"I heard you say it," Corvino said.

Mosca, dressed like a gentleman, walked into the courtroom.

The Fourth Judge said, "Here comes the gentleman; make way for him."

The Third Judge said, "Get him a stool to sit on."

The Fourth Judge thought about Mosca, *He is a handsome man, and if Volpone were dead, he would be a fit husband for my daughter.*

"Give him room," the Third Judge said.

The disguised Volpone whispered, "Mosca, I was almost lost. Voltore the advocate had revealed everything, but now it is all recovered. All's on the hinge and moving smoothly again. Tell the Judges that I am living."

Mosca said loudly about the disguised Volpone, "What interfering, meddling knave is this man?"

He then said to the Judges, "Most reverend Fathers, I would have arrived sooner to wait on your grave pleasures except that my order for the funeral of my dear patron required me —"

The disguised Volpone whispered, "Mosca!"

Mosca said, "— whom I intend to bury like a gentleman."

The words "like a gentleman" were ambiguous. They could refer to Volpone or to Mosca, or both. Like a gentleman, Mosca could bury Volpone like a gentleman.

Also, the words "bury like a gentleman" were ambiguous. Did he mean to bury Volpone like a gentleman, or at some later date have a gentleman's burial for himself?

Volpone thought, *Yes, you would like to bury me like a gentleman — so quickly that I am still alive — and cheat me out of everything.*

"This is even stranger!" the Second Judge said. "It is very intricate!"

"And come about again!" the First Judge said.

Volpone had been declared dead by Corvino and then alive by Voltore and now was declared dead again by Mosca.

The Fourth Judge thought, *Volpone is dead. I have a husband for my daughter. She shall marry this man who has been called a parasite but who is now a gentleman.*

Mosca whispered to the disguised Volpone, "Will you give me half of all your wealth?"

"First, I'll be hanged," the disguised Volpone said.

"I know," Mosca whispered. "I heard you, your voice is good, cry out not so loudly."

"Let us question the advocate," the First Judge said.

He then asked Voltore, "Sir, didn't you affirm that Volpone was alive?"

Instead of Voltore, the disguised Volpone answered the question, "Yes, and he is."

He pointed to Mosca and said, "This gentleman told me so."

He whispered to Mosca, "You shall have half of my wealth."

Mosca said loudly about Volpone, "Whose drunkard is this man? Speak, someone who knows him. I have never seen his face before now."

He whispered to Volpone, "I cannot now afford to help you so cheaply."

Even if Mosca were to get Volpone's promise to give Mosca half his wealth, what would prevent Volpone from reneging on his promise later?

"No!" the disguised Volpone said.

The First Judge said to Voltore, "Answer the question. What do you say in answer to it?"

Voltore pointed to Volpone, who was still disguised as a police officer, and said, "This officer told me that Volpone is still alive."

"I did, grave Fathers," the disguised Volpone said, "and I will maintain he lives with my own life."

He pointed to Mosca and said, "And I maintain that this creature told me that Volpone is still alive."

He thought, *I was born with all good stars as my enemies.*

"Most grave Fathers," Mosca said, "if such insolence as this is allowed to be inflicted upon me, I am silent. I hope that this is not the reason for which you sent for me."

Referring to the disguised Volpone, the Second Judge said, "Take him away."

The disguised Volpone shouted, "Mosca!"

Referring to the disguised Volpone, the Second Judge said, "Let him be whipped."

The disguised Volpone said to Mosca, "Will you betray me? Cheat me?"

The Third Judge said, "And let him learn how to bear himself toward a person of a gentleman's rank."

"Take him away," the Fourth Judge ordered.

Some police officers seized the disguised Volpone.

Mosca said, "I humbly thank your Fatherhoods."

The disguised Volpone thought, *Hold on! Wait! Whipped! And lose all that I have! If I confess, I cannot be punished much more harshly.*

In hopes of getting his daughter wed to a wealthy man, the Fourth Judge asked Mosca, "Sir, are you married?"

The disguised Volpone thought, *Mosca and the Fourth Judge's family will be allied soon through Mosca's engagement to the Fourth Judge's daughter. I must be resolute. The Fox shall here and now remove his disguise.*

He took off his disguise and revealed himself to all present.

"Patron!" Mosca said.

Volpone said to him, "Now my ruin shall not come alone. Your wedding match I'll certainly hinder. My wealth shall not allow you to attach yourself to a family or worm yourself into one."

"Why, patron!" Mosca said.

"I am Volpone, and this is my knave," Volpone said, pointing to Mosca.

He pointed to Voltore and said, "This man is his own knave."

He pointed to Corbaccio and said, "This man is avarice's fool."

He pointed to Corvino and said, "This man is a chimera of wittol, fool, and knave."

A wittol is a contented cuckold.

A chimera is a mythological monster that has the head of a lion, the body of a goat, and the tail of a snake.

Volpone continued, "And, reverend Fathers, since all we can hope for is nothing but a sentence, let's not now despair of receiving it. You hear me ... brief."

A brief is a begging petition. Volpone was not begging; this was as close to a begging petition as the Judges would get from him. He was also speaking only briefly so the Judges could get on with their sentencing.

Corvino, who was willing to beg, began, "May it please your Fatherhoods —"

A police officer ordered, "Silence!"

The First Judge said, "The knot is now undone by a miracle. All is clear."

"Nothing can be more clear," the Second Judge said.

The Judges could see that Volpone, who had been reputed to be dying for the last three years, was a vigorous, healthy man. The Judges were also aware of the many gifts that Volpone had received from the legacy-hunters. Intelligent people, the Judges could figure out what had happened.

"Nothing can more prove these two — Bonario and Celia — innocent," the Third Judge said.

Volpone was certainly healthy enough to attempt to rape Celia.

"Give them their liberty," the First Judge ordered.

"Heaven could not long let such gross crimes be hidden," Bonario said.

The Second Judge said, "If this is held to be the highway to riches, I hope I may be poor!"

"This is not gain, but torment," the Third Judge said.

"These possess wealth, as sick men possess fevers, which more truly may be said to possess them," the First Judge said.

The Second Judge said, "That parasite is dressed like a gentleman. Take that clothing off him."

Police officers stripped Mosca of his gentleman's robe.

Corvino and Mosca said together, "Most honored Fathers!"

The First Judge asked, "Can you plead anything to stop or pause the course of justice? If you can, speak."

Corvino and Voltore said, "We beg favor."

Celia, who was very forgiving, added, "And mercy."

The Judges were not forgiving.

The First Judge said to Celia, "You hurt your innocence by begging for the guilty. Stand back."

He then said, "First we will judge the parasite."

He said to Mosca, "You appear to have been the chief agent, if not plotter, in all these wicked impostures, and now, finally, you have with your impudence abused the court and worn the clothing of a gentleman of Venice, although you are a fellow of no noble birth and no noble blood."

For a non-gentleman to wear the clothing of a gentleman was a serious crime in Venice.

The First Judge continued talking to Mosca, "For which our sentence is that first you will be whipped and then you will live as a perpetual prisoner in our galleys — our Venetian ships."

"I thank you for him," Voltore said.

Just minutes previously, Mosca had seemed to be a very wealthy gentleman.

Mosca snarled at Volpone, "Bane to your wolvish nature!"

Wolfbane is a poison.

The First Judge ordered, "Deliver him to the police officers."

A bailiff took Mosca over to some police officers who escorted him out of the courtroom.

The First Judge said, "Thou, Volpone, who are by blood and rank a gentleman, cannot fall under a similar censure."

The First Judge's use of the word "thou" — and his use soon of the word "thee" — was that of a superior talking to someone much lower on the social scale. It was an insult.

He continued, "But our judgment on thee is that all your wealth be immediately confiscated and forfeited to the Hospital of the Incurabili — the Hospital of the Incurables.

"And since the most of your wealth was gotten by imposture, by feigning lame, gout, palsy, and such diseases, you are to lie in prison, cramped with irons, until you are sick and lame for real."

He ordered, "Remove him."

Volpone said, "This is called mortifying a Fox."

Even in these circumstances, he was capable of wit. "Mortifying" was a multiple pun that meant these things:

- Humiliating. Volpone was publicly humiliated.
- Subjecting the body to discipline intended to subjugate bodily desires so that spiritual desires would be dominate.
- Giving wealth to charitable causes, aka disposing of wealth by mortification. Volpone's wealth would go to the Hospital of the Incurables.
- Hanging up a dead game animal to let it become tender. Volpone would at least metaphorically be hung up in chains.
- Wasting away. Volpone would waste away in prison.
- Becoming gangrenous. Volpone's chains in prison could very well cause gangrene.
- Causing death. Volpone would die in prison.

Volpone was taken over to some police officers, who escorted him out of the courtroom.

The First Judge said to the advocate, "Thou, Voltore, to take away the scandal thou has given all worthy men of your profession, are banished from their fellowship and from our state."

He then said, "Corbaccio!"

He ordered the bailiff, "Bring him near to me so he can hear me!"

He then said to Corbaccio, "We here give thy son possession of all your estate, and we confine thee to the monastery of San Spirito, where, since you didn't know how to live well here, thou shall be taught how to die well there."

Corbaccio said, "Ah! What did he say?"

A police officer said, "You shall know soon, sir."

The First Judge said, "Thou, Corvino, shall be immediately embarked from your own house, and rowed round about Venice, through the miles-long Canal Grande, wearing a cap with very long asses' ears instead of horns."

The asses' ears would show that he is a fool. The cap had no horns because the court had determined that Celia was innocent of committing adultery.

The First Judge continued, "And then you will climb, with a paper describing your crimes pinned on your breast, to the pillory —"

The pillory was a wooden device that restrained a criminal's hands and head. Often, people would torment the criminal while he was in the pillory.

"Yes," Corvino said, "and I will have my eyes beaten out by all the things people will throw at me — stinking fish, bruised fruit, and rotten eggs. This punishment is good. I am glad that I shall be blind and shall not see my shame."

The First Judge said, "And to expiate thy wrongs done to your wife, you are to send her home to her father, with her dowry trebled."

He said to Voltore, Corbaccio, and Corvino, "And for your crimes, these are all your sentences —"

Voltore, Corbaccio, and Corvino pleaded, "Honored Fathers —"

The First Judge continued, "— which may not be revoked.

"Now you begin, when your crimes are done and past, and when you are to be punished, to think what your crimes are."

He said to the police officers, "Take them away! Let all who see these vices thus rewarded, take them to heart and love to study them! Evil deeds feed like beasts, until they are fat, and then they bleed."

EPILOGUE

Volpone says this to you the readers:

The seasoning of a play — and a book — is the applause.
Now, although the Fox is punished by the laws,
He yet does hope, there is no suffering due,
For any crime that he has done against you.
If there is, censure him; here he full of fears stands.
If not, fare jovially, and Jovially, and clap your hands.

***

In astrology, the planet Jupiter is associated with mirth and humor.

APPENDIX A: NOTES

Cast: ANDROGYNO, a Hermaphrodite

True hermaphrodites exist.

Here is the beginning of the Wikipedia article on "True Hermaphroditism":

True hermaphroditism, now clinically known as ovotesticular disorder of sex development, is a medical term for an intersex[1] condition in which an individual is born with ovarian[2] and testicular[3] tissue. More commonly one or both gonads is an ovotestis[4] containing both types of tissue.

https://en.wikipedia.org/wiki/True_hermaphroditism

Here is the beginning of a first-person account of a true hermaphrodite:
I Am a True Hermaphrodite

We Do Exist

People say that true hermaphroditism does not exist in humans; I can tell you for definite that it does. It's true that you cannot have a fully functional and complete set of both genitals together, but I was born with one ovary and one testicle, and that makes me a hermaphrodite.

http://www.experienceproject.com/stories/Am-A-True-Hermaphrodite/2663037

Fast and Loose (1.2)

This con game can be performed in various ways. Here is a YouTube video explaining one way to perform it:

Scam School: Fast and Loose!

---

1. *https://en.wikipedia.org/wiki/Intersex*

2. *https://en.wikipedia.org/wiki/Ovary*

3. *https://en.wikipedia.org/wiki/Testis*

4. *https://en.wikipedia.org/wiki/Ovotestis*

https://www.youtube.com/watch?v=1-zL3_F0lHw

"unprepared antimony" (2.2)

This is a quotation from John Man's *The Gutenberg Revolution: How Printing Changed the Course of History* (2010), p. 130:

Antimony deserves respect. The silvery ore was much used in antiquity for make-up and as a means of chemical purification. It was said that monks, impressed by its chemical effects, swallowed it to purify their bodies. Unfortunately, antimony is deadly poisonous, so the only things they purified, if anything, were their souls. Almost certainly this is a piece of nonsense based on a false etymology that derives the metal's name from anti/monos — 'anti-monk'. In popular parlance it was 'monks bane'.

Source: http://tinyurl.com/y7anl882

Four Humors and Four Elements (2.2)

The society of *Volpone* believed in the theory of elements, which are earth, air, water, and fire, and the theory of humors, which are blood, phlegm, choler, and black choler.

Every physical thing, including the bodies of human beings, is made up of the four elements, each of which has associated qualities.

Earth is cold, heavy, and dry.

Air is hot, light, and wet.

Water is cold, heavy, and wet.

Fire is hot, light, and dry.

Doctors in this society believed that each of the human body's four humors, or vital fluids, made a contribution to the personality, and for a human being to be sane and healthy, the four humors had to be present in the right amounts. If a man had too much of a certain humor, it would harm his personality and health.

Blood was the sanguine humor. A sanguine man was optimistic.

Phlegm was the phlegmatic humor. A phlegmatic man was calm.

Yellow bile was the choleric humor. A choleric man was angry.

Black bile was the melancholic humor. A melancholic man was gloomy.

When a man was ill, doctors would try to get the four humors back into balance by purging him, often through bloodletting or through the use of laxatives. Mountebanks sold "medicines" that were supposed to bring the four humors into the correct balance.

"He shall come home, and minister unto you / The fricace for the mother" (2.5)

The "mother" is "hysteria." Doctors (mountebanks were quack doctors) would give women genital massages to make them orgasm as a treatment for hysteria.

The below is an excerpt from a *New York Times* review of this book: Rachel P. Mains, *The Technology of Orgasm: "Hysteria," the Vibrator, and Women's Sexual Satisfaction.* The Johns Hopkins University Press. 1999. Revised Ed. 2001.

In 1653 Pieter van Foreest, called Alemarianus Petrus Forestus, published a medical compendium titled Observationem et Curationem Medicinalium ac Chirurgicarum Opera Omnia, *with a chapter on the diseases of women. For the affliction commonly called hysteria (literally, "womb disease") and known in his volume as* praefocatio matricis *or "suffocation of the mother," the physician advised as follows:*

"When these symptoms indicate, we think it necessary to ask a midwife to assist, so that she can massage the genitalia with one finger inside, using oil of lilies, musk root, crocus, or [something] similar. And in this way the afflicted woman can be aroused to the paroxysm. This kind of stimulation with the finger is recommended by Galen and Avicenna, among others, most especially for widows, those who live chaste lives, and female religious, as Gradus [Ferrari da Gradi] proposes; it is less often recommended for very young women, public women, or married women, for whom it is a better remedy to engage in intercourse with their spouses."

As Forestus suggests here, in the Western medical tradition genital massage to orgasm by a physician or midwife was a standard treatment for hysteria, an ailment considered common and chronic in women.

This is the review:

Sarah Boxer, "Batteries Not Included: A social history of the vibrator." *New York Times*. 21 March 1999

http://www.nytimes.com/books/99/03/21/reviews/ 990321.21boxert.html

Note: Doctors hated doing this, largely because of the time it took, and so they often had midwives do this. In the 1880s, the vibrator was invented so that doctors wouldn't have to perform genital massages on females.

"pull the pillow from his head" (2.6)

When people were dying, their pillows were taken away from under their heads to make it easier to die. The sixteenth-century *Shiltei Hagiborim* by R. Joshua Boaz argued against what he regarded as a form of what we would probably call euthanasia:

"There would appear to be grounds for forbidding the custom, practiced by some, in the case of someone who is dying and his soul cannot depart, of removing the pillow from underneath the goses [someone who is expected to die within 72 hours] so that he will die quickly. For they say that the bird feathers in the bedding prevent the soul from leaving the body."

Horned Flood (3.7)

The below is from Sophocles' *Trachiniae* (*Women of Trachis*):

My suitor was the river Achelöüs, who took three forms to ask me of my father: a rambling bull once — then a writhing snake of gleaming colors — then again a man with ox-like face: and from his beard's dark shadows stream upon stream of water tumbled down. Such was my suitor.

Source: *The Women of Trachis and Philoctetes*. A new translation in verse by Robert Torrance. Houghton Mifflin. 1966.

Pearls — Lollia Paulini and Cleopatra (3.7)
The below is from Pliny's *Natural History*:
Pliny the Elder, *The Natural History*. John Bostock, M.D., F.R.S., H.T. Riley, Esq., B.A., Ed.

I once saw Lollia Paulina, the wife of the Emperor Caius — it was not at any public festival, or any solemn ceremonial, but only at an ordinary wedding entertainment — covered with emeralds and pearls, which shone in alternate layers upon her head, in her hair, in her wreaths, in her ears, upon her neck, in her bracelets, and on her fingers, and the value of which amounted in all to forty millions of sesterces; indeed she was prepared at once to prove the fact, by showing the receipts and acquittances. Nor were these any presents made by a prodigal potentate, but treasures which had descended to her from her grandfather, and obtained by the spoliation of the provinces. Such are the fruits of plunder and extortion! It was for this reason that M. Lollius was held so infamous all over the East for the presents which he extorted from the kings; the result of which was, that he was denied the friendship of Caius Cæsar, and took poison; and all this was done, I say, that his grand-daughter might be seen, by the glare of lamps, covered all over with jewels to the amount of forty millions of sesterces! Now let a person only picture to himself, on the one hand, what was the value of the habits worn by Curius or Fabricius in their triumphs, let him picture to himself the objects displayed to the public on their triumphal litters, and then, on the other hand, let him think upon this Lollia, this one bit of a woman, the head of an empire, taking her place at table, thus attired; would he not much rather that the conquerors had been torn from their very chariots, than that they had conquered for such a result as this?

Nor, indeed, are these the most supreme evidences of luxury. There were formerly two pearls, the largest that had been ever seen in the whole world: Cleopatra, the last of the queens of Egypt, was in possession of them both, they having come to her by descent from the kings of the

East. When Antony had been sated by her, day after day, with the most exquisite banquets, this queenly courtesan, inflated with vanity and disdainful arrogance, affected to treat all this sumptuousness and all these vast preparations with the greatest contempt; upon which Antony enquired what there was that could possibly be added to such extraordinary magnificence. To this she made answer, that on a single entertainment she would expend ten millions of sesterces. Antony was extremely desirous to learn how that could be done, but looked upon it as a thing quite impossible; and a wager was the result. On the following day, upon which the matter was to be decided, in order that she might not lose the wager, she had an entertainment set before Antony, magnificent in every respect, though no better than his usual repast. Upon this, Antony joked her, and enquired what was the amount expended upon it; to which she made answer that the banquet which he then beheld was only a trifling appendage to the real banquet, and that she alone would consume at the meal to the ascertained value of that amount, she herself would swallow the ten millions of sesterces; and so ordered the second course to be served. In obedience to her instructions, the servants placed before her a single vessel, which was filled with vinegar, a liquid, the sharpness and strength of which is able to dissolve pearls. At this moment she was wearing in her ears those choicest and most rare and unique productions of Nature; and while Antony was waiting to see what she was going to do, taking one of them from out of her ear, she threw it into the vinegar, and directly it was melted, swallowed it. Lucius Plancus, who had been named umpire in the wager, placed his hand upon the other at the very instant that she was making preparations to dissolve it in a similar manner, and declared that Antony had lost — an omen which, in the result, was fully confirmed. The fame of the second pearl is equal to that which attends its fellow. After the queen, who had thus come off victorious on so important a question, had been seized, it was cut asunder, in order that this, the other half of the entertainment, might serve as pendants for the ears of Venus, in the Pantheon at Rome.

Source: *The Natural History*. Pliny the Elder. John Bostock, M.D., F.R.S. H.T. Riley, Esq., B.A. London. Taylor and Francis, Red Lion Court, Fleet Street. 1855.

http://tinyurl.com/yavx8otp

Panthers' Breath (3.7)

The below is from Pliny's *Natural History*:

CHAP. 23.—PANTHERS.

The panther and the tiger are nearly the only animals that are remarkable for a skin distinguished by the variety of its spots;[15] whereas others have them of a single colour, appropriate to each species. The lions of Syria alone are black. The spots of the panther are like small eyes, upon a white ground. It is said that all quadrupeds are attracted in a most wonderful manner by their odour,[26] while they are terrified by the fierceness of their aspect; for which reason the creature conceals its head, and then seizes upon the animals that are attracted to it by the sweetness of the odour. It is said by some, that the panther has, on the shoulder, a spot which bears the form of the moon; and that, like it, it regularly increases to full, and then diminishes to a crescent. At present, we apply the general names of varia[37] and pard, (which last belongs to the males), to all the numerous species of this animal, which is very common in Africa and Syria.[48] Some writers distinguish the panther, as being remarkable for its whiteness: but as yet I have not observed any other difference between them.

---

5. *http://www.perseus.tufts.edu/hopper/*

   text?doc=Perseus%3Atext%3A1999.02.0137%3Abook%3D8%3Achapter%3D23#note1

6. *http://www.perseus.tufts.edu/hopper/*

   text?doc=Perseus%3Atext%3A1999.02.0137%3Abook%3D8%3Achapter%3D23#note2

7. *http://www.perseus.tufts.edu/hopper/*

   text?doc=Perseus%3Atext%3A1999.02.0137%3Abook%3D8%3Achapter%3D23#note3

8. *http://www.perseus.tufts.edu/hopper/*

   text?doc=Perseus%3Atext%3A1999.02.0137%3Abook%3D8%3Achapter%3D23#note4

1⁹ Pliny, in B. xiii. c. 15, speaks of "tables of tiger and panther pattern," as articles of ornamental furniture among the Romans, named from the peculiar patterns of the veins in the citrus wood, of which they were formed. — B.

2¹⁰ This, though mentioned by Aristotle, Hist. Anim. B. ix. c. 8, is probably incorrect; and still more the addition made by Ælian, Anim. Nat. B. v. c. 40, that this odour is grateful to man. It has, however, induced some to conjecture, that the animal here described might be the civet but the description given is inapplicable to that animal; nor, indeed, does the civet appear to have been known to the ancients. For further information, see the remarks of Cuvier, Ajasson, vol. vi. p. 420, and Lemaire, vol. iii. p. 386. Pliny, in B. xxi. c. 18, says that no animal, except the panther, has any odour.—B.

3¹¹ Meaning the "spotted" or "parti-coloured" female.

4¹² Xenophon, in his Cynegetieon, *says, that the pard is found on Mount Pangæus, in Macedonia; the truth of which is denied by Aristotle, who says that it is not to be found in Europe.*

Source: Pliny the Elder. *The Natural History*. John Bostock, M.D., F.R.S. H.T. Riley, Esq., B.A. London. Taylor and Francis, Red Lion Court, Fleet Street. 1855.

https://tinyurl.com/y7sunuct

Mummia (4.4)

This is an excerpt from the Wikipedia article on MUMMIA:

---

9. http://www.perseus.tufts.edu/hopper/

text?doc=Perseus%3Atext%3A1999.02.0137%3Abook%3D8%3Achapter%3D23#note-link1

10. http://www.perseus.tufts.edu/hopper/

text?doc=Perseus%3Atext%3A1999.02.0137%3Abook%3D8%3Achapter%3D23#note-link2

11. http://www.perseus.tufts.edu/hopper/

text?doc=Perseus%3Atext%3A1999.02.0137%3Abook%3D8%3Achapter%3D23#note-link3

12. http://www.perseus.tufts.edu/hopper/

text?doc=Perseus%3Atext%3A1999.02.0137%3Abook%3D8%3Achapter%3D23#note-link4

Mummia, mumia, or originally *mummy* referred to several different preparations in the history of medicine[13], from "mineral pitch[14]" to "powdered human mummies[15]". It originated from Arabic[16] mūmiyā "a type of resinous bitumen[17] found in Western Asia[18] and used curatively" in traditional Islamic medicine[19], which was translated as pissasphaltus (from "pitch" and "asphalt") in ancient Greek medicine[20]. In medieval European medicine[21], mūmiyā "bitumen" was transliterated[22] into Latin as mumia meaning both "a bituminous medicine from Persia" and "mummy". Merchants in apothecaries[23] dispensed expensive mummia bitumen, which was thought to be an effective cure-all[24] for many ailments. Beginning around the 12th century when supplies of imported natural bitumen ran short, mummia was misinterpreted as "mummy", and the word's meaning expanded to "a black resinous exudate[25] scraped out from embalmed Egyptian mummies". This began a period of lucrative trade between Egypt and Europe, and suppliers substituted rare mummia exudate with entire mummies, either embalmed[26] or desiccated[27]. After Egypt banned the shipment of mummia in the 16th century, unscrupulous European apothecaries began to sell fraudulent mummia prepared by embalming and desiccating fresh corpses. During the Renaissance[28], scholars proved that

13. https://en.wikipedia.org/wiki/History_of_medicine

14. https://en.wikipedia.org/wiki/Pitch_(resin)

15. https://en.wikipedia.org/wiki/Mummies

16. https://en.wikipedia.org/wiki/Arabic

17. https://en.wikipedia.org/wiki/Bitumen

18. https://en.wikipedia.org/wiki/Western_Asia

19. https://en.wikipedia.org/wiki/Medicine_in_the_medieval_Islamic_world

20. https://en.wikipedia.org/wiki/Ancient_Greek_medicine

21. https://en.wikipedia.org/wiki/Medieval_medicine_of_Western_Europe

22. https://en.wikipedia.org/wiki/Transliterated

23. https://en.wikipedia.org/wiki/Apothecaries

24. https://en.wikipedia.org/wiki/Cure-all

25. https://en.wikipedia.org/wiki/Exudate

26. https://en.wikipedia.org/wiki/Embalmed

27. https://en.wikipedia.org/wiki/Desiccation

*translating bituminous mummia as mummy was a mistake, and
physicians stopped prescribing the ineffective drug. Lastly, artists in the
17th and 18th centuries used ground up mummies to tint a popular
oil-paint called mummy brown[29].*

Source: https://en.wikipedia.org/wiki/Mummia
Tortoise (5.4)
John S. Weld wrote this about the tortoise scene:

*The meaning of this scene is emphasized and perhaps Jonson's choice of
symbol is explained by Erasmus's interpretation of the proverbial* quam
curat testudino muscas: *"the mind fortified with virtue and philosophy
fears the assaults of Fortune no more than a tortoise fears flies."* —
Opera, *II. 662.*

Source: John S. Weld, "Christian Comedy: 'Volpone.'" *Studies in Philology.*
Volume 51. 1954. P. 183. Footnote 17.
"vomits crooked pins" (5.12)
Witches were said to make people do this.
The below is an excerpt from a late seventeenth century account of
witchcraft:

*In the Town of Beckenton, in Somersetshire, liveth one William Spicer,
a young Man about eighteen Years of Age. As he was wont to pass by the
Alms-house (where lived an Old Woman, about Four score) he would
call her Witch, and tell her of her Buns; which did so enrage the Old
Woman, that she threatened him with a Warrant; and accordingly did
fetch one from a Neighbouring Justice of the Peace. At which he was
so frightened, that he humbled himself to her, and promised never to
call her so again. Within a few days after, this Young Man fell into
the strangest Fits that held him about a Fortnight. When the Fits
were upon him, he would often say that he did see this Old Woman
against the Wall in the same Room of the House where he was, and*

---

28. *https://en.wikipedia.org/wiki/Renaissance*

29. *https://en.wikipedia.org/wiki/Mummy_brown*

that sometimes she did knock her Fist at him; sometimes grin her Teeth, and sometimes laugh at him in his Fits. He was so strong, that three or four Men could scarce hold him; and when he did call for Small Beer to drink, he would be sure to bring up some Crooked Pins to the Number of Thirty, and upwards.

In the same Town liveth one Mary Hill, about the same Age of this Young Man; who meeting with this Old Woman, demanded the Ring she borrowed of her, with a threatening from the Old Woman that she had been better to have let her kept it longer. About a Week before the said Mary was taken with Fits, she met this Old Woman in the Street; who taking her by the hand, desired her to go with her to Froom, to look after some Spinning Work. The said Mary being afraid, refused to go with her. About four days after she met the Old Woman again, who begged an Apple of her, which she refused to give her.

The Sunday following, she complained of a pricking in her Stomack; but on Monday, as she was Eating her Dinner, something arose in her Throat, which was like to have Choaked her; and at the same time she fell into Violent Fits, which held her till Nine or Ten a Clock at Night. The Fits were so strong and violent, that Four or Five Persons were scarce able to hold her, and in the midst of them, she would tell how she saw this old Woman against the Wall, grinning at her, and that she was the Person that had bewitcht her.

The Wednesday following, she began to throw up Crooked Pins, and so continued for the space of a Fortnight. After this, she began to throw up Nails and Pins. And then she began to throw up Nails again, and Handles of Spoons, several pieces of Iron, Lead, and Tin, with several clusters of Crooked Pins; some tied with Yarn, and some with Thread, with abundance of Blood. She threw up in all, above Two Hundred Crooked Pins.

The People of the Town seeing the sad and deplorable Condition of the said Mary, did cause this old Woman to be brought near the House where the Mary Lived, and being gathered together above an Hundred People, the said Mary was brought forth into the open Air, who immediately fell into such strong Fits, that two or three men were scarce able to hold her, and being brought upon the Hill by the Church, and the old Woman brought near her (notwithstanding there were four men to hold the said Mary in a Chair) she mounted up over their Heads into the Air; but the men, and others standing by, caught hold of her Legs, and pulled her down again.

This old Woman was ordered to be searched by a Jury of Women, who found about her several purple Spots, which they prickt with a sharp Needle, but she felt no pain. She had about her other Marks and Tokens of a Witch, and she was sent to the County Jayle.

This old Woman was had to a great River near the Town, to see whether she could sink under Water. Her Legs being tied, she was put in, and though she did endeavour to the uttermost by her Hands, yet she could not, but would lie upon her Back, and did Swim like a piece of Cork. There were present above Twenty Persons to Attest the Truth of this. She was had to the Water a second time, and being put in, she swam as at first; and though there were present above Two Hundred People to see this Sight, yet it could not be believed by many. At the same time, also, there was put into the Water, a Lusty young Woman, who sunk immediately, and had been drowned, had it not been for the help that was at hand. To satisfy the World, and to leave no Room for doubting, the old Woman was had down to the Water the third time, and being put in as before, she did still Swim. At this Swimming of her, were present, such a Company of People of the Town and Country, and many of them, Persons of Quality, as could not well be Numbered; so that now, there is scarce one Person that doubts of the Truth of this thing.

It is full Ten Weeks ago that this young Woman was first seized with these Terrible Fits, yet she continues to be often seized with terrible Fits, and to bring up both Nails and Handles of Spoons, and is still remaining an Object of great Pity.

Source: "She threw up crooked pins." *Shakespeare's England: Everyday Life in Seventeenth Century England.* Accessed 16 August 2017

http://www.shakespearesengland.co.uk/2012/09/17/she-threw-up-crooked-pins/

The website notes that the old woman — the "witch" — died in prison.

APPENDIX B: FAIR USE

§ 107. Limitations on exclusive rights: Fair use

Release date: 2004-04-30

Notwithstanding the provisions of sections 106 and 106A, the fair use of a copyrighted work, including such use by reproduction in copies or phonorecords or by any other means specified by that section, for purposes such as criticism, comment, news reporting, teaching (including multiple copies for classroom use), scholarship, or research, is not an infringement of copyright. In determining whether the use made of a work in any particular case is a fair use the factors to be considered shall include —

(1) the purpose and character of the use, including whether such use is of a commercial nature or is for nonprofit educational purposes;

(2) the nature of the copyrighted work;

(3) the amount and substantiality of the portion used in relation to the copyrighted work as a whole; and

(4) the effect of the use upon the potential market for or value of the copyrighted work.

The fact that a work is unpublished shall not itself bar a finding of fair use if such finding is made upon consideration of all the above factors.

Source of Fair Use information:

<http://www.law.cornell.edu/uscode/17/107.html>.

APPENDIX C: ABOUT THE AUTHOR

It was a dark and stormy night. Suddenly a cry rang out, and on a hot summer night in 1954, Josephine, wife of Carl Bruce, gave birth to a boy — me. Unfortunately, this young married couple allowed Reuben Saturday, Josephine's brother, to name their first-born. Reuben, aka "The Joker," decided that Bruce was a nice name, so he decided to name me Bruce Bruce. I have gone by my middle name — David — ever since.

Being named Bruce David Bruce hasn't been all bad. Bank tellers remember me very quickly, so I don't often have to show an ID. It can be fun in charades, also. When I was a counselor as a teenager at Camp Echoing Hills in Warsaw, Ohio, a fellow counselor gave the signs for "sounds like" and "two words," then she pointed to a bruise on her leg twice. Bruise Bruise? Oh yeah, Bruce Bruce is the answer!

Uncle Reuben, by the way, gave me a haircut when I was in kindergarten. He cut my hair short and shaved a small bald spot on the back of my head. My mother wouldn't let me go to school until the bald spot grew out again.

Of all my brothers and sisters (six in all), I am the only transplant to Athens, Ohio. I was born in Newark, Ohio, and have lived all around Southeastern Ohio. However, I moved to Athens to go to Ohio University and have never left.

At Ohio U, I never could make up my mind whether to major in English or Philosophy, so I got a bachelor's degree with a double major in both areas, then I added a Master of Arts degree in English and a Master of Arts degree in Philosophy. Yes, I have my MAMA degree.

Currently, and for a long time to come (I eat fruits and veggies), I am spending my retirement writing books such as *Nadia Comaneci: Perfect 10*, *The Funniest People in Dance*, *Homer's* Iliad: *A Retelling in Prose*, and *William Shakespeare's* Othello: *A Retelling in Prose*.

By the way, my sister Brenda Kennedy writes romances such as *A New Beginning* and *Shattered Dreams*.

APPENDIX D: SOME BOOKS BY DAVID BRUCE

Retellings of a Classic Work of Literature

Arden of Faversham: *A Retelling*

Ben Jonson's The Alchemist: *A Retelling*

Ben Jonson's The Arraignment, or Poetaster: *A Retelling*

Ben Jonson's Bartholomew Fair: *A Retelling*

Ben Jonson's The Case is Altered: *A Retelling*

Ben Jonson's Catiline's Conspiracy: *A Retelling*

Ben Jonson's The Devil is an Ass: *A Retelling*

Ben Jonson's Epicene: *A Retelling*

Ben Jonson's Every Man in His Humor: *A Retelling*

Ben Jonson's Every Man Out of His Humor: *A Retelling*

Ben Jonson's The Fountain of Self-Love, or Cynthia's Revels: *A Retelling*

Ben Jonson's The Magnetic Lady, or Humors Reconciled: *A Retelling*

Ben Jonson's The New Inn, or The Light Heart: *A Retelling*

Ben Jonson's Sejanus' Fall: *A Retelling*

Ben Jonson's The Staple of News: *A Retelling*

Ben Jonson's A Tale of a Tub: *A Retelling*

Ben Jonson's Volpone, or the Fox: *A Retelling*

Christopher Marlowe's Complete Plays: Retellings

Christopher Marlowe's Dido, Queen of Carthage: *A Retelling*

Christopher Marlowe's Doctor Faustus: *Retellings of the 1604 A-Text and of the 1616 B-Text*

Christopher Marlowe's Edward II: *A Retelling*

Christopher Marlowe's The Massacre at Paris: *A Retelling*

Christopher Marlowe's The Rich Jew of Malta: *A Retelling*

Christopher Marlowe's Tamburlaine, Parts 1 and 2: *Retellings*

Dante's Divine Comedy: *A Retelling in Prose*

Dante's Inferno: *A Retelling in Prose*

Dante's Purgatory: *A Retelling in Prose*

Dante's Paradise: *A Retelling in Prose*

The Famous Victories of Henry V: *A Retelling*

From the Iliad *to the* Odyssey: *A Retelling in Prose of Quintus of Smyrna's* Posthomerica

George Chapman, Ben Jonson, and John Marston's Eastward Ho! *A Retelling*

George Peele's The Arraignment of Paris: *A Retelling*

George Peele's The Battle of Alcazar: *A Retelling*

George's Peele's David and Bathsheba, and the Tragedy of Absalom: *A Retelling*

George Peele's Edward I: *A Retelling*

George Peele's The Old Wives' Tale: *A Retelling*

George-a-Greene: *A Retelling*

The History of King Leir: *A Retelling*

Homer's Iliad: *A Retelling in Prose*

Homer's Odyssey: *A Retelling in Prose*

J.W. Gent.'s The Valiant Scot: *A Retelling*

Jason and the Argonauts: A Retelling in Prose of Apollonius of Rhodes' Argonautica

John Ford: Eight Plays Translated into Modern English

John Ford's The Broken Heart: *A Retelling*

John Ford's The Fancies, Chaste and Noble: *A Retelling*

John Ford's The Lady's Trial: *A Retelling*

John Ford's The Lover's Melancholy: *A Retelling*

John Ford's Love's Sacrifice: *A Retelling*

John Ford's Perkin Warbeck: *A Retelling*

John Ford's The Queen: *A Retelling*

John Ford's 'Tis Pity She's a Whore: *A Retelling*

John Lyly's Campaspe: *A Retelling*

John Lyly's Endymion, The Man in the Moon: *A Retelling*

John Lyly's Galatea: *A Retelling*

John Lyly's Love's Metamorphosis: *A Retelling*

John Lyly's Midas: *A Retelling*

John Lyly's Mother Bombie: *A Retelling*

John Lyly's Sappho and Phao: *A Retelling*

John Lyly's The Woman in the Moon: *A Retelling*

John Webster's The White Devil: *A Retelling*

King Edward III: *A Retelling*

Mankind: *A Medieval Morality Play* (A Retelling)

Margaret Cavendish's The Unnatural Tragedy: *A Retelling*

The Merry Devil of Edmonton: *A Retelling*

The Summoning of Everyman: *A Medieval Morality Play* (A Retelling)

Robert Greene's Friar Bacon and Friar Bungay: *A Retelling*

The Taming of a Shrew: *A Retelling*

Tarlton's Jests: A Retelling

Thomas Middleton's A Chaste Maid in Cheapside: *A Retelling*

Thomas Middleton's Women Beware Women: *A Retelling*

Thomas Middleton and Thomas Dekker's The Roaring Girl: *A Retelling*

Thomas Middleton and William Rowley's The Changeling: *A Retelling*

The Trojan War and Its Aftermath: Four Ancient Epic Poems

Virgil's Aeneid: *A Retelling in Prose*

William Shakespeare's 5 Late Romances: Retellings in Prose

William Shakespeare's 10 Histories: Retellings in Prose

William Shakespeare's 11 Tragedies: Retellings in Prose

William Shakespeare's 12 Comedies: Retellings in Prose

William Shakespeare's 38 Plays: Retellings in Prose

William Shakespeare's 1 Henry IV, aka Henry IV, Part 1: *A Retelling in Prose*

William Shakespeare's 2 Henry IV, aka Henry IV, Part 2: *A Retelling in Prose*

William Shakespeare's 1 Henry VI, aka Henry VI, Part 1: *A Retelling in Prose*

William Shakespeare's 2 Henry VI, aka Henry VI, Part 2: *A Retelling in Prose*

William Shakespeare's 3 Henry VI, aka Henry VI, Part 3: *A Retelling in Prose*

William Shakespeare's All's Well that Ends Well: *A Retelling in Prose*

William Shakespeare's Antony and Cleopatra: *A Retelling in Prose*

William Shakespeare's As You Like It: *A Retelling in Prose*

William Shakespeare's The Comedy of Errors: *A Retelling in Prose*

William Shakespeare's Coriolanus: *A Retelling in Prose*

William Shakespeare's Cymbeline: *A Retelling in Prose*

William Shakespeare's Hamlet: *A Retelling in Prose*

William Shakespeare's Henry V: *A Retelling in Prose*

William Shakespeare's Henry VIII: *A Retelling in Prose*

William Shakespeare's Julius Caesar: *A Retelling in Prose*

William Shakespeare's King John: *A Retelling in Prose*

William Shakespeare's King Lear: *A Retelling in Prose*

William Shakespeare's Love's Labor's Lost: *A Retelling in Prose*

William Shakespeare's Macbeth: *A Retelling in Prose*

William Shakespeare's Measure for Measure: *A Retelling in Prose*

William Shakespeare's The Merchant of Venice: *A Retelling in Prose*

William Shakespeare's The Merry Wives of Windsor: *A Retelling in Prose*

William Shakespeare's A Midsummer Night's Dream: *A Retelling in Prose*

William Shakespeare's Much Ado About Nothing: *A Retelling in Prose*

William Shakespeare's Othello: *A Retelling in Prose*

William Shakespeare's Pericles, Prince of Tyre: *A Retelling in Prose*

William Shakespeare's Richard II: *A Retelling in Prose*

William Shakespeare's Richard III: *A Retelling in Prose*

William Shakespeare's Romeo and Juliet: *A Retelling in Prose*

William Shakespeare's The Taming of the Shrew: *A Retelling in Prose*

William Shakespeare's The Tempest: *A Retelling in Prose*

William Shakespeare's Timon of Athens: *A Retelling in Prose*

William Shakespeare's Titus Andronicus: *A Retelling in Prose*

William Shakespeare's Troilus and Cressida: *A Retelling in Prose*

William Shakespeare's Twelfth Night: *A Retelling in Prose*

William Shakespeare's The Two Gentlemen of Verona: *A Retelling in Prose*

William Shakespeare's The Two Noble Kinsmen: *A Retelling in Prose*

William Shakespeare's The Winter's Tale: *A Retelling in Prose*